THE NIGHT WATCHER

ALSO BY TARIQ ASHKANANI

Welcome to Cooper

Follow Me to the Edge

The Midnight King

THE NIGHT WATCHER

TARIQ ASHKANANI

Published by Thomas & Mercer, Seattle

www.apub.com

Amazon, the Amazon logo, and Thomas & Mercer are trademarks of Amazon.com, Inc., or its affiliates.

EU Product Safety contact:
Amazon Publishing, Amazon Media EU S.à r.l.
38, avenue John F. Kennedy, L-1855 Luxembourg
amazonpublishing-gpsr@amazon.com

ISBN-13: 9781662528019
eISBN: 9781662528002

Cover design by Dan Mogford
Cover image: © Stephen Mulcahey / ArcAngel Images; © Songquan Deng © Daniel Gale / Shutterstock

Printed in the United States of America

For Isaac

You are a night stalker.

You drift along the edge of the road like flotsam, coaxed forever forward, caught in the eddies of passing cars.

You are a lone woman.

Your whole adult life you have been a lone woman, and before that you were a lone girl. Brief moments of companionship, of intimacy. You remember the warm embrace of your mother. The way she would run her fingers through your hair. The way she would hum a tune, the way she would rock you to sleep. You remember the electric fizz of the young boy who lived down the street. You remember the way he slid out of his clothes. You remember the way he took control.

You are an addict.

You have hardened yourself to this way of life. To the urges, to the endless need. A single path lies ahead of you now and so you walk it; you follow it wherever it goes. Deep into this hard world. This dark world. There are glimpses of who you used to be and of who you have become. You see it in the angry stares of hotel managers. You see it in the dead eyes of a child's doll, left on the back seat of their father's car. Sometimes, as you freshen up in an en-suite bathroom, as you listen to the sound of him undressing or pacing the room, sometimes you can even see it in yourself. And afterwards, when he is done with you, you return to the cold streets where you unload everything for pennies, for a few hours' peace, for nothing. The single path is your future. It is all you will ever walk. A route charted by the star-like constellations of track marks on your skin.

You are waiting.

Watching the car slow as it approaches. It is dark blue. You do not know the model but you know it is expensive. A tinted window slides down. The driver is smiling, he is motioning with his head. Cocky. Confident.

Rich.

Where are you going? the driver asks you.

Wherever you are, you tell him. I'm going wherever you are.

You are a passenger.

The car is quiet and calm as it moves off.

This is nice, you say.

It's an electric, the driver tells you. I just got it the other week.

The radio is playing a strange weather forecast. You listen to the words and numbers but you do not understand them. You gaze around the cabin, see nothing out of place. No coffee cups in the holders, no takeaway wrappers in the footwell. In the distance you see the lights of the Queensferry Crossing. It is like some great alien structure, pulsing softly in the dark.

You must be freezing dressed like that, the driver says. How long were you waiting?

A while, you say.

Well, I hope you're careful, he says. There's a lot of dangerous people out there.

In the darkened cabin he slides his hand on to your thigh. You wrap your fingers around his. You think you know what he wants.

Why don't we pull in up ahead, you tell him. I know a quiet spot.

I want to go somewhere private, he says. Somewhere we can take our time.

You start to speak – Baby, it's triple if I stay overnight – when you feel a sharp scratch on your wrist. You look down to see a thin line of blood running across your pale skin.

It's a hypodermic syringe, he tells you. Spring-loaded. Don't worry, it shouldn't take long.

Chapter One

A half-hour before dawn, Callie stands outside her front door and smokes.

Her street is only part-formed; a haar settled during the brief night. She can feel the cold sea fog in her throat every time she inhales. She imagines it filtering down into her chest, her insides slowly fading away.

Abbeyhill stirs around her. Bathroom windows light up, their glow faint and scattered, shadow figures moving behind mottled glass. Somewhere a car door slams and an engine coughs weakly. The distant sound of traffic going slow along London Road.

Some part of her, she is sure, would have liked to be truly alone this morning, even if only until she finished her cigarette. The small part of her that has always liked being alone, that finds it a strange sort of comfort. A retaliation, perhaps, against the chaos of her childhood.

Most of her, however, is selfishly glad to know she isn't the only asshole up at this time.

Two doors down, a man stoops in his pyjamas and yawns as his dog takes its morning shit. Their eyes meet, and he nods. Callie lifts her cigarette and blows smoke.

Behind her come footsteps. Slow and plodding. She checks her watch as Richard swings open the front door.

'Thought you'd have gone by now,' he says.

'Just about to.'

'I can pop the kettle on if you've got time.'

Callie takes one last, long drag and drops the end into the chipped mug by her feet. She exhales slowly then turns around, shaking her head. ''Fraid not.'

'I can put it in a flask.'

'I'm fine.'

'You had breakfast?'

'Coco Pops. What are you doing up so early?'

Richard shrugs. He is shivering a little, standing in the open doorway. His skinny arms wrapped around his ratty t-shirt. His gaze goes behind her to the foggy street. 'Jesus, look at that.'

'I know. Listen, I'm sorry if I woke you.'

'You didn't.' He looks back at her and grins. 'Last night was fun.'

'It was.' She smiles back. A heartbeat too late maybe, she can see it in his eyes. She bends down and picks up the half-filled mug. Wrinkles her nose at the smell. 'I'll be inside in a moment. Close the door, it's freezing.'

She pads down the steps from her two-floor upper colony flat and out on to the little street. She knows Richard will be analysing their brief conversation. Picking it apart, stress-testing it. She wasn't lying when she told him last night was fun – it had been fun – but they've been doing this dance for a while now: Richard wanting to get closer while something in her gut tells her to stay back.

She walks the short distance to the row of multicoloured bins, tosses the collection of cigarette ends into the landfill container, and then, taking a tentative look at the inside of the mug, tosses that too.

When she gets back, Richard is in the small kitchen. It is painted turquoise blue. An exciting colour choice that everyone always praises her for, and which was already there when she moved in.

'You going back to bed?' she asks him.

He is fiddling with his watch. A large, chunky thing with a silver metal strap. An expensive present he bought for himself, which has now given him a skin rash. 'Nah, might go to the gym. Need to swing by my place before work anyway. You get your report printed off okay last night?'

Callie picks it up from the dining room table. 'Twenty pages of pure gut-punch, complete with pictures.'

She flicks through the report. Grant Miller: a thick, beefy man with a ruddy complexion and a niggling suspicion that his wife is having an affair. A couple of weeks' surveillance was enough to confirm it: Amy has been engaging in multiple late-night hook-ups with her also-married Asda supervisor. Callie even managed to snap a few pictures of them after work, rutting in the back seat of a cramped Fiat 500. The couple had parked in the furthest-away spot they could find. Callie needed a zoom lens.

'At least you're getting paid today,' Richard says.

'Not nearly enough, the stuff I had to watch.'

'Hey, you want to see a magic trick?'

'What?'

Richard grins and reaches for his wallet. Opening it, he pulls out a tenner and smooths it out on the kitchen counter. 'Have you got a pen?' he asks.

'Richard . . .'

'Come on, it's a good one. It'll cheer you up.'

Callie pulls a biro from her bag and hands it over. Richard leans forward and draws a doodle of a small dog on the banknote. He folds it up and closes his fingers around it. Then he moves his hands behind his back, makes a face like he's concentrating deeply, and presents both fists for her to inspect.

'Where's the tenner?' he asks.

'Richard . . .'

'You don't want it back?'

She taps his left fist. Richard opens it, to show it's empty.

'Try again,' he says.

She taps his right fist. Again, empty.

'Okay, where is it?' she says.

Richard pats himself down, his brow furrowed. Then he clicks his fingers and says, 'Check your purse.'

She does: the tenner is inside. Tucked away, next to her loose change. When she unfolds it, the same doodled dog is on one side. Callie laughs.

'Very good,' she says. 'When did you hide this in my purse?'

'When you were having a smoke. Told you it would cheer you up.' Richard puts the kettle on and leans back against the counter. 'What's your plans for later?'

'Nothing much.'

'Fancy a takeaway?'

Callie packs the Miller report into her leather bag and slides it on to her shoulder. 'Sure. Yours or here?'

'Here, if that's alright?'

'That's fine.'

They kiss, briefly, before Callie checks her reflection in the hallway mirror, opens her front door and steps back out into the fog.

The Marksman opens its doors early. Six a.m., to catch the night workers coming off shift. Gone are the days when an Edinburgh pub could be open twenty-four hours, but there's still a decent number of places left where you can get a pint in before your kids start school.

Grant Miller works as a security guard at a hostel on York Place. Callie knows he comes off shift at five a.m., wanders slowly down Leith Walk via Storries for a macaroni pie before arriving at Duke Street around five-thirty. There, he falls in with the area's resident shift workers and alcoholics until The Marksman opens its doors. If it's cold, the owner sometimes takes pity and lets them start their tab early.

By eight o'clock Miller will be half-cut. Callie wants to break the bad news before he gets started – really started – on his morning session. She doesn't want any trouble. Most importantly, she just wants to get paid.

The fog fills the streets on the way to the pub. It's not far from her flat – a twenty-minute walk. Longer, maybe, in this weather. But the thought of striding into the freezing mist in the near-dark isn't appealing, so she drives her small, three-door Mini Cooper slowly down deserted roads instead. Her headlights are near-useless. They reflect back at her, make her squint. The edges of parked cars fade in through the mist as she passes them.

Outside The Marksman, Callie wonders how early the owner ushered people inside. Away from the cold fog and into the warm embrace of Tennent's lager and Famous Grouse. She parks on a single yellow line and hopes the traffic warden isn't out in this weather. Picking up her report, Callie takes a breath and heads inside.

Grant Miller is sat at the bar. Hunched forward and alone. A half-empty pint in front of him, his thick fingers knuckle-deep in a packet of crisps and his eyes on nothing. Callie slides on to the stool next to him and places her report on the bar.

'Morning, Grant.'

He turns at her voice. His eyes are glassy. Maybe from the booze, maybe from crying. Callie tries to picture the guy bawling his heart out in a bathroom stall.

It's definitely the booze.

Three older men sit round a table in the corner. Each one's nose bigger and redder than the one before. A couple of students argue over the jukebox, trying to keep their night out going just that little bit longer. The barman half watches them from across the room as he thumbs through his phone.

'Wondered when you were going to show up,' Grant mutters. He leans his head back and drains his glass. Motions for another. Callie wonders what number this is.

'I've finished looking into your case,' she says. 'Thought I'd try and catch you after work.'

'Well, if you were trying to catch me sober, you're too late.'

The barman places a fresh pint of Tennent's in front of him. Glances over at Callie. 'I get you anything, hen?'

Before she can speak, Grant says, 'She's fine.'

A brief look passes across the barman's face and he raises his eyebrows at Callie. She shakes her head. He shrugs and wanders back to his phone. Laughter by the jukebox as the *Ghostbusters* theme tune starts up.

'Fuck me,' Grant says.

Callie taps the report on the bar. 'Listen, I don't want to keep you. I've got some news, and I'm afraid it's not what you were wanting to hear.'

'Amy's fucking her boss at work. I know.'

'What? When did you find out?'

'Last week.'

'Last week? And you didn't think to tell me?'

Grant finally focuses on her properly. His stubble is scraggly, he hasn't shaved in days. Doesn't look like he's washed his hair in a while, either. For the first time, Callie notices light stains down his jumper – mayonnaise from his nightly kebab. She wonders how much he had to drink before he got here. Couple of cans on the way down the road, maybe.

He snorts like he's getting ready to spit. Says, 'Funnily enough, you weren't at the top of my list.'

'I've been working two weeks on this, Grant. You should've told me.'

'You should've worked harder. I found out in half the time. Looked at her phone, didn't I? Bet you didn't even think of that. Fucking private investigator my arse. You're fucking shit, love.'

'Fine. Let's just settle up and I'll go.'

Grant is lifting his beer when she says that. If he'd been swallowing, he'd probably have choked. He lets out an angry cry and bangs his glass down so hard that liquid spills over the sides. 'Are you having a laugh? I'm not paying you anything, you daft bitch. For telling me what I already know?'

Callie knows goading him is a mistake. But pissed or not, he's got her back up now. Two weeks she's wasted on this grimy case. Two weeks following a woman to and from work. An entire Wednesday evening sat freezing in her car with the engine off and the window down, watching two devastatingly unattractive people dogging in a supermarket car park. It took three showers before she stopped feeling grubby.

'Guess these were a waste of film, then,' she says, flicking open the folder and scattering lewd photographs of Grant's wife next to his pint. They're grainy but they get the job done.

Grant pushes them away violently. Just about knocks over his beer. 'Oh, fuck off—'

'You know I spent the whole of last night working out how to break this to you nicely? I actually felt sorry for you.'

'I swear to God—'

'Look, I think you might find this shot interesting. It's called an orgasm.'

Even as the words leave her mouth, Callie knows she's taken it too far. Grant stands up fast, his barstool flying. His face is dark red, his mouth twisted into a snarl. Callie is halfway to her feet when his fist comes swinging into her stomach. She stumbles backwards,

11

exhaling hard and clutching at the bar, her eyes watering. Someone starts shouting.

'Grant!'

Callie breathes through the pain. Short, sharp bursts of air. She swallows it down and stands up straight. Shifts her weight off centre, sets her arm like she's doing a push-up. Elbow behind her wrist, shoulder behind her elbow. Aims just above Grant's wet lips and fires the heel of her hand into his nose. Once, twice. Second time sends a squirt of blood across her jacket. Grant pinwheels and falls on his arse.

Everyone in the pub goes silent. The only sound is *Ghostbusters*, still playing on the jukebox. Their whole exchange took less than a minute.

Callie bends down and wipes her bloodied palm on Grant's jumper. He's cradling his nose and moaning. She reaches into his jeans pocket and pulls out his wallet. The guy must have been planning a big session. She thumbs out two hundred quid. It isn't even half of what he owes.

'This is for my services,' she says, then thumbs out another fifty. 'And this is for my fucking jacket.'

She tosses his wallet on to his chest and leaves.

Chapter Two

Callie falls through her front door. Her stomach aches and her wrist throbs. She climbs the stairs to her bedroom and goes into the en-suite. Swallows a couple of paracetamol, drinks ice-cold water straight from the tap. Then she kicks off her shoes, drops her bloodstained jacket on the floor and collapses face down on to her bed.

When she wakes it's early afternoon. Her stomach still hurts but her wrist feels better. She thinks about Grant Miller's face as he fell ass-backwards clutching his nose. Thinks about the noise he made as he lay on the floor. It helps with the pain.

A smoke, another couple of painkillers and a mug of black coffee. She drinks it sitting at her dining room table, her laptop open. She scrolls through her emails. Flicks through the handful of other cases she's currently working. A deceased's estate trying to track down a distant relative. An insurer who suspects a payout was fraudulently claimed. She doesn't have the energy for them just now.

The two hundred and fifty quid is sat next to her. She'd been expecting over twice that for the amount of work she put in. Reaching into her purse, she pulls out Richard's folded tenner from this morning and adds it to the pile. The lopsided dog stares up at her, wagging its little tail.

Two-hundred and sixty quid now. Just enough to cover last month's overdue council tax.

It isn't enjoyable, living like this. But Callie learned a long time ago to keep her complaints to herself. About this job, about a lot of things. A side effect of growing up in the foster system; everyone has their own shit to deal with, and no one expects any help in doing so. Most of the time that suits Callie just fine. She's always been isolated, for as long as she can remember. Always had to look out for herself, always had to scrap and fight for every small piece of whatever she could get her hands on. It didn't matter to the crowds of people that circled her life. Officials, foster parents, other children. Not one of them ever gave a real fuck about her. A childhood spent surrounded by others, and yet forever alone.

And Richard . . . Richard thinks he knows what she needs. A stable life, a routine. A job that pays a monthly salary, like she hasn't already tried that. Hasn't sat in an office, hasn't stood behind a bar. An easier life in some ways, but a wasted one in so many others. Being an investigator is the only life Callie knows – truly knows. The only life in which she has total control. The only life that one day might answer the biggest question of all.

What happened to her parents?

The bruise wraps itself around Callie's stomach. It's bright red, the blood pooling beneath her skin still wholesome and new. She knows it will soon lose its colour. It will darken as the blood starves and the cells rot. Reabsorbed to be used again. There is something Callie finds strangely calming about this. How the hurt always fades. How the human body is able to recycle such ugliness.

She is swallowing another couple of painkillers when she hears the front door opening. Richard is here. She listens to him unzip his jacket and kick off his shoes. He calls her name as he climbs the stairs. Callie reaches over and quietly locks the bathroom door.

'Callie?'

They have been together for nearly six months now. On and off, never quite managing to stay in sync. She knows it's her fault; she refuses to let him get close. A character flaw, she is quite sure. But opening herself up to someone means putting the darkness inside her on full display. All the shameful things she has done, all the violent acts.

Not that Richard doesn't have his own demons to deal with: a wretched childhood spent watching his father beat his mother on a near-daily basis. Callie has seen it on his face: when he drinks too much, when he's running late, when he drives – aggressively, muttering under his breath. A knot that appears in his forehead, a little curve of skin that bulges just above his right eye. She sees it, and more than most might, she understands it, too.

Perhaps that's why she returns to him, time and again. When common sense tells her to pull back, when she knows she is making a mistake. That shared pain, it connects them in a way she does not fully understand.

But Callie is not ready to open up to him. Not tonight. And so she leans her head against the mirror and pictures the bruise – the blood vessels bursting and spilling their contents under her skin. She pictures Grant Miller. Sat at the bar with a face as red as her stomach is now. Red from the drink, from the shame, from the anger that simmered inside him, stewing his guts and boiling his bones. Just like all the boys she grew up with. Just like Richard. Just like Callie herself.

The door handle jiggles.

'Callie? Are you alright?'

She pictures Grant Miller's face after it was over. He hadn't expected her to fight back. They never do.

'I'm fine,' she says.

'You fancy a Chinese? I liked that crispy beef we got last time.'

'Chinese sounds great,' she says, her voice level.

'Alright then. Hurry up, I'm making gin and tonics.'

Callie waits until he's retreated from the bedroom and his footsteps have descended the stairs. Then, breathing out slowly, she pulls her t-shirt down over the bruise, tucks a stray strand of reddish-blonde hair behind one ear, and unlocks the bathroom door.

Later, when she has finished eating greasy chow mein and drunk three bottles of Moretti and Richard has gone home, Callie lies in bed alone and finds that she cannot sleep.

She snatches at it, holds it briefly in her hands. Never enough to piece together into anything whole. Flashes of The Marksman, of Grant Miller's expression as he swung his fist. His words, so casually cruel: *you daft bitch.*

Callie wonders how often he has used that phrase. Against a woman, against his wife. For the first time she wonders about Amy Miller. What she's had to put up with. How she's managed to cope. Maybe her Asda supervisor's a decent man – Callie doesn't know. It wasn't her job to find out.

She worries about the chain of events she may have set in motion. Grant Miller going home at ten a.m., boozed up and bloodied and two-hundred-odd quid down. She decides, lying there in the dark, to check on Amy Miller in the morning.

When tomorrow comes, it somehow feels like the day before never left. Outside, the mist has gone but its chill remains. Callie can feel it as she crosses her small bedroom to the en-suite, where the overhead lights flicker and make her squint. She inspects herself in the mirror. Shadows under her eyes and her face pale. Lifting her shirt, she sees her stomach is starting to heal. The bruising already turning a shade darker. The blood cells dying beneath her skin.

Grant and Amy Miller live in a sixties housing estate in Corstorphine. A stone's throw from Edinburgh Zoo. Callie glances at it as she drives past; she hasn't been since she was a girl. A primary school trip one afternoon. She remembers a polar bear that paced its cage, over and over. This wild beast, trapped and driven mad. Standing by herself, her forehead pressed against the glass, the rest of the class off in their little groups, she thought she understood what the bear felt.

Turning into the estate, it is suddenly obvious that she is too late. In the fading dark, the silent strobe of blue from two parked police cars lights up the entire street. White and blue tape that reads *Do Not Cross* is stretched out across the driveway of the Millers' small, semi-detached house.

Chapter Three

Callie parks two houses down and kills the engine. Climbing out, she scans the street. Spots people at their windows or craning their necks out their front doors. No one has summoned the nerve to go up to the tape yet. She knows this won't last.

Past the tape she can see the house. Pebble-dashed walls, a small garden out front. Through the windows she can see figures in white boiler suits moving around. Gliding silently through the living room, masks over their faces, their hoods pulled tight.

A single officer watches her approach. He holds a clipboard, his radio crackling constantly. 'Excuse me, ma'am, but you'll have to move away.'

'What happened here?'

'I'm sorry but I can't say.'

'I need to speak with your DCI, or whoever is in charge.'

A voice from off to one side: 'Can I help you?'

Callie turns to see a young man with brown, swept-back hair smiling at her. He ducks under the police tape and extends a hand from the pocket of his overcoat. 'DS Mackenzie Reid.'

She shakes it. The detective's hand is cold. She wonders how long he has been standing outside. 'My name is Callie Munro,' she says. 'I'm a private investigator. Grant Miller hired me to look into his wife, Amy.'

DS Reid's eyebrows rise slightly. 'You're the woman who gave Miller his broken nose?'

'Yeah, well, it turns out he likes beating on women. And I'm betting I wasn't the first.'

'It's alright, I'm not interested in arresting you for assault, Ms Munro.' He pulls out a notebook and flips it open. 'I am going to need to ask you some questions, however.'

'Has something happened to Amy?'

'You'll understand that I'm not—'

'Oh, don't give me that. This is a crime scene. You've got a forensics team working the house already. She's dead, isn't she. He fucking killed her.'

The detective hesitates. Unsure how much he should say, perhaps. 'We don't know,' he settles on finally.

'You don't know?'

'She's missing.'

'Since when?'

'Since yesterday night.'

'Is there any sign of a struggle?'

DS Reid cocks his head. 'Okay, that's enough. My turn to ask the questions.'

But before he can begin, an older woman emerges from the house and calls his name. 'Mac! Chief's on the radio. He wants an update.'

'Yes, ma'am.'

'In person, I'm afraid.'

Callie glances over at her. The woman has paused by the doorway to watch them as she peels off her blue overshoes and gloves.

Reid snaps his notebook shut. He hasn't even written anything down yet. He gives Callie a short smile. 'I need to deal with this, but then I want to speak with you.'

19

'Fine with me.'

'Good. I'm heading back to the station, we can talk there. You alright to follow me?'

He leaves her waiting for nearly forty-five minutes. Out front, at least. A small lobby by the reception desk. A big officer with a ginger moustache sitting behind it, catching up on some paperwork. This time of day, this part of the city, it's quiet. Enough to let Callie run through everything again. Enough to let the sliver of worry she experienced last night blossom into full-blown guilt. That she got Grant Miller riled up before sending him home to his cheating wife. That whatever has happened to Amy is her fault.

When DS Reid finally shows up again, he looks flustered. For the first time she notices his poorly ironed shirt and the shadows under his eyes. The young detective doesn't look like he's been sleeping much either.

'I'm sorry for the wait,' he says, holding a door open for her. It leads into the back of the station. 'Let's have that chat.'

They walk down a twisty corridor. Through interlocking doors and beyond the interrogation rooms. She glances in them as she passes. Grant Miller is sitting alone in the last one – side on, facing the wall, his hands clasped on the table in front of him. He's wearing the same stained jumper that he had on in The Marksman. His hair is ruffled and Callie is pleased to see the bruising around his swollen nose. He turns, perhaps sensing movement at the door. Callie darts on quickly before their eyes meet.

She follows the detective into a small, open-plan office. A handful of officers mill about, typing reports or talking quietly on the phone. There is the smell of instant coffee and sweat. A badly hung TV plays BBC News. Reid motions to a messy desk against one wall.

'Please, have a seat.'

'Everything alright with the chief?'

'Hmm?'

He barely seems to hear her as he moves folders off his desk, digging out his keyboard and dropping his notebook next to it.

'You were with the chief for nearly an hour. Everything alright?'

'Everything's fine.' The detective smiles and sweeps his hair back, scratching at his scalp. 'Can I get you a coffee, Ms Munro?'

'Is it instant?'

''Fraid so.'

'Then no, thank you. And please, call me Callie.'

'Fine.' Reid starts flipping through his notebook. 'I want to start with Grant Miller. He hired you to investigate his wife?'

'He suspected her of cheating on him.'

'And was she?'

'Yeah. With her supervisor at work. I . . .' She falters a little. 'I met him yesterday morning to hand over my report. Told him what I'd discovered.'

'That was at The Marksman? In Leith?'

'Yes.'

'This was where you got into an altercation with him?'

'If you mean where he sucker-punched me, then yeah.'

Reid nods, his head down as he scribbles notes. 'I guess the guy didn't like finding out his wife was sleeping around.'

'He already knew. And she wasn't sleeping around, Detective, she was having an affair. Given who she's married to, can you blame her?'

'I—'

'You know what, don't answer that. Have you interviewed either man yet?'

'Not yet. We're waiting until we finish a preliminary search of the house.'

'Jesus, how long is that going to take? Amy's out there somewhere. She might be hurt.'

'We know what we're doing, Callie.' Reid stops writing for a moment and looks up at her. He says it in a way that is perhaps supposed to be reassuring. It is the sort of phrase that Callie has heard all her life.

Mind your place.

Just relax.

Do what you're told.

A sudden urge to get to her feet and walk out. She forces herself to remain seated. Behind her, a babble of raised voices draws the detective's attention. She turns to see a bald man in a cheap, ill-fitting grey suit talking angrily to another officer.

'Miller's lawyer,' Reid says, almost to himself as he returns to writing.

'What's got him so worked up?'

'God knows. Now, after you left the pub, did you see or hear from him again?'

'No.'

'So what made you come down to their house this morning?'

Callie glances away. 'A . . . feeling, I guess. I was worried about what he might do.'

'You thought he might hurt Amy?'

'I was right, wasn't I?'

Reid is quiet as he finishes writing in his notebook. 'If you're blaming yourself for whatever's happened here, don't. You said it yourself, Callie. He already knew.'

'Yeah, but I really pissed him off.' She flashes a small smile. 'I have a habit of doing that.'

The detective smiles back. He rubs at his tired eyes. In the corner of the room, Miller's lawyer is finally leaving. The officer he'd been talking with blows air out the side of his mouth.

'What was the house like?' Callie asks.

Reid watches her for a moment before answering. 'Messy.'

'Were there signs of a struggle?'

Another pause, then, 'Yes.' The detective's mobile rings. He checks the screen before answering. 'Ma'am.'

Callie wonders if it is the older woman from the Miller house. Reid's partner, perhaps. Her attention drifts. It is after eleven a.m. now, and she is suddenly aware of how hungry she is. She skipped breakfast this morning, and greasy noodles only get you so far.

DS Reid ends the call and gets to his feet. Callie does the same. 'Is that it?' she asks.

'That's it,' he says. 'For now, anyway. We're going to speak with Grant Miller and see what he has to say for himself.' He reaches into a drawer and pulls out a small stack of business cards. Peels the top one off and hands it over. 'Take this. If you remember anything else, give me a call. Do you want me to show you out?'

Callie slips the card into her pocket. 'I can remember the way.'

She is halfway to the door when Reid says, 'Oh, I forgot to ask you. In the pub, when you broke Miller's nose . . .'

'What about it?'

'How many times did you hit him?'

'Twice.'

'Closed fist?'

'Open palm.'

'Did you scratch him?'

'No. Why?'

The detective shrugs. 'No reason. Take care, Callie.'

Chapter Four

The events of that morning haunt Callie for the rest of the day. She sits in a small cafe and eats lunch and thinks about Amy Miller. Spoonfuls of lukewarm tomato soup as she tries to reframe her. Wife, adulterer, victim. Like the woman has to have a label so she can be filed away. Callie remembers scattering Amy's intimate photographs across a dirty bar and she pushes her soup away, half finished.

The disgust stays with her. In her belly, pressed up against her bruising. She takes painkillers and tries to focus on her caseload. A positive response from her contact in the Crown Office, though not the one her client will be looking for: formal identification of a John Doe that was fished out of the Union Canal six months ago. She busies herself with the admin of it all. Emails, filing, invoicing. She tries to lose herself in the work, and it's so monotonous that she almost succeeds.

She's not long home when Richard calls. It's the early evening. He makes small talk until even he can tell that something's wrong. She tells him about her day.

'Jesus,' he says. 'Why didn't you phone me?'

'And say what?'

'I dunno, just to talk about it.'

'I don't think I do want to talk about it.'

There's an uneasy silence.

Richard says, 'Do you want to do something tonight?'

'Like what?'

'Cinema? Get some dinner?'

Callie closes her laptop. Maybe going to see a film would be a good idea. It might take her mind off everything – help pass the time until the police have something more concrete. She gets to her feet, wincing slightly at her stomach, and pads through to the living room. She makes a mental note to take some more painkillers after this call.

'Sure,' she says. 'I'd be up for that. What's on at the moment?'

'I think the new *Spider-Man* is still playing.'

'Oh, is that Andrew Garfield? I like him.'

Richard laughs down the line. 'Andrew Garfield? Christ, Callie, he hasn't been Spider-Man for like, ten years or something.'

'Alright, calm down.' Callie gingerly lowers herself on to the sofa. Already she is losing interest in going out. She hates it when Richard gets like this. Acting all superior, like a childhood spent reading comic books is somehow not embarrassing anymore.

'Sorry. I could pick you up about seven? Get some food after?'

'I'll just meet you there. I need to finish up some work first.'

Afterwards, she swallows two paracetamol and sets her alarm for six-thirty, then stretches out on her sofa and sleeps.

She wakes to the local news. Groggy, half asleep. She's reaching for her phone when she hears the name Amy Miller coming from the TV.

The reporter is stood at the end of Amy's street. He's halfway through his piece. Behind him, Callie can see the house she went to this morning. Same police cars, same blue tape. She was right about the rubberneckers; they're all there now. Some of them are dressed for a night out; make-up and high heels. A chance to be caught on the evening news overriding any sort of respect for a missing woman.

'Police have confirmed that after a day spent questioning Amy's husband,' the reporter is saying, 'they've now ruled out Grant Miller as a potential suspect and fully expect him to assist in their ongoing search.'

Callie stares at the television.

Grant Miller is no longer a suspect.

The realisation takes a while to trickle through her. It has to fight through her mental defences. That she heard it wrong, that she's still waking up. That the police must have made a mistake.

Twenty minutes later she's still sat on her sofa. The news has moved on to the next story but Callie is trawling the internet for anything new. An Edinburgh subreddit title catches her eye.

Is Amy Miller another victim of the Night Watcher?

She clicks on it, opening a thread filled with armchair detectives spouting theories about Amy's disappearance. That she ran away, that her husband did her in. That she was taken by someone in the night while she slept.

Callie reads the comments, hunched forward, her back starting to ache. There's so little information on Amy's vanishing to go on, but that doesn't stop the conjecture. People toss around the names of other women, names that Callie has never heard reported before. A warning in her head starts to sound, slow and steady.

Her phone rings – Richard calling to find out where she is. Callie lets it ring out, then sends him a text saying she's not feeling well.

Let me know how Andrew Garfield is, she types, using humour to try to soften the stab of guilt she feels for standing him up like this. *Takeaway tomorrow?*

Sliding her phone back into her pocket, her fingers brush against a business card. DS Mackenzie Reid's contact details. Callie spends a long moment considering whether or not she should call him. Ask the detective directly how the hell someone like Grant Miller is a free man. If the Night Watcher moniker means anything.

In the end, she decides against it.

The next few hours pass in a blur of cigarettes, news websites, Reddit threads and social media posts. Richard messages back but she barely reads it. She pauses to order pizza, then shortly after to answer the door when it arrives, and before she's finished her first slice she's decided on a course of action.

She's a private investigator, after all. Investigating people is what she does.

Chapter Five

Martin Walsh is a short, bald man of around fifty, maybe fifty-five. Callie has never been good with ages. The baldness doesn't help matters, but with Martin it's all about the walk. The stooped gait, the shuffling steps. He moves like his very bones are liable to break at any moment. He reminds Callie of that Samuel L. Jackson character in *Unbreakable*. The line comes to her every time she sees him. *They called me Mr Glass.*

'Come in, Callie, come in,' Martin says, swinging open the door to his Grassmarket flat.

It's a small, pokey place. Three floors up, overlooking the thrall of pubs, cafes and shops that always seem to draw crowds of tourists no matter the time of year. Callie wonders how the hell he copes, living here during the festival. Single glazing, too. She can't begin to imagine the noise at night.

'How are you?' he asks her, slowly sidling past to close and triple-bolt his door. 'How's work?'

'Work's fine,' she says.

'How'd you like the zoom lens?'

Callie holds up the padded bag and he takes it from her, motioning for her to follow him. 'It was good,' she tells him. 'Stuff I had to shoot, I was glad not to have to get too close.'

'What was it again? An affair?'

'It's complicated.'

'Affairs are always complicated.'

She makes a non-committal noise as they weave through the tight corridor and into the spare bedroom. Martin has set this up as his home office. Every wall is lined with the latest surveillance equipment: cameras, recording devices, GPS trackers. He's the go-to contact for most of the private investigators in the local area. Probably the go-to contact for most of the ones further afield, too. He set up shop nearly ten years ago now. Figured out early on that this equipment was expensive as hell, and he could make a decent living off renting it out to people, piece by piece.

For Callie, Martin has been a godsend. She'd never have been able to get off the ground if she'd had to stump up for some of the items she's borrowed from him. Plenty of cases that would have been far more tricky, if not impossible, without a radio microphone or hidden camera. And it's not just the physical gear, either. Martin has contacts. Runs registration numbers and carries out disclosure searches if you ask him nice. For a fee, of course.

It was a smart business move on Martin's part. The guy is in high demand. Callie figures he must have made over five times what he paid on most of this stuff by now.

Of course, that success brings problems of its own. Storing close to a hundred grand's worth of surveillance equipment in a cheaply built Edinburgh tenement flat makes you an easy target. Hence the security cameras filming up and down the street. The motion sensors in the stairwell. The triple bolts on the reinforced steel front door. Not for the first time, Callie takes it all in and knows it's not a life she would want. Money be damned.

Martin drops awkwardly into a large, leather seat. The computer monitor behind him is displaying a camera feed – an awkward angle of a street somewhere.

'Anything good?' she asks him.

He taps his keyboard and the window minimises. 'If it was filmed with my kit, it's always good,' he says, then he starts opening the padded bag she's brought him. 'You format the SD card this time?'

'Yeah. Even recharged it for you and everything.'

'I don't give out a discount for that.'

'You should. Cost of electricity these days.'

Martin smiles as he lifts out the SLR camera and spins it around, checking it over. Satisfied, he puts it to one side and swivels to face her. 'So, what else can I do for you today, Callie. You want a pocket mic? A GPS tracker? I got a nifty folding periscope that no one's tried yet. Oh, shit, you ever thought about using a drone before?'

Callie takes a seat and crosses her arms. 'I need to know what you've got in the way of remote covert surveillance,' she says.

Martin grins.

It's getting dark when Callie arrives back at the Millers' estate. But for what she's about to do, it's probably not quite dark enough.

She spends a while sitting in her car. Parked far enough down the street that she's not an obvious target for any twitching curtains, but close enough for her to keep an eye on the Miller house.

If Grant's inside, he's keeping his head down. Every light is off, every curtain pulled tight. Callie isn't sure if he's working his usual security shift tonight at the hostel – she isn't sure if he's still got a job there. For a moment she considers phoning them and asking . . . what? The name of the guy currently manning the front door? The amount of media attention Grant Miller's had in the last twenty-four hours, she'd be amazed if he was working tonight.

And shit, Grant's got a serious daily drinking target. Callie would bet good money that he's sat on his sofa right now, cradling a six-pack or a bottle of something dark, his bruised head rocking forward on to that stained jumper. Or perhaps he slipped out the back door a couple of hours ago. Made his way to a pub. Somewhere nearby he can walk to, just not somewhere he's known.

Finally, Callie judges that it's dark enough. She's been sat there for over an hour now, and aside from a couple of dog walkers and a Deliveroo man on a bike, there's been no movement in the street. Lifting her small backpack, she climbs out of her car and closes the door – pressing it shut gently to keep the noise down.

She walks quickly, keeping her head up. She tries not to make it obvious – not that she thinks she's being watched, but you never know. A neighbour glancing out of their window sees someone with a hood up, hunched forward and scurrying through an estate, they might call the police. They see someone walking like they live there, maybe they give her a pass.

Callie already knows where she's going to plant the cameras. She has two of them – one for the front and one for the back. She slips her backpack off a shoulder as she approaches the junction box that sits opposite the Miller house. Crouching down next to it, she slides out the first camera.

'It's genius,' Martin told her excitedly. 'Biggest problem with an outdoor camera is hiding the damn thing. But with this?'

Callie smiled, despite everything. 'Very clever,' she said. 'Keep it in plain sight.'

'Exactly.'

The device is a small, grey box, about ten centimetres across and maybe half as thick. *DANGER*, it reads in bold, yellow text across the front, *230 VOLTS*. A small lightning bolt underneath to drive the point home.

31

'You fit this in the right place,' Martin said, 'no one will touch it. They won't even give it a second thought.'

'What about recharging?'

'Battery lasts a month. Maybe three weeks, this time of year.'

'How do I access the footage?'

'App on your phone. Like watching your own personal YouTube.'

It takes her under thirty seconds to fix the camera against the wall, next to the junction box. Pausing to look at it, she has to admit that Martin was right. The device just seems like part of the furniture.

Crossing the street, she watches the Miller house as she approaches. Still nothing. With a bit of luck, Grant is passed out in front of the TV. With a bit more luck he's getting his head kicked in across town. She feels momentarily bad for thinking that. But only momentarily.

The Millers' car is sat in the driveway. A red Audi A3. Callie looks it over as she slips past, then she's at the wooden fence that leads around the back of the house and into the garden. Without pausing, she gently lifts the metal latch and opens the gate just wide enough to squeeze through.

'Now the garden, that's easier.'

Martin showed her a variety of cameras for this. All of them fairly small – no bigger than her closed fist – and yet she was expecting something more.

Callie turned them over in her hands. 'Don't you have any of those tiny spy cams I keep seeing advertised on YouTube?'

'Course I do. I got cameras so small you can thread them through your buttonhole. I got a camera you can put inside a fake dog shit, swear to God. You just slap the thing on the pavement and people leave it alone.'

'So why don't you give me a couple of them?'

'Because you need to power the damn things, Callie. You want them running for more than a couple hours at a time. And you need them to record at night, in infrared. And unless you're happy with a day's worth of footage, max, then—'

'Alright, alright, point made.'

The Millers' garden is nice. A small patch of lawn next to a patio big enough for a table and chairs; a little shed against the far wall. Callie stands in the shadow of the house and stares up at the darkened windows. Blinds down, curtains drawn tight.

She crosses the lawn in four quick steps. The second camera is already in her hands. She fixes it securely underneath the overhang of the shed roof. It's hard to tell, but she's confident there'll be enough shade to keep it hidden during the day.

One last glance over at the quiet house, then she leaves the garden the same way she came in. As she passes the red Audi, she crouches down and places the GPS tracker under the rear wheel arch. It connects magnetically with a satisfying clunk.

Then Callie is walking back down the street. She takes the long route – looping around the block to approach her car from the rear. Just in case that same someone who maybe spotted her on the way in spots her again on the way out. It wouldn't look good. And besides, you never can be too careful.

Callie is dead tired when she finally gets home. It's late now and all she can think about is crawling into bed and closing her eyes. Her stomach is aching again. Couple of painkillers and eight hours' sleep ought to help.

She has to drive the narrow streets a bunch of times before she finds a parking spot. 'Every fucking time,' she murmurs to herself. She ends up leaving her car a few streets over. Squeezed tight between a lamp post and a badly parked motorcycle that's taking up nearly two spaces. Callie tries to be thankful she drives a Mini and not a Land Rover like her next-door neighbour. Poor bastard's been too scared to move the thing for nearly six months now, in case he loses his parking spot.

Still, just because it's routine doesn't make it any easier, and she finds herself resenting the walk more than usual tonight. She resents the shooting pain each step sends up her belly. She resents the owner of the Great Dane who never picks up his dog's shit, leaving her to navigate it by smell alone in the near-dark. She resents the cold, she resents the tiredness. She resents the craving for a cigarette.

And the universe responds in turn: when she finally reaches her gate and looks up at her front door, the man waiting there appears to resent her, too.

Chapter Six

'Richard?'

She pauses at the gate. Keys in her left hand. She briefly considers sliding them between her fingers.

'Where have you been?' he asks her. His voice is quiet; maybe because he's angry, maybe just because it's late. Callie realises that she doesn't know him well enough yet to tell.

'I've been working,' she says. Climbing the stairs now. 'How long have you been waiting here?'

'About as long as I've been phoning.'

Callie feels for her mobile. Pulls it out. Sees she has – Jesus – thirteen missed calls. She holds up the phone. 'Must have had it on silent.'

'Uh-huh.'

'Are you pissed off at me?'

'I was worried about you, Callie. I thought something had happened. I thought maybe you'd done something.'

It's an odd phrase. Callie is near the top of the stairs now. This close, even in the dim light from her neighbours' flats, she can tell Richard is stressed. His forehead is knotted. The little curve of skin bulging above his right eye. His tell-tale marks.

Trying to keep her voice calm, despite everything, she says, 'What did you think I might do?'

'Can we talk inside?'

Callie wants to say no. She knows she should say no. That this man should turn up outside her front door after dark and wait for her to return home is insanely creepy. She knows she should tell him to leave. That she's within her rights to call the police, and that if he isn't gone in the next ten seconds that's exactly what she'll do.

'Please, Callie,' he says. 'I was just worried about you.'

'Why? Because I wasn't answering my phone at night?'

'Christ, no. Because I saw the news.'

It takes her a moment to work out what he means. 'Grant Miller,' she says finally.

Richard nods, quickly. Empowered by her response. 'That's the guy you were working for, wasn't it? Whose wife was cheating on him.'

'Yeah, that's him.'

'And now she's missing and he's no longer a suspect.'

'Yes, Richard, I understand you watched the news. What I'm struggling with is why you're here.' She shifts her weight from one foot to the other. Her stomach tenses. 'You thought I might – what? – confront him?'

'I . . . I don't know. Or maybe he would come after you. You know, blame you for—'

'For what, Richard?'

'I don't know, alright! But I was worried! And you still haven't answered my question, Callie. Where were you tonight?'

'I already told you, I was working.'

Callie is getting angry herself now. She can feel it sparking. Solar flares in her fists, same as with Grant Miller in the pub. Same as it's always been.

'Working where?' Richard presses.

'Working none of your damn business,' she snaps. 'Not everyone had the time to go sit in a cinema, watch fucking Tobey Maguire—'

'Jesus, Callie, it's—'

'Oh, I don't care who it is, Richard! I'm tired. I'm going to bed.'

'What's wrong with you?'

'What's wrong with me? You stand around outside my house in the dark and you ask me that?'

'No, I mean—'

'What the fuck's wrong with you, Richard?'

'I mean what's wrong with your stomach?'

She's been holding it, she realises now. Cradling it, almost. One hand wrapped around it. Like she's protecting herself. She lets her arm fall to her side. Stands up straight. But she can't hide the wince and Richard spots it. Jumps on it like it's vindication.

'That!' he crows, pointing. 'I knew something was wrong the other night. What happened to your stomach?'

'I fell.'

'You fell?'

'Yes, Richard, I fucking fell.'

'Where?'

'In the street.'

'What street?'

'Fuck off, Richard!'

'Fine, so show me your stomach then.'

'No.'

'Come on, Callie, just lift your shirt.'

'No.'

The penny finally seems to drop. Richard's face shifts. The tension fades, his features flattening as he steps back. 'You're right,' he says, 'I'm being an idiot.' His words are half formed; they stumble and trip on their way out. 'I'll go. Of course I'll go. I'm sorry. I'll call you in the morning?'

'Whatever,' Callie mutters. She has already moved away and is unlocking her door. Pushing it open as Richard turns, and for a moment – a crazy, credible moment – she thinks he is about to force his way into her flat.

But of course he doesn't. He is turning to leave, his footsteps quiet as he pads down the stairs. Callie doesn't look back as she closes the front door and slides the bolt home.

Chapter Seven

In the cold November morning, the events of the previous night almost seem like a dream. And not just the fight with Richard. All of it. Creeping through Grant Miller's back garden and fixing a camera to the roof of his shed. Attaching a GPS tracker to his car.

Callie rolls over and picks up her mobile phone from her bedside table. Unplugs the charging cable. She has three WhatsApp messages from Richard. All of them variations on a theme. *I'm sorry. I was being stupid. I was just worried about you.* She swipes away the notifications, irritated.

She logs into the remote camera software. It takes thirty seconds or so to connect, and then two boxes pop up on her screen. Each shows a live image – one from the camera by the junction box, the other from the back garden.

In both feeds the house looks completely normal. The curtains are open, the blinds are raised. The red Audi still sits in the driveway.

Starting with the front camera, Callie slides the progress bar to the left. Scrubbing backwards in time. She watches cars reverse and children skip homewards in their school uniforms. Then, around an hour ago, she sees the ambling figure of Grant Miller at each window of his house, lowering the blinds.

She stops. Hits play. Watches it all again, only this time going in the right direction. When she's done, she repeats the exercise with the rear camera. She picks up her notebook and scribbles down a few trite thoughts. Then she clambers out of bed and stretches. Her stomach is feeling better again today, which is good. It's nearly eight a.m., and she's got a full day ahead of her.

◆ ◆ ◆

She spends the rest of the morning in her car. Parked two blocks down from the Miller house. Her phone running both camera feeds simultaneously, plugged into a battery pack to keep it going.

She isn't sure what she's going to do. Doesn't have much of a plan. Every so often she sees Grant on the cameras, moving around inside the house. Guy can't seem to sit still. She considers waiting until he leaves and then breaking in to search the place. Using the GPS tracker to make sure she's gone before he returns. Callie knows the police have already worked the house over, but if Grant really does have anything to do with Amy's disappearance then he would have covered his tracks.

Now it's different. He's been cleared as a suspect. He might have gotten sloppy, left something lying around he shouldn't have.

Callie cracks open her flask of coffee and takes a sip. It's bitter, the instant granules burnt. Still, it's better than nothing – and besides, she's got plenty of adrenaline to fuel her today. That early case buzz that always seems to kick in around now. Her body tingles with it. With the thrill of what might be to come. With the possibilities.

It's the second-best part of her job. The best, of course, being when she actually wraps a case up. When she snaps the perfect picture, records the killer conversation. Sometimes it's as mundane as tracking down the beneficiary of an estate. But there's a satisfaction to it all. To the closing of a file, to the opening of something new. A satisfaction that Callie never thought she'd find.

Growing up, Callie didn't give much thought to the future. When she was fifteen, she was in her fifth home and just about everyone around her – Callie included – was counting down the days until she could leave.

She'd never particularly excelled at school, never had an obvious career path like some of the other kids. At times it seemed like everyone but her was being handed out pointers; hints about what they could do and where they could go, and how they could use their skills – the ones who loved animals or tinkering with car engines or reading history books. With Callie, the only thing she'd ever been good at was surviving. An innate skill of being able to read someone and know instinctively whether to swing a punch or slip out of the room. A talent for lying in bed at night, listening to the sound of another kid crying and still managing to go to sleep.

But being able to blend into the background when needed served its purpose as she went through life. People talk when they don't think you're paying attention. When they underestimate you, they let their guard down. She would overhear things – comments from the older children, discussions between the adults, secrets told in whispers and glances – and it would give her a power of sorts. A shield, a layer of protection.

Not that she had it particularly rough. Like everyone else, she knew the stories. About the kids placed in houses, different houses, dark houses, where they'd lie awake at night listening for the sound of footsteps on the stairs. She'd even met a few of them growing up. Taken one look in their eyes and known how lucky she was.

But still. Just because you're not jamming a chair against your bedroom door every night doesn't mean you have it easy. Pain is relative. It's personal. It doesn't like to be pinned down.

Three hours in, things finally get moving.

Grant steps out of his front door, pulling on a coat. Callie can't tell for sure on the camera what kind of lock he's got, but it looks like a simple Yale. Those are good, she's popped them before. All she needs is a bit of plastic and a little slack in the door frame.

He's headed for his car. Callie has a choice. She weighs up the options as she watches him climb into the red Audi and start it up. She glances out her window at the streets around her. A little traffic and a pair of mums walking down the pavement pushing prams. It's not much, but it's probably too risky to try breaking into the house right now.

She loads her GPS tracker app and watches the pulsing blue dot moving slowly through the estate towards the main road. Callie sets down her coffee and starts up her Mini.

Chapter Eight

Callie follows him for nearly thirty minutes. Halfway, she realises where they're headed. Along Ferry Road, towards Seafield and the long row of car showrooms. Derek Leckie lives out this way. A little bungalow in Portobello, just a street back from the promenade. It's a nice house; Callie looked it up a few weeks ago. Too nice to afford on an Asda manager's salary, but Derek's wife is an accountant. Works long hours and spends every other weekend down in London. Maybe she didn't know her husband was cheating on her. Maybe she didn't care. Shit, maybe she was doing the dirty herself twice a month in some Kensington penthouse.

It's easy, tracking someone like this. Callie hangs five cars back. She doesn't try to jump the lights or take a hard corner. She lets the GPS do the hard work. When Grant finally pulls in, she parks at the end of the street. Winds down her window just enough to fit the zoom lens of her rented SLR through.

Grant seems wired. Antsy. It takes him a moment to work the gate; she wonders if his hands are shaking. Why is he coming here? Callie watches him pound on the door with a closed fist and she wonders how much she should let this play out. She's not sure she's prepared to watch Derek Leckie get his head kicked in just to maintain her cover.

The door opens. Amy's manager squints out at Grant. Callie almost doesn't recognise him with his trousers on. She brings her eye to the viewfinder and starts snapping pictures. At this distance it's impossible to hear what's being said, but thanks to the zoom lens she can make a pretty good guess.

Derek's face whitens.

You're Amy's husband.

Grant steps closer, his bulky frame nearly filling the doorway.

And you're the bastard who's been screwing her.

There's a sudden scuffle; Grant shoves Derek against the door. Callie jumps slightly. The camera skitters against the glass. She keeps taking pictures.

Through the viewfinder, the closing shutter gives everything a jerky, strobe-like effect. Derek raising his hands to his face. Grant grabbing him by the throat. A right hook to his stomach that Callie feels all over again.

Derek falls to the floor, out of shot. Callie snaps a picture of Grant hunched forward, both hands gripping the front door, his right heel mid-stomp. Again. Again.

'Jesus, he's going to kill him.'

Callie yanks the camera inside the car and dumps it on to the passenger seat. She starts the engine and pulls out, not checking her mirrors and nearly slamming into a passing car. The driver leans on the horn and yells at her.

Grant hears the commotion. Callie watches him slip away from the property, his head bowed. He's wise enough not to look over and show his face. Callie's not sure what she would have done if he'd spotted her.

By the time she gets over, the front door is closed and there's no sign of Derek Leckie. According to her phone, Grant's car is halfway along Seafield already. Guy must be doing fifty in his rush to get home.

She glances over at the door one last time. Debates going and knocking on it. To check if he's alright, to ask him some questions of her own. It's a strange move on Grant's part, coming here. It draws attention – and for what? To maintain the illusion that he doesn't know where she is? That he's a broken man, desperate to find his wife? Callie doesn't think Grant Miller is smart enough to play that game. Judging by the state of his clothes, he's barely smart enough to work the washing machine.

Callie drives back to her flat. Slow, letting herself manage the car almost on autopilot, her mind working it all over. She starts to think that maybe Grant Miller didn't have anything to do with Amy's disappearance. She starts to think that maybe she's lost focus, let this get personal. She told herself she was following her gut but her gut's bruised and bloodied, and half filled with preconceptions and notions of payback. She thinks back to her internet research. To that subreddit thread. What was it they called him?

The Night Watcher.

She knows it's time to take the blinkers off. To stop letting confirmation bias funnel her down the wrong path. She needs to set everything out properly and ask herself the big question: if Grant Miller didn't take Amy, then who did?

Chapter Nine

It feels good. Working the case like this. Working it proper.

Callie shifts the coffee table in the living room to one side and sits on the floor, cross-legged. She lays out everything she has so far in front of her. Most of it is from her initial investigation into Amy's affair. Information pulled from the internet and social media, an itinerary of her movements over the previous two weeks, photographs of her going about her days. Callie takes the pictures of Amy and Derek in the car together and puts them to one side, face down.

Derek Leckie is too obvious a suspect. So obvious that she's sure the police will have already spoken to him. It's the classic set-up: married man has affair with woman, woman threatens to tell man's wife, man strangles her to death to keep her quiet. Callie thinks back to the scuffle she witnessed earlier today. She flicks through the photos on the camera's screen. Derek barely puts up a defence, to the point where she wonders if the man has ever been in a fight before. It's not a criticism, most people haven't, but still, it's important. Does Derek seem like the type of person capable of killing a grown adult and getting rid of the body?

Callie smokes and drinks beer and makes notes. She scours social media, comes across a handful more posts about the Night Watcher. It's not much; the dedicated posting of a determined few. A list of missing women who apparently vanished under similar circumstances to Amy Miller. From their beds, as they slept. Women from all walks of life; some who had fallen on hard times, others who had struggles with addiction. She considers the moniker and the implications that it brings: that there is a person out there watching women, stalking women, then taking them and either keeping them prisoner or murdering them outright. A serial abductor – likely serial killer – stalking the streets of Edinburgh. It all just sounds a little far-fetched.

It gets late. By the time her stomach reminds her she hasn't eaten since breakfast, it's dark outside. She gets up to raid the kitchen for a ready meal and sways a little on the way through. Three bottles of Moretti is a lot on an empty stomach.

She eats microwaved katsu curry on the sofa. Watching the news, her legs drawn up beneath her. There's a story about Amy Miller. Nothing much, it's still too early for anything formal like a police conference. Instead a woman is speaking to a gaggle of reporters on the steps of Corstorphine station.

Callie recognises the woman. It's the officer who emerged from the Miller house. DS Reid's partner. The caption says her name is DI Sandra Dawson. She has an unfortunate hard look about her that Callie cannot pin down. A sharpness around her mouth, perhaps. It's a feature not helped by her hair: a fiercely cut bob that stops just below her ears.

'We're still in the preliminary stages of our investigation,' she says. Her voice is slow and steady, no-nonsense. She glares at the reporters in front of her. 'We're currently asking for members of the public to come forward if they have any information that may be of assistance.'

Cameras flash. The air is filled with the constant clicks of their shutters. Someone asks whether the police think Amy left on her own or if there's any evidence that she was taken during the night.

Dawson purses her lips for a moment before speaking. 'There are a number of theories that we're presently working on,' the detective says carefully. 'Nothing has been ruled out at this point.'

The news moves on. Callie slides rubbery chicken around her plate, suddenly not hungry. Her mobile rings from underneath a pile of papers. When she finally finds it, she stares at the name on the screen – Richard – and debates whether or not to answer.

Chapter Ten

'I've been roasting this lamb all day,' Richard says, bending to squint at the open pot inside his oven. 'It should be just about ready to eat with a spoon.'

Callie sits at his dining room table and takes a drink of red wine. 'It does smell good,' she says. 'I've not had a proper home-cooked meal in a while now.'

'Well then,' Richard says, drifting over towards the table and refilling his glass, 'allow me to change that.'

He smiles and offers to top hers up too. She shakes her head. The wine is nice, but she wants to make sure she's fully present tonight. Not because she thinks he'll try anything, more because she doesn't want to do anything she'll later regret.

Like coming here for dinner, for instance. Richard's call the previous evening caught her at a moment of weakness. Slightly tipsy, with glimpses into a missing woman's rather depressing life scattered across her living-room floor. Then, after agreeing to give him another chance, she woke up this morning with a heavy feeling on her chest. Booze or regret, or maybe both. The rest of the day was spent wondering whether she should cancel tonight or just get it over with. A (very) small part of her trying to rationalise that she had nothing to lose.

Maybe that part of her was right. Maybe Richard would win her round. Callie considers this will likely be difficult, however. She can still see him, standing outside her front door, ordering her to lift up her shirt.

'So tell me,' Richard says, returning to the cooker to stir frozen peas into a pan sizzling with garlic and pancetta, 'how's your work going?'

'It's going alright,' Callie says, a little warily. 'I guess it's like any other job, you know? It has its ups and downs.'

'Such an interesting profession. Do you prefer the term "private investigator" or "private detective"?'

'"Investigator", I think. "Detective" makes me sound like a cop.'

'Did you ever want to be a cop?'

'God, no. I didn't want to be anything.'

'Not much inspiration where you grew up, I imagine.'

It's an off-hand comment, and honestly Callie doesn't think he means anything by it. She makes a non-committal noise and takes a sip of wine.

Richard looks over and says, 'What was it really like? Growing up in the foster system, I mean.'

'It was difficult sometimes. There wasn't much stability. Most houses I stayed in were crowded and noisy. There wasn't any privacy. Just trying to do your schoolwork was a nightmare.'

'Sounds like living with my brothers.'

Callie stares into her glass. She can see them, even now. The ghosts of the other children.

'Everyone was just hanging on, you know? Until they turned sixteen and they could leave, get out into the world. Nobody really had much aspiration beyond that.'

'Do you mind me asking why you were there? I mean, what happened to your parents?'

'You're very inquisitive tonight,' Callie says, keeping her tone light. 'Did you ever want to be a cop?'

Richard laughs. 'I don't think I would last five seconds as a police officer. Honestly, the shit they have to deal with? I'd end up throwing half of Edinburgh in jail.' He bends down to check the flame on the hob. 'What's going on with that woman, anyway?'

'What woman?'

'The one you were looking into. Amy Miller.' He straightens up and looks over. 'Have they found her yet?'

Callie shakes her head. 'I was reading a theory about it online. Apparently there's a serial killer out there, stalking women. Goes by the name of the Night Watcher.'

'Oh really? Seems a little . . .'

'Far-fetched?'

Richard shrugs, turns to the island and begins drizzling olive oil on to a green salad. 'I was going to say too simple.'

'I don't follow.'

Richard pauses, sets the bottle of oil down. 'You know about my mum. My dad would hit her, for the slightest thing he'd hit her, and he'd taunt her while he did it. He'd tell her to leave if she hated him so much.' He falters a little, staring into the salad bowl. 'And I used to look back and think why the fuck did you stay? And of course, it was for me. She stayed for me.'

'Richard, I didn't mean to—'

'I just think people get caught up in violence for so many reasons, you know? Maybe they get trapped. Or maybe they look the wrong way at some random psycho on the bus home. But mainly? Mainly I think they choose it for themselves.' He sighs and shakes his head, then turns and looks at her. He laughs awkwardly. 'Sorry, that got a bit heavy.'

'It's fine. It's . . . interesting.'

'Well, enough of my rambling for the time being. Would you mind setting the table? Dinner's just about ready.'

As predicted by the smell, Richard's cooking is excellent.

She sits back in her chair and lets out a contented sigh. Richard – mopping up his plate with a piece of bread – laughs. He is clearly delighted that she has enjoyed her dinner so much. Callie knows that he has pulled out all the stops for her tonight. An expensive cut of lamb and a full day spent prepping it. If she had a single criticism it's that the joint was overcooked, the meat far too dry, but plenty of gravy and the creamy-cheese sauce of the dauphinoise potatoes covered it well. And besides, it didn't take away from the effort. He even bought her favourite ice cream for dessert, and from her favourite place, too; the delightfully named Joelato, a little venture that she first discovered during lockdown.

'I never knew you were such a good cook,' Callie says.

'There's a lot about me you don't know,' Richard says.

'Is that right?'

'Oh, absolutely.'

Callie lifts her glass and finally finishes her wine. She watches Richard refill it. The part of her from before, the part with doubts, is starting to fade into the background.

'So tell me,' she says.

Richard stretches out in his seat and smiles. 'Let's see. I used to play ultimate frisbee at university.'

'You played ultimate frisbee?'

'Well, I went to a couple of meet-ups.'

'In the pub?'

'I think we had beers on the field once.'

'Uh-huh. What else.'

'I was deputy head boy at high school.'

Callie snorts. 'That sounds about right.'

Richard watches her now, his mouth moving like he's working out how to phrase what's coming next. Or maybe he's just got a piece of lamb stuck in his teeth.

'I really am sorry about the other night,' he says at last. 'I swear, I'm not normally like that.'

Callie lowers her glass and cradles it in her lap. It's her turn to watch Richard now. For the meaning behind the words, for the truth in his eyes. She knew this conversation was coming at some point tonight, of course she did. If he hadn't brought it up she was planning to herself. Does he get credit for being the one to raise it? Maybe. She's not sure.

'I didn't like being accosted on my doorstep in the dark,' she says quietly. 'That sort of shit can't happen anymore.'

'I know,' he says. 'Believe me, I know. You want the truth?'

'Always.'

'I was upset.'

Callie shifts in her seat and her stomach tenses slightly. A strand of reddish hair falls loose, tickling her cheek. 'With me?'

'Yes.'

'Because I cancelled on you?'

'You cancelled on me at the last minute, Callie. Like, the literal last minute. They were showing the trailers.' Richard sniffs and sets his glass down on the table, hunching forward. 'I didn't go and see it, by the way. I just went home. I'd paid for the tickets and everything. And then when I saw on the news the next day about that missing woman . . .'

'Amy Miller.'

'When I saw about her, and I remembered what you'd said about her husband, that he was a drunk and a brute—'

'I didn't call him a brute—'

'Something like that. Anyway, that's not the point. The point is I was concerned and I couldn't get hold of you, and I swear I hadn't been hanging out at your door or anything. I was worried, that's all. And I think I was probably right to be, wasn't I?'

His eyes move to her stomach. Callie imagines he can see the bruising, even through her clothes. Perhaps in his head it's worse. She knows how he must see her now: as a woman who needs saving. As a stand-in for his mother. For every female victim of assault or domestic abuse.

She reaches over and takes his hand.

'I get it,' Callie says. 'And for whatever it's worth, I am sorry for cancelling on you. That would've annoyed me as well. I'm not the best communicator sometimes, but you need to know that in my line of work, I don't always work office hours.'

'Something for us both to work on, then?'

'Yeah, I guess so.'

Richard smiles broadly and sinks back a little, exhaling loudly. 'So, a fresh start?'

'That depends on what flavour of ice cream you've got in the freezer.'

'Stracciatella.'

Callie raises her glass. 'Fresh start,' she says. 'I just need to go use the bathroom.'

'Great, I'll get some bowls and meet you in the living room.'

Callie gets up from the table and leaves the room. She can hear Richard in the kitchen, opening a fresh bottle of wine. She feels a little better than she'd been expecting to, after that. She wonders if tonight has been a big step for them – for her. Setting boundaries, accepting flaws. She wonders if it's time to lower her defences, just a touch, and let Richard in a little more.

Things change in the bathroom. She is standing at the sink when it happens. She is washing her hands, checking her teeth in the mirror, letting her eyes drift around the room. Fancy glass walk-in shower; large green plant by the door. And there, in the corner of the room, a washing basket. One of Richard's shirts must be near the top, as a white sleeve is hanging over the rim.

A white sleeve covered in blood.

Callie pulls out her phone and loads up the camera feed from Grant Miller's house. She knows what to expect as she scrubs through the footage. Deep in the pit of her gut she knows, and yet still the violence somehow catches her off guard.

She sinks against the glass shower screen, one hand over her mouth, one hand gripping her phone, shaking. With shock, with rage, with wild fury.

Chapter Eleven

'You fucking psycho.'

Richard looks up sharply. He's bent over the kitchen counter, scooping ice cream into bowls. A look of confusion on his face as he watches Callie burst back into the room.

'What?'

Callie holds up the bloodied shirt. She sees Richard's eyes go to it, sees understanding dawn.

'You went through my washing?'

'You did a shit job of hiding the evidence.'

'What are you talking about?'

Callie throws the shirt at him. He drops the ice cream scoop and catches it awkwardly. The stained sleeve hangs down from his arm.

'Don't lie to me,' she says, her voice low, her words rippling with fury. She's so angry she can barely keep it together. 'Where's my fucking coat.'

'You're leaving?'

'Of course I'm leaving!'

'Can you let me explain?'

But Callie can barely hear him. She roams the small, trendy flat, hunting out her belongings. Coat, bag, shoes. Putting them on feels like armour. Against Richard, against the world.

He talks as she dresses. 'It's wine, Callie. Do you hear me? It's red wine. I spilled a bottle of it all over myself yesterday when I was cooking. Look, I still have the empty bottle somewhere.'

Callie listens to his protests. Or, at least, she does a good job of pretending. She watches his mouth move, his hands gesticulating wildly. Towards the end he points at the recycling box in the corner of the room.

She waits until he's finished, then pulls out her phone. Without saying a word, she repeats the exact same steps she did just a few minutes ago. When she was in Richard's bachelor-pad bathroom, all glass and polished chrome. When that horrible, sick feeling was building inside her. The feeling that she was being played, that he was taking her for a fool – no, worse, that she was a fool. For believing him, for giving him a second chance, for not trusting her gut.

She presses play on the footage again. Richard frowns at her phone – his face cycling through a range of emotions as realisation dawns. Bemusement, concern, and finally, resignation.

Callie lets the video play. She turns the volume up.

Together they watch Richard hammer on Grant Miller's back door. He uses his left hand; the right he keeps down by his side, twisted slightly in a way so it never quite happens to be in shot. But when Grant answers the door – wearing that same godawful stained jumper – it becomes obvious what Richard's holding.

A metal wheel wrench.

He swings it upwards; a glancing blow, but with enough force to knock Grant backwards. Richard follows it up with a better-aimed jab. Grant crumples.

'That's enough,' Richard says. Here, now, in the kitchen.

Grunts from the phone as he continues swinging the wrench. Grant is a huddled, pixelated mess on the floor. He has stopped crying out. At this distance, all the camera can pick up is the occasional *thwump* as the hard metal hits soft flesh.

'I said that's enough!' Richard shouts. He hurls the ice cream scoop across the room. It crashes into a lamp. The flat darkens.

Callie pockets the phone silently. 'How did you know what he'd done?' she asks him.

Richard stares at her. He is panting, standing there. His face red, his chest heaving, his eyes wild. That little curve of skin above his right eye pulses like crazy. He's like a cornered beast.

'Richard?'

'I went to The Marksman,' he says. 'Barman told me what happened.'

'And you thought you'd teach him a lesson? On my behalf?'

'I did it for you, you ungrateful . . .'

He trails off. His hands are trembling.

'Finish the sentence, Richard,' Callie says coolly. She steps forward. Feels the old familiar heat flooding through her. 'You ungrateful what? Bitch? Is that what I am? An ungrateful bitch? How about a mad cow, hmm? Or maybe I'm a silly, stupid cunt?'

She drives the last word home. Hard enough to make Richard flinch.

'Did the barman tell you what I did to Grant Miller?' she asks. 'Did he tell you how I already handled it?'

'He said you gave him as good as he got.'

'But you wanted to give him better. Because you think you are better, don't you, Richard.'

'Listen, Callie—'

'No thanks. Delete my number from your phone. Don't ever come round to my house again. If I see you in my street I'll call the police.'

She storms out of the kitchen. Throws open the front door before turning round to add, 'For your sake, you better hope Grant Miller isn't dead. And by the way, your lamb was dry as fuck, you silly, stupid cunt.'

Chapter Twelve

Callie lights up and drives fast. Window down. The wind making her eyes stream while her lungs fill with warm, wonderful smoke. She knows it's bad for her, but since when has that ever stopped anyone? And besides, maybe that's why she likes it.

She's glad she only had the one glass of wine. Figures she's probably still over the limit – you can barely look at a beer without being over the limit these days in Scotland – but it'll be close. Tight enough to have dropped back under by the time a doctor takes her bloods. Worth the risk, in other words, tonight of all nights.

Richard's flat is near Haymarket. One of those fancy new apartments in the old deaf school. This time of night, she makes the drive to Corstorphine in just under ten minutes. Each one of them playing out a different future in her head. Grant Miller bleeding out on his kitchen floor. Detectives knocking on Richard's door. Grant waking up and following Richard home one night before breaking his legs.

If Callie's honest with herself, she doesn't really know why she's this worried. About Grant Miller of all people. Richard said she'd called him a brute and she can't remember saying that, but that doesn't mean it's not true. Grant is a brute, and she's still got the bruises to prove it.

Maybe it all comes back to the labels: wife, adulterer, victim. Maybe Amy Miller isn't the only person to have these labels. Maybe she's not the only victim in all this.

Callie is convinced she knows what sort of person Grant is, but people have been just as convinced about her all her life. It churns her up sometimes. As a kid, staring through the banister rails at the top of the stairs, listening to the adults talk about her as if they knew her – as if they really knew her.

She's a tricky one.

You need to be careful with her.

Talking about her like she was livestock. Like she was property. And she was, in a way. Callie was never sure how much each foster family got paid to look after her, but it must have been a lot. The dads would always drive the nicest cars.

The Miller house is dark when she arrives. No lights, the curtains drawn. Callie parks her Mini outside. It has started to rain; an old man in the distance carries an umbrella.

She rings the doorbell. Gives it a few moments, then rings it again. She lifts the letterbox flap and peers through, but all she can make out is the warped glass of a vestibule door. She pictures Grant lying face down somewhere, and debates yelling his name before she tries the handle.

The door swings open. Callie steps inside, carefully, like it is an old tomb lined with traps. There is light beyond the patterned glass. Twisted and refracted; coming from the kitchen, perhaps. Spilling out into the hallway ahead of her.

She pushes open the second door and calls Grant's name. Nothing. She moves deeper into the house, towards the light. Still announcing herself, babbling near-nonsense about who she is and why she's here – anything to create some kind of noise in this deathly quiet space.

By the time she nears the light – which is the kitchen – she can finally hear something. A faint, rapid, gasping sound. Callie quickens her pace and turns, blinking, into the room.

Grant Miller is sitting on the floor. Propped up against the oven. His hands in his lap, his head rocking to one side. Dried blood covers his chest, his arms, his legs. It is splashed up the walls and speckled across the cabinets. Callie can tell from the blood trail left behind that he has dragged himself here from the back door.

But it is Grant's face that is the worst. His forehead is split open. One eye has already started to swell shut. His nose is off at one angle, and Callie realises that was probably her, and all of a sudden she feels like an asshole. The man's breathing is coming in quick, shallow spurts. His good eye is staring at her in disbelief.

'The fuck . . .' he mumbles.

Callie looks around the room for a dishcloth. Finds one draped on a small plastic hook by the sink. She grabs it and runs it under the tap, waiting until the water goes warm. When she is close enough, Grant reaches out and snatches it from her.

'I'll do it,' he says.

'We need to get you to a hospital,' Callie says. 'You've lost a lot of blood.'

'No. No hospital.'

'Grant—'

'No fucking hospital!'

She holds her hands up in defeat. 'Can I at least do something about that cut in your forehead? Do you have any superglue?'

Grant glares at her for a moment, then nods out of the room. 'Bathroom,' he says.

Callie leaves, going back into the darkened hallway. She turns on lights as she goes. The place is a mess. Either the Millers have been living in squalor or the SOCOs did a real number on it.

She finds the bathroom, and locates a little tube of superglue in the bottom drawer. Digging through the cabinet, she takes out packets of paracetamol and ibuprofen as well. Pops a couple of tablets from their foil wrappers into her palm as she returns to the kitchen. Grant is still sitting where she left him, but he's mopped up some of the blood from his face. The dishcloth is dripping with red.

'Here,' Callie says. She hands him the pills and checks cupboards for glasses, fills one and hands him that, too. Then she rinses out the cloth. It takes a long while for the water to go clear.

'Help me up,' Grant says. 'I'm going to bed.'

'Wait,' she tells him. 'And hold still.'

She crouches down beside him and carefully runs a thin line of glue along the split in his forehead. Then, ignoring his moans of protest, she forces the skin together and holds it in place. A trick she picked up in her third house, after a girl ran a breadknife across her own forearm. As a cry for help it went largely unanswered – an older boy glued the wound closed, saving their foster parents an awkward trip to the hospital and earning himself an extended curfew in the process. Poor guy barely got to use it in the end; the girl stepped into traffic six weeks later and finished the job.

'Not my finest work,' she mutters, 'but it should do.'

'Fine, now help me up.'

'Is there anyone I can call?'

'Just help me to bed and then fuck off.'

Callie shifts her balance as Grant puts an arm awkwardly over her shoulders. She stands slowly, tensing, and together they start to hobble out of the room.

It takes them nearly a full minute to navigate through the small house to the bedroom. Thankfully it's on the ground floor; Callie doesn't know how they would have managed the stairs.

Once inside, Grant falls away from her with a grunt and collapses on to the bed. He leaves behind a smear of red down her blouse. *That's two outfits ruined with his blood*, she thinks to herself.

The room itself is freezing. Callie can feel goosebumps catch across the tops of her arms. She glances at the window. A small square of cardboard is taped across one pane.

'You can go now,' Grant grunts, rolling on to his back. 'I'll be fine in the morning.'

'What happened to your window?' Callie asks.

'What?'

'Your window.' She gestures towards it, but when she glances down at Grant she can see he's already falling asleep. Or at least she hopes it's sleep.

'Nothing happened,' he murmurs, his breathing slowing and becoming deeper. 'They told me not to say anything.'

Callie frowns. 'Who told you?'

'Nobody.'

'Grant? Who told you?'

But he's gone. His eyes are shut, and only one of them on purpose. She leans down and presses two fingers against his stubbled throat. Satisfied that he isn't dying, she straightens up and stares at the patch of cardboard.

She crosses the room towards it. Clearly it wasn't fitted by anyone official. The edges are roughly torn, the Sellotape clumsily applied. One corner of it is loose and jutting open. Callie takes hold of it and lifts the square away, revealing what appears to be a perfectly cut circle in the glass.

'Someone broke in here,' she says quietly to herself. She thinks of the internet forums. She thinks of the Night Watcher. She

63

thinks back to yesterday's news report. DI Sandra Dawson glaring at reporters from her station's steps. One of them asked if Amy Miller was taken in the night. How did Dawson respond to that again? *A number of theories.*

The police never mentioned the window. Why would they ask Grant to keep it quiet?

The question stays with her. As she securely re-tapes the cardboard, as she quietly leaves the house through the back door. She goes to the shed at the bottom of the garden and retrieves the hidden camera. The GPS tracker from the red Audi, too. Crossing the road to the junction box, she glances around to make sure she's alone and then pulls up the second camera.

She's dumping it all in the boot of her car when she's struck by an idea. One born from her constant worry about a neighbour seeing her sneaking around the Miller residence at night. Callie turns slowly and studies the front of each house in the street. Nearly all of them have a doorbell camera.

No doubt the police have already asked for the footage, but Callie has the distinct impression that the police know more than they're letting on. And maybe there's a perfectly good reason for that – in fact, there's almost certainly a good reason for that – but Callie is intrigued now. She's invested in this. She needs to see it through.

She closes the boot of her Mini and heads towards the first house.

Chapter Thirteen

Of the three houses closest to the Miller residence, Callie only finds success at one. The neighbour across the street to the right isn't in – or isn't answering – while the old man directly opposite tells Callie to get lost before he 'calls the cops', as though they have somehow been transported to a crime-riddled American city. An unfortunate attitude, given the view his Ring doorbell must have.

The young woman who lives next door is more helpful. She's happy to show Callie the recordings from her doorbell camera. A little too happy, maybe. From her wide eyes and excited chatter, she's clearly rather caught up in everything. Callie gets the impression it's all she's talked about ever since the police strung tape around her neighbour's front garden. Probably took the day off work to go stand next to it. Callie swallows down her instinctual indignation.

They watch it together, stood on the woman's front step. It's a series of clips. The doorbell camera is motion-activated, and it must have a hair trigger because it's recorded everything. Twenty-four hours of slow estate living. Callie swears one video is of a plastic bag blowing down the street. She asks if she can take a copy of it all, and of course the woman agrees. Knows exactly how to share the footage, too. Says the police helped her do it the previous day.

Later, at home, Callie sits and watches it again on her laptop. Slowly this time. Noting down everything the camera picks up in case it's important. She smokes as she goes through it. Hunched forward, cigarette dangling, lips parting just enough to blow out smoke.

She's halfway through her second cigarette when she spots it. A white Volvo driving into the estate a little after one a.m. the night Amy Miller went missing. Forty-five minutes later it drives back out. Might be nothing, but Callie isn't taking any chances. She notes down the registration and sends it to Martin, along with a request for an owner check.

In the time it takes to finish her cigarette, Martin texts back.

Vehicle belongs to Philip Joyce. Just what have you gotten yourself involved in?

Callie, frowning, grinds the cigarette butt out. She types the name into Google.

'Holy shit,' she says.

Chapter Fourteen

DS Mackenzie Reid drives a blue VW Golf. It has an outdated tax sticker on the windscreen and a long dent across the driver's-side door. Callie watches it pull into the police station car park.

It's another early start. Not quite The Marksman early, but still. Early enough. She takes long, slow drags on her second cigarette of the day. She shivers in the cold morning air. She wraps her arms around herself and stamps her feet to keep warm.

DS Reid gets halfway to the station door before he spots her. Callie sees surprised recognition on his face.

'Callie Munro,' he says as he nears. 'How are you?'

'Cold. You?'

The detective grins. He's wearing a long, woollen overcoat that's buttoned up to his neck, and a pair of leather gloves. 'If you're looking to keep warm, I'd recommend layers rather than inhaling hot smoke.'

'Yes, but then where would I get my cancer?'

He frowns. 'What can I help you with today?'

'Can we talk inside?'

'Sure.'

Callie tosses the remainder of her cigarette as she follows him in. The waiting room is empty. Reid nods to the man behind the front desk and pushes through the double doors. He leads her through the same narrow, twisty corridor as last time, pulling off his coat and gloves as he walks.

'Is this to do with Amy Miller?' he asks.

'Yes,' she says. 'I've uncovered something I want to run past you.'

'You're working the case?'

'You sound surprised.'

He shrugs. 'Just figured you'd want to put some distance between it, after what happened with her husband.'

DS Reid is referring to the altercation at The Marksman. He doesn't yet know about Richard's assault on Grant. Callie briefly wonders if Grant will report it, then decides she doesn't care if he does.

Inside the main office, nothing much has changed. The same messy desks, the same badly mounted TV showing BBC News. Reid motions for her to sit down. He throws his coat and gloves over the back of his chair.

'Can I get you a coffee?'

'Is it still instant?'

The detective pulls open a drawer and rummages around. 'It is for most people. But for you . . .' He holds up a couple of small pods. 'I would be happy to grant access to the Nespresso machine.'

Callie smiles. 'Go on then.'

'Milk, sugar?'

'Just milk, please.'

When Reid returns a few minutes later, he brings with him two flat whites. He places one down on the desk in front of her.

'Thank you, DS Reid,' she says.

'Call me Mac,' he says. 'And you're welcome.'

From a desk off to one side, an older man leans over and shouts, 'Hey, Mac! How come you never let me use your fancy Nespresso machine?'

'Because you hate coffee, Neil.'

'Aye, right enough,' the man says, giving Callie a wink as he turns away.

Reid – Mac – settles down into his chair. His face has flushed a little. 'Alright,' he says, taking a sip. 'So what's this all about, then?'

'Philip Joyce.'

The detective frowns. 'What about him?'

Callie reaches into her bag and pulls out a couple of sheets of folded paper. She passes them over for Mac to open.

'Yesterday, I spoke with one of the Millers' neighbours,' she says. 'I was able to obtain a copy of her doorbell camera footage.'

'Yes, we've already seen it,' Mac says, unfolding the pages. He looks down at the printouts. The white Volvo, entering and exiting the estate. He smooths the paper flat with his palm.

Callie asks, 'Did you run that registration number?'

'Did you?'

'Of course not. Private investigators don't have access to the DVLA.'

'Uh-huh.'

'But I have a contact . . .'

Mac snorts and leans back in his chair. 'Let's skip ahead here, Callie. You want to know whether or not we followed up on this vehicle.'

'I want to know why your chief inspector was hanging out in Amy Miller's estate for nearly an hour the night she went missing.'

She holds his gaze until he turns away. From under a pile of papers he pulls out his notebook and starts flicking through it. She takes a sip of coffee. It's delicious.

'Alright, let me see . . .' Mac sets his notebook down and taps at a page. 'My partner raised this with Chief Inspector Joyce when we came across his car on the doorbell footage.'

'Your partner? DI Dawson?'

'That's right.'

'And what did Joyce say?'

'His wife was driving the vehicle. They have friends in the estate, she was giving them a lift home.'

'Did it take her forty-five minutes to find the right house?'

'They invited her in, she had a cup of tea.' The detective closes the notebook. 'I get it. On the surface, it seems like something. But it's not.'

'Did DI Dawson speak with Joyce's wife?'

'No. I did. And before you ask – yes, she corroborated his statement, down to the letter.'

'What about the friends? Did you speak with them?'

Mac moves his coffee to one side and leans towards her. 'I didn't have any reason to,' he says. 'I know the chief inspector, Callie. I know his wife. Trust me, this is a red herring.'

Callie takes another sip. Maybe he's right. Still, Joyce wouldn't be the first police officer to be involved in something like this. Not by a goddamn long shot.

'Fine,' she says, mentally making a note to follow up on the lead herself when she leaves. 'But there's something else I wanted to ask.'

'Ask away,' Mac says, picking up his coffee.

'The glass.'

Mac pauses, the coffee halfway to his mouth. He sets it down. 'What glass.'

Callie feels the atmosphere change. In the detective's body language, in the lack of inflection in his question. 'The bedroom window at the Miller house,' she says. 'There was a perfect circle cut into the glass. Someone told Grant to keep it quiet. Was that you?'

For a long moment, Callie thinks she's not going to get an answer. Then Mac gets to his feet. He lifts his coat.

'Come with me,' he says.

Chapter Fifteen

He leads her outside. Back through the twisty corridor, back through the station's main entrance. Pulling on his coat as they go. Holding the door open for a passing colleague with a tight smile.

The whole time, he doesn't speak. Not when they're going down the main steps, not when they're moving across the car park towards his blue Golf. The hazards flash as he unlocks it.

'Get in,' he says.

'What is—'

'Trust me.'

He climbs in without waiting for her answer. Callie glances around, though she's unsure what she's looking for, then follows. She reaches for her seat belt and Mac stops her.

'Don't worry, we're not going anywhere.'

'Then what the hell am I doing here?'

'I just didn't want to talk in there.'

'In the station?'

Mac looks at her dead on. 'How did you know about the glass?'

'Am I not meant to know about it?'

'You can't tell anyone. Not yet.'

'Why not?'

'I need to know how you found out.'

'I saw it. I asked Grant about it. Why wasn't he supposed to tell anyone?'

'You were in his house?'

'Jesus, Mac. It's a long story. Nearly as long as this one. Can we move things along?'

Callie glares at the young detective. He sinks back and props his elbow against the door rest, rubbing at his forehead.

'What I'm about to tell you can't leave this car,' he says. 'Do you understand?'

'Yes – fucking yes,' Callie snaps. 'Hurry up with it.'

'We decided to keep certain parts of Amy Miller's disappearance quiet from the media,' Mac says. 'The circular hole in the bedroom window is one example.'

'Why?'

'A couple of reasons. Mainly it's good to keep something in your pocket to rule people out. If they know about the window, it legitimises them as a suspect.'

'We've all seen *Line of Duty*, Mac. That's Police Work 101. You didn't need to drag me to your car to tell me that. Why am I really here?'

'Because . . . the method used to access Amy Miller's bedroom? This isn't the first time we've encountered it.'

Callie blinks. It takes her a moment to work through what he's telling her. When it does, she feels the awful knowledge in her chest. A physical weight.

'Jesus Christ,' she says. 'The fucking Night Watcher is real?'

'God I hate that name.'

'But this has happened before?'

'Yes.'

'How many times?'

'Two before now. Amy Miller makes three.'

'All women? All missing?'

'All women, all missing.'

'How long a period are we talking about here, Mac?'

The detective glances out the windscreen. Callie can see the turmoil on his face. He's wondering how much he should tell her, how much he should keep back. Shit, the guy's in this deep already, he might as well go all the way.

'We think the first victim was taken just over eighteen months ago,' he says.

'Eighteen months?'

'That's right.'

'Do you have any idea if Amy is still alive?'

'This long since her abduction, and given the other women, our working theory is that she's dead.'

Callie closes her eyes. The weight in her chest intensifies. It wants to drag her into the footwell, curled up in a little ball. 'Just so I'm clear on all this,' she says, 'are we talking about what I think we are?'

'Depends what you think we're talking about.'

'A serial killer.'

'In my view? Yes.'

'In your view?'

'Not everyone in the department agrees. The idea that this man, this . . . Night Watcher is really out there, most people refuse to see it.' Mac gives one final glance around the car park, then reaches for the door handle. He pops open the door and freezing air rushes inside. 'But that's where you come in.'

'What?'

She's climbing out now, too. Meeting his gaze across the roof of the Golf.

He smiles sadly at her. 'I need help on this. Someone who can follow up on this theory without drawing the department's suspicion.'

'And you think that someone is me?'

'Callie, you're already working the case. All I'm offering is my support.'

'Unofficially.'

'Unofficially. If you're in, I'll get you copies of our files on the other missing women. If not, then we never have to see each other again.'

He almost makes it sound like she has some sort of choice.

You are filth.

You peel dirty gloves from your swollen, red hands. Gloves caked in grime and sludge and foul-smelling matter. Thin gloves, useless gloves. Another rip in the plastic; a putrid smear and a band of thick, black hair coiled around your fingers. You wash it all away under scalding water but the feeling remains. Around your knuckles, the skin is blistered and cracked.

You are trapped.

It is nearly four a.m. and you have barely even started. You push a trolley with a broken wheel down a brightly lit corridor. Another cubicle, another pair of gloves. Another coating of muck. It makes you gag, this stench. You fight to keep it down but today it is too much, today you are too weak and you vomit thin, stringy bile into the toilet, the toilet you just cleaned and now must clean again.

You are a day drinker.

You hide it well. From your co-workers, from your family. You sneak it into coffee cups and half-empty cans of Coke. You empty water bottles and refill them with clear spirits. Your pockets bulge with mints, your car's glove compartment is stocked with Listerine. When you finally arrive home it is morning, and as your children eat breakfast in front of the TV you take a shower, swallowing mouthfuls of vodka from your shampoo bottle.

You are not alone.

You think you are. You feel like you are. And later – much later – you will wish that you were. Crawling into bed, you do not notice the man stood across the street. You did not notice him on your drive home, and you did not notice him sat in his car outside your work. You did not notice him yesterday, or the day before that, or the day before that.

You are awake.

A breeze on your skin even though the window is closed. The curtains swell with it, drifting apart at the peak to let in a sliver of daylight. Over and over, this rhythmic movement. You lie with your eyes closed and listen to the sound of it. The rustle of fabric against the radiator as the curtains rise and fall. The wind, growing and fading with each passing moment. It almost sounds like a ventilator machine, or perhaps a desk fan, oscillating back and forth. It almost sounds like someone is standing over your bed, breathing heavily.

Chapter Sixteen

Callie's head buzzes. It feels like it's filled with static. Sitting in her car, trying to remember how to start the engine, Mac's words swirling around inside her.

Three women.

Three women who were taken from their beds as they slept. Three women over a period of eighteen months. She knows Mac is probably right. The chances of whoever took them going to the effort of keeping them alive all this time is slim to none. Wherever these women are, Callie knows they're most likely dead.

It's an info dump almost too big to process. Callie pulls out of the station car park on autopilot. She needs to focus on something else right now, at least until Mac sends her the files on the missing women. Once she has them, everything else will go on pause. She can feel it, the pull of it. The secrets and the lies, the connections, the coincidences. She'll sink into this case completely.

But not yet.

She's driving the route before she even realises where she's going. Pulling up at the Corstorphine estate. Knocking on Grant Miller's front door. After an age he answers, squinting a little through the chain gap.

'What the hell are you doing here?'

'I wanted to see how you were getting on.'

'Did you fuck.'

'Can I come in?'

Grant stares at her for a long moment. In the sliver between the door and the frame, Callie struggles to get a read on him. The hallway behind him is dark, and the sun is on the wrong side of the house. All she can really see are his eyes. Bloodshot and glassy, like they'd been at The Marksman. She wonders if he's been drinking this morning.

'Fuck off,' he says, and closes the door.

Callie can hear his footsteps walking away, heavy and slow. She says, 'I know about the window,' and they stop. A long heartbeat later, they return.

The door opens a crack. Grant's face at the chain gap once more, those red eyes wide. 'What did you say?'

'I said I know about the window. He uses a glass cutter to get inside. Detectives told you to keep it quiet. You know why?'

'I know why.'

'Then let me in so we can talk.'

He makes tea. Asda's own brand with not enough milk. They sit at the kitchen island, across from one another, and Callie tries not to overthink how strange it is to be sitting here, drinking tea with the man who sucker-punched her less than a week ago.

Grant sniffs and shifts his weight on his stool. He's looking better this morning. The swelling on his eye has reduced. Amazing what a shower and a set of clean clothes can do.

He reaches up and taps at the superglued cut on his forehead. It will likely leave an ugly scar. 'Neat trick,' he says gruffly. 'Where'd you learn to do that?'

Callie cradles her mug. The heat begins to burn her palms but she doesn't move them. 'I grew up in foster care,' she says, a little surprised at how easily she answers him. 'We learned pretty quick how to fend for ourselves.'

'Foster care? Shit. Is it as bad as they make it out on TV?'

'Some of it.' Callie finally lifts her tea and blows steam off the surface. 'Some of it is worse.'

'How'd you end up there then?'

Callie starts to deflect the question, reaching for her stock response. Then she figures *screw it*, and says, 'My folks abandoned me at a homeless shelter when I was a baby.'

Grant's eyebrows lift a little. 'Seriously?'

'They left me on the doorstep and rang the bell.'

'Jesus. You ever track them down?'

'It's why I became a private investigator.'

'And?'

Callie shakes her head. 'Nothing. I don't know if I was registered, I don't know if I was born in a hospital. I don't know what I don't know.'

'What about the – what did you say it was? – a homeless shelter?'

'It was a long time ago, Grant. They didn't keep the best records. I thought I got close once, but . . .'

She lapses into silence, a lump forming in her throat. She takes a sip of tea to swallow it down.

Grant lets out a grunt. 'Listen,' he says. 'About the other day. I shouldn't have, you know . . .'

'Can we not talk about that right now?'

'Fine. Let's talk about Amy instead.'

Callie takes another sip of tea and nods. She pulls out a notebook and pen from her pocket and sets them down on the island. 'Tell me about the night she was taken.'

'Not much to tell, really.' Grant sniffs again, wipes his palm across his mouth. 'I was working my usual night shift at the youth hostel, then I went for a couple beers at The Marksman.'

'I remember. After that?'

'I went home.'

'What time did you get home?'

'About nine-thirty, ten a.m.'

'Were you expecting Amy to be here?'

Grant shakes his head. 'No, she's usually gone to work by the time I get back. But it was obvious something wasn't right. The place was a mess, you know?'

'Like there'd been a fight?'

'Yeah. Her bedside drawers were overturned and there was a crack in the wardrobe mirror.'

Callie makes a note of everything Grant says. She mentally chides herself for not spotting the cracked mirror last night. 'Did you try and contact her? Ring her phone?'

Grant's gaze is back on his tea. 'Nah. I was hammered, wasn't I? I mean, I knew something wasn't right, but I was too drunk to think it through. I passed out on the bed, woke up sometime in the afternoon.'

'What did you do then?'

'I called her phone but it was still in the house. Was lying under the bed. I couldn't get into it, but I could see she had a bunch of missed calls from work.'

'Did you phone them back?'

'They told me she hadn't turned up for her shift. After that I called the police.'

Callie's throat is dry. She pauses scribbling to take another sip of tea. 'What did they tell you about the window?'

'They said it looked like someone had . . .' Grant trails off. When Callie glances up, she sees the man is gripping his mug so tight, the tea is trembling. 'Like someone had used the window to break in.'

'They tell you why they wanted that part kept quiet?'

'Don't want to start a panic, do they? Folk hear that this Night Stalker guy's going around snatching people in their sleep.'

'Night Watcher. And did they phrase it like that? About starting a panic?'

'Younger one did. Don't think his partner was very happy about it though.'

'Do you know anyone that might have wanted to target Amy?'

Grant's face is dark now. He cannot meet her gaze. 'I don't just work as a bouncer for a youth hostel,' he says. 'I've done . . . other work, on the side.'

Callie pauses writing and sets her pen down quietly. 'Other work?'

'Here and there. Cash-in-hand stuff.'

'What sort of work, Grant?'

'Debt collection. For people you don't ever want to be owing money to.'

'I need a name,' Callie says. 'Who did you work for?'

Grant stands up. The screech of his stool on the tiled floor makes Callie flinch. His jumper shifts and she sees a set of deep scratches across his collarbone. He notices, pulls the fabric away to give her a closer look.

'You want to take a photo?'

'How did you get those, Grant?'

'Our cat doesn't like being picked up when she's sleeping.'

'Listen—'

'Eddie McCall,' he says. 'That's who I used to work for. But I never met the guy. Always spoke with one of his boys.'

Callie notes the name down. She's heard of McCall, of course she has. An Edinburgh gangster. The sort of man that's made himself rich by flooding the streets with drugs and women, and who likely has half the police in the city either paid up or blackmailed into silence. She says, 'You think McCall might have wanted to hurt Amy?'

Grant shrugs. He's standing over by the sink now, staring out the window. Outside, there's the sound of children laughing as they ride scooters up and down the street. 'Maybe I pissed McCall off,' he says, still gazing away. 'Maybe someone I roughed up wanted to get back at me. I don't tend to make many friends, doing what I do.'

Callie closes her notebook. She isn't sure how best to phrase the next question. It is the question that has been driving her for some time now. Sitting in her head, watching every action and colouring every thought. Wife, adulterer, victim. She needs to get past the labels.

'What was Amy like?' Callie asks gently.

Grant doesn't answer, his eyes still fixed out the window. Staring at some distant view, the children's laughter fading as they scoot off. They leave behind a growing silence.

Callie shifts uncomfortably on her stool. 'Grant—'

'She was funny,' he says quietly. His voice low. 'She made me laugh. She'd make an arse of herself if it made me laugh. She knew when to tell me to get over something and she knew when to say nothing, when to just be there, you know? She got a Pikachu tattoo on her shoulder when she was younger and the guy coloured him in green, and she loved it. She'd show it to people all the time. She was kind and she was smart, and she was brave, in ways I wasn't. She didn't like me working for Eddie McCall, but only because I didn't like working for Eddie McCall. I could have emptied the

82

bins for a living, so long as it made me happy. That's all she really wanted. For us both to be happy.' Grant finally turns away from the window and Callie can see tears in his eyes. The man still cannot look at her. 'I ruined everything,' he says. 'I pushed her away and now she's gone.'

Callie leaves shortly after that. Her tea is half drunk. She packs away her notebook and pen, and Grant walks her to the front door. This close to the sunlight and the sound of traffic, she feels like a diver coming up for air.

Grant moves past her to unlock the door, and then stops. 'You know, at first I thought you were just doing all this to keep me from hurting your boyfriend,' he says.

'What?'

'I know who beat me up, Callie. The twat kept saying your name as he was swinging the wrench.'

Fucking Richard.

Callie can feel her face harden. 'For what it's worth, we're not together. Not anymore.'

Grant laughs. It is a guttural, horrible sound. 'I understand why he did it. I don't even blame the guy. Believe me, if I ever get my hands on whoever hurt Amy, I'll probably do a lot worse.'

Chapter Seventeen

Mac shows up at Callie's door that night. He gives her a tired smile and holds up a Tesco carrier bag. 'Brought you some shopping,' he says.

Inside her living room, he removes the copied police reports and sets them down on her coffee table. Callie brings through two bottles of Moretti and passes him one.

'So what are we looking at?' she asks him.

The detective leans against the arm of the sofa. 'Their names are Jennifer Patton and Gail Hart,' he says. 'And in my view, they're his first victims.'

'That we're aware of.'

'Sure, that we're aware of.'

Callie sits cross-legged on the floor by the coffee table. She takes a long drink. Leaning forward, she begins to flick through the files.

'Jennifer Patton,' she says, studying the photo on the top page. It shows a short, squat woman with long dark hair braided down one shoulder. It shows her wearing a green and white chequered shirt. It shows her smiling. 'What's her story?'

Mac slides down on to the floor beside her. 'Jennifer Patton,' he repeats. 'Married, with two young kids. Worked as a cleaner for a financial company. Shift work in a fancy West End office, scrubbing toilets and emptying bins overnight. Hard graft for not much pay. She was taken eighteen months ago.'

Callie nods as he talks, reading slowly through the file. There isn't much to go on, and of course the word *taken* never appears once. That isn't the official line, after all.

'She was last seen by her husband and kids on the morning of her disappearance,' Callie says, turning pages.

Mac takes a drink. 'That's right. She'd just finished working a shift. Usually she'd come home as her husband was leaving for work and her kids to school. She'd then go to bed and get some sleep.'

'She was gone when they got back later that afternoon?'

'Kids came home to find the back door open and their mother missing. They waited until their father got in from work and he called the police shortly after.'

'They take it seriously?'

'At first. But aside from the circle cut into the kitchen window, there wasn't any sign of foul play.'

'That's a pretty big sign, Mac.'

'You know what I mean. No signs of a struggle, no obvious motive.'

'So what, they thought she just finished work one day and decided to leave her life behind?'

Mac shrugs and takes another drink. 'I reckon they took one look at her life and wondered why she hadn't done it sooner.'

Callie snorts and picks up the second file. 'Gail Hart,' she reads. 'Tell me about her.'

'Similar in a lot of ways. Around the same age as Jennifer Patton. No kids, but a partner who raised the alarm when she went missing.'

'They live together?'

'No. After Gail went dark, her girlfriend went round to check and found her gone. Again, no indication of a struggle, and no obvious motive. Police figured she'd left, maybe even taken her own life somewhere, and stuck her file on a shelf. That was six months ago.'

'If Amy's his third victim, that means he's picking up steam,' Callie says. 'He went a year between Jennifer and Gail. Only managed half that before he took Amy.'

Mac nods. 'Assuming there aren't any other victims we're missing.'

'It says here she worked for a law firm, some kind of business support role.'

'She was laid off shortly before she was taken,' Mac says. 'The pandemic made a lot of employers realise that if they don't need an office, they probably don't need an office manager.'

Callie studies Gail's photo. She is tall and slim, with blonde hair shaved short on one side. She is leaning against a bar somewhere, laughing. Christmas decorations hang from the ceiling; tinsel running between the beer taps.

'So what's the next step?' she asks Mac. 'You happy for me to just work the case?'

'Sure,' Mac says, getting to his feet. 'Work the case, however you see fit. Keep in touch, let me know how you're getting on.'

'What kind of support can I expect?'

'From me?'

'No, Father Christmas.'

Mac rolls his eyes as he drains his beer. 'I'll do whatever I can to help, alright? Obviously I need to be careful though. If anyone finds out I've given you those files . . .'

'Don't worry. Your secret's safe with me.'

He grunts in response, pulling on his coat. At the front door, he turns around and says, 'Oh, you think I could get that Tesco bag?'

'The one you brought the files in?'

'Yeah. I need to pick up some shopping on the way home and I'm not paying for another.'

Callie stares at him for a moment before she retrieves the bag. 'You tight fucker,' she says, handing it over. 'It's ten pence.'

'Thirty pence now.'

'Those bastards. Would you like another? I've got about a hundred stuffed under the sink.'

'No, this will do me fine. Goodnight, Callie. Thanks for the beer.'

'Goodnight, Detective.'

Chapter Eighteen

After Mac leaves, Callie opens another beer and spends an hour reading through both files. There isn't much to go on, the thinness of each folder showing just how little police time was devoted to finding these women.

She expands her search a little. Scrolls through their Facebook and Instagram profiles. She checks to see if there's any obvious connective tissue between them. Any shared friends or followers, any groups they're both members of. In a moment of desperation, she even checks Gail Hart's LinkedIn.

Nothing jumps out.

Sighing, Callie looks at her watch. It's a little after eight p.m. She figures it's not too late and dials the number for Jennifer Patton's husband. His name is Euan. Thinning brown hair and some middle-aged spread, according to his Bluesky profile.

He answers on the third ring. Says 'Hello?' and his voice is like treacle. Like she's caught him mid-yawn.

'Mr Patton?' she asks.

'Yes. Who's this?'

'My name is Callie Munro. I'm sorry to call you out of the blue like this, but I'm a private investigator, and I'm hoping you could—'

'You're a what?' Euan's voice has sharpened. He's awake now.

'A private investigator. I'm—'

'Is this to do with Jen?'

Callie pauses. 'It is,' she answers carefully. 'Mr Patton, it would really assist me if we could meet.'

'I'm not interested in talking with you,' Euan says. 'You understand me? Don't call here again.'

The line goes dead. Callie stares at her phone screen for a moment, unsure of whether she could have handled that better. She rubs at her face. Maybe it was too late to call. Her thumb hovers over the number again. Feels an urge to blurt out the fact another woman is missing as soon as Euan answers. Anything to get his attention.

'Screw it,' she mutters, and calls him.

It rings once, then clicks through to voicemail. Callie has dealt with enough of these to know that Euan has blocked her number.

'Shit,' she says.

The next morning is still bitterly cold. Callie has her usual smoke outside her front door. It warms her up from the inside, and even though she knows they're bad for her, that knowledge doesn't stop her enjoying the hell out of it.

By nine a.m. she's sat at her dining room table. A freshly made Americano next to the police files and her notebook. Callie didn't sleep much last night. Her mind going over it all – not just the paperwork, but what Grant Miller told her, too. About Amy. About Eddie McCall.

When she finally drifted off it didn't last. Just long enough for the swirling thoughts inside her to coalesce. Dreams of violence, of women's screams. When Callie woke she felt vulnerable and alone, hearing the sound of a sharpened blade running across glass. She had to check the windows before trying to sleep again.

But now it's morning, and everything always seems better in the light. She sips her coffee and reads through her notes one last time. At ten past nine she dials the number for Nicola Mosley. She's Gail's partner, and Callie is hoping to have more luck than she had the night before.

'Hello?'

Nicola answers and straight away Callie can tell the woman is stressed. Heavy breathing, a clipped tone. It sounds like she's walking briskly down a busy street.

'Ms Mosley? My name is Callie Munro. I'm looking into the disappearance of Gail Hart, and I have a new line of investigation I'd like your help with.'

'You're looking into Gail?'

Nicola has stopped walking. Her breathing has changed. It's still fast, only now it has a strained quality to it. Emotions clamping down on the woman's throat.

'I am,' Callie says. 'I just have a few questions. Would you have any time to talk today?'

'I'm sorry, who is this exactly? Are you with the police?'

Callie pauses before answering. Scared to get the same reaction she got from Euan Patton last night.

'No,' she says at last. 'No, I'm not. I'm a private investigator, and I'm looking into the disappearance of another woman under similar circumstances to your partner's.'

Nicola is silent for a long moment. Callie chews her lip, waiting for the line to go dead or to be told to get lost. Both outcomes equally possible, she knows only too well.

'Yes, of course,' Nicola says at last. 'I'm at work for the rest of the day, unfortunately, but—'

'Where do you work?'

'Oh, just a small cafe over in Marchmont. Near Sciennes Road.'

'I can pop by this morning if that's alright? We could chat there?'

'Sure. It normally doesn't pick up until lunchtime, so I could talk.'

'Great. Let me know the address.' Callie glances over at her empty mug. 'I could do with a good coffee right about now anyway.'

Nicola Mosley is a slight, awkward-looking woman. She's stood nervously behind the counter, watching people pass by the large windows for anyone who might be about to enter. Callie zeroes in on her moments after entering the cafe. Nicola's eyes are already on her.

The cafe is quiet. A young man in the corner wearing headphones and typing on a laptop; a mother rocking a pram back and forth with her foot while cradling a mug like it's the Holy Grail. Judging by how tired the poor woman looks, maybe it is.

Nicola smiles and half raises her hand in greeting. She steps out from behind the counter, turning to say something to her co-worker on the way. Callie slides into a corner booth. Nicola joins her, pulling off her apron.

'I've taken my break early,' she says, folding the apron neatly in half and placing it on the table. She smooths the fabric down with the palm of her hand. A nervous gesture, maybe. 'And I'm sorry, I've forgotten your name.'

'Please, don't apologise. It's Callie. Callie Munro.'

'It's nice to meet you, Callie. You're a private investigator?'

'That's right.'

'And you're looking into Gail?'

'I am.'

'I don't understand. I thought you had to be hired by someone. At least, that's what it's like on TV. Did Gail's family contact you?'

Callie shakes her head. 'Like I said on the phone, I've been working another case.'

'Another missing woman?'

'That's right.'

Nicola hesitates for a moment, then nods. 'Well then. Anything I can do to help.'

Callie pulls out her notebook and flips to a fresh page. She's about to start asking questions when Nicola's co-worker arrives to take their order. A flat white for Callie and a glass of iced water for Nicola.

'I wanted to ask about the night Gail went missing,' Callie says when they're alone. 'You didn't live together, am I right?'

'You are,' Nicola says. 'We'd been talking about it for a while though. I was going to rent out my little flat and move in with her. Gail lived in a nice terraced house over in Liberton. She had more space.'

'She was reported missing on May third. A Saturday. When was the last time you saw her?'

'The day before. We'd been out with friends on the Thursday night, and I stayed over at Gail's. I worked a double shift on the Friday. We were doing a dinner service so I didn't get back to my flat until early Saturday morning.'

'Were you in contact with Gail on the Friday?'

'On and off. Text messages whenever I got a break. I think the last one I got from her was just before midnight. She was off to bed, said that I should just come round to hers after my shift. I never did.'

'Why not?'

'I was knackered. I just wanted a shower and my own bed, you know?' Nicola trails off then, her gaze going distant. 'I still wonder, though . . .'

Callie studies the woman. 'What would have happened if you'd gone round?'

'Yeah. Maybe I would have been able to prevent whatever happened.'

'Or maybe you'd be missing too.'

Their drinks arrive. Callie downs half her coffee in one go. She's finally starting to feel herself again. 'Tell me what happened on the Saturday morning.'

Nicola sips her water and shrugs. Her gaze is still a hundred miles away. 'Not much to say, really. I woke up late, saw she hadn't responded to my last message and so I sent her another. I got dressed and made myself some breakfast, and after a while, when she still hadn't responded, I tried calling but she never picked up.'

'Is that when you went round to her house?'

'That's right.'

'What did you find?'

'Nothing. It was like she'd just upped and left. The place looked the same as it had when I'd been there the day before.'

'How did you get into the property? Did you have a key?'

'I had a key, but I didn't need to use it. The front door was open.'

'Open or unlocked?'

'Unlocked, sorry.'

Callie grunts as she notes all this down. Her hand is starting to ache a little. She sets her pen down, massages her fingers and then takes another drink.

'This case you're working . . .' Nicola says, leaning in across the table, her voice low. Her palm is still smoothing the folded apron, the creases long gone. 'This other woman. How similar is it to Gail's?'

Callie weighs it all up before answering. 'There's a lot that's the same,' she says eventually. 'Not everything, but a lot.'

'Like what?'

'Like a circle cut out of a downstairs window. That ring a bell?'

Nicola nods. 'The police found something just like that in Gail's house. In her kitchen.'

'What did they say about it?'

'They didn't say anything about it.' Nicola sits back a little. She takes another sip of water. The level in the glass looks untouched. Callie wonders if the woman just needs something to do, like a nervous habit. 'They noted it down, but then everything went quiet. I called them every couple of days to find out how the investigation was going, and every time I got the same answer.'

'Which was?'

'I don't know, some stock phrase about how they were still following up leads. Then one day, maybe a month or so after Gail went missing, they told me that they didn't have anything further to go on, and without any new evidence it was unlikely they'd be able to find her.'

'They tell you what they thought had happened?'

Nicola snorts. Colour has appeared in her cheeks. 'They thought that Gail had maybe run away. Or worse, that she'd gone somewhere to kill herself, on account of her financial situation.'

Callie thinks back to the police file. 'Gail had recently been let go at work.'

'Yeah. The law firm she was working at was downsizing, so they sacked her. She tried to get a job elsewhere but every company was closing down their offices and an office manager was the last person they wanted to hire.'

'How was she making ends meet?'

'She wasn't. She was behind on her mortgage, and I was having to loan her money. She finally swallowed her pride and signed on the dole, but she hated it. The way people on the street would look at her when she came out. Like she was being judged, like she was a failure, you know?'

'I know.'

'She even . . .'

Nicola stops talking and glances away. Callie's eyes snap up from the notebook. 'She even what, Nicola?'

'She even borrowed money from people. Just a little, just to help her make ends meet.'

'What people?'

'I don't know. I didn't want to know. But they gave her it in cash, in a Primark carrier bag. The whole thing was dodgy as hell.'

Callie thinks back to her conversation with Grant Miller. What did he call it? Debt collection. 'Nicola, did Gail borrow money from a man named Eddie McCall?'

Nicola presses herself into her seat. Her gaze is still downwards, on the table. On the ice inside her glass. 'I think that might have been his name,' she says quietly.

Callie nods, then finishes writing. She stares at the pages of scribbled notes, massaging her hand absent-mindedly. Deciding how best to ask the next question.

'What do you think happened to Gail?' she says.

Nicola takes another minuscule sip and says, 'I think someone took her. I think someone cut a hole in her kitchen window, climbed in, and snatched her. I mean, what do you think happened?'

'I think you're probably right,' Callie admits. 'Do you know if Gail had any sort of intruder alarm? Anything that might have needed to be disabled to gain access?'

'Christ. Yeah, she had an intruder alarm, but she never used it. I don't think I ever saw her punch a code into that keypad by her front door the whole time we were together. You know how frustrating that is? For her to have an alarm system and never use it?'

Callie nods but says nothing.

'I just keep thinking . . .' Nicola says, and closes her eyes. As she's been talking, she's sunk lower and lower into herself. Now, she's practically curled up into a ball in her seat. 'I just keep thinking that if I'd went round there after work she might still be here.'

Callie surprises herself a little by reaching over for Nicola's hands. She takes hold of them and squeezes. The woman's fingers are frozen from being pressed up against the water glass for so long. 'You can't think like that,' Callie says. 'You hear me? You'll drive yourself crazy thinking like that. You'll never get past it.'

'Speaking from experience?'

'Sure. Now, listen, I want you to take my card.' Callie lets go of Nicola's hands to pull a business card from her purse. She slides it across the table. 'You take this, and if you think of anything else, you give me a call, alright?'

'Alright. Thank you, Callie.'

'Don't mention it.'

Chapter Nineteen

Back in her Mini, Callie takes ten minutes to read over her notes. She annotates in the margins, expanding on answers and clarifying illegible scribbles. By the end, she's become fixated on one thing. One piece of information, one name that Nicola confirmed for her.

Eddie McCall. The same man that Grant Miller used to work for. Did terrible things for. Callie isn't stupid, she knows that McCall is a gangster. She knows he's involved in plenty of bad shit. But now his name has cropped up twice, in connection with two different missing women. That may just be a coincidence, but Callie has always hated coincidences.

She starts her car and pulls out. Punches an address into Google Maps and then dials Grant's number. He answers on the second ring.

'Didn't think I'd be hearing from you so soon,' he says.

'I didn't think so either.'

'You find something already?'

'Maybe. But I need to ask for a favour.'

Grant snorts down the line. Callie hears the sound of a can being cracked open in the background. She wonders if he's drinking. She glances at the clock. It's barely ten-thirty.

'What's the favour?' he asks.

'You told me that you used to work for McCall,' Callie says. 'As an enforcer or whatever.'

'Yeah?'

'So I think I'm going to need to speak with him. Can you arrange a meeting?'

Grant goes quiet. She taps the steering wheel impatiently. Finally he says, 'Callie, are you sure you want to dip your toe into this world? Into his world? Once you do . . .'

'Once I do, I'm forever tarnished with the stink of the underworld, doomed to forever be the target of police investigations and mob assassinations. I get it.'

'It's not funny.'

'All right, I'm sorry. But his name's come up, Grant. His name's come up and I need to look into it.'

'Fine. I'll see what I can do. Just don't hold your breath, okay?'

'Thank you.'

Callie pulls in and ends the call just before she kills the engine. She's parked outside a small, semi-detached house in Newington. Taking a breath, she climbs out and approaches the front door.

The front garden is a little unkempt. Scattered weeds and half-dead plants. Parts of the wooden fencing have started to collapse, and glancing upwards she can see a number of cracked or missing roof tiles. The blinds in the living-room window hang crooked, and an alarm box reading *Vangelis* sits above, flashing blue.

She rings the doorbell and spots it a moment later. The little plate set just above the letterbox with the family name. *Patton*.

Footsteps approach and then the door swings open. A man stands there, dressed in joggers and an old t-shirt. His clothes are peppered with what looks like paint. He frowns at her.

'Can I help you?'

Callie recognises his voice immediately from her brief phone call the night before. Still, it seems rude to presume.

'Mr Patton?'

'Yes, what's this about?'

Callie jumps straight to the point. 'Mr Patton, I'm sorry to drop in on you out of the blue like this. I'm a private investigator, and I'm—'

'Fuck me,' Euan Patton says. He curls his upper lip at her in disgust. 'You're that woman who phoned last night.'

'That's right. My name is—'

'I don't give a fuck what your name is! I told you already, I don't want anything to do with you. Jesus, I'm trying to move on. Do you understand that?'

'I do understand that, Mr Patton, but if you'll just let me explain—'

'No,' he says firmly. 'I won't, and if I see you around here again, you'll regret it.'

He steps back and slams the door in her face.

Callie sighs. She retreats to her car, glancing back as she reaches the street to see the dark figure of Jennifer Patton's husband standing at the living-room window, watching from behind those lopsided blinds.

Chapter Twenty

Callie goes to bed late.

She spent the evening reading old news reports on Jennifer and Gail's disappearances, hunched over her laptop, eating tasteless scrambled eggs and drinking the last of her Morettis.

She smokes a cigarette outside her front door before bed. It's become her usual spot. There's something about standing here, in this quiet bubble of colony houses, that Callie finds relaxing. In the summer it catches the last of the afternoon sun, and often she will take a chair from the dining room and place it at the top of the steps, and she will sit and smoke and read a book and feel the warmth on her face.

But even now, in the dark, it's relaxing. Around her she can feel the presence of others: her neighbours, her community. And in the air, the relentless rhythm of passing cars along London Road. It's like a heartbeat. It is white noise in the still. It fills the quiet street and calms her in a way that she does not fully understand.

Only it doesn't help her sleep. Not tonight. When she goes to bed she lies and stares at the ceiling because she knows that if she closes them she will see their faces. Those missing women. Taken from their beds, one in broad daylight. Taken by a man who sliced his way through glass to reach them. A man who knew when they would be alone. Who knew the people they lived with and knew their schedules. A man who knew that the best women to vanish are those who are halfway gone already.

The Night Watcher.

All of it points to a horrifying level of preparation. Of education, of planning. None of these women were attacked on the spur of the moment or in a jealous rage. They were selected – carefully selected. Maybe because of how they looked or where they lived or where they worked. Maybe it was a combination of all three, or maybe it was something else entirely. The police know so very little, and what little they do know is enough to keep Callie awake.

She hears it then. A gentle scrape. The sound of something metal moving against a hard surface. Holding her breath, she strains to hear past the noise of her pulse thudding in her ears. For a brief second she wonders if she's imagined it. Her mind playing tricks.

And then she hears it again. Stronger, this time. It's coming from downstairs. Someone is trying to unlock her front door.

Chapter Twenty-One

Rising quickly from her bed, Callie snatches her phone up and moves towards the bedroom door. She rolls her bare feet across the carpet; these old houses shift and creak so easily. She grabs a hoodie from the back of a chair and pulls it on over her pyjamas.

Outside the bedroom, the landing is freezing. Callie wishes she wasn't wearing shorts. She wishes she was wearing anything other than her pyjamas.

At the top of the stairs, she pauses to listen. The steps curve away from her into darkness, but there is no mistaking the sound now. Someone is stood on the other side of her front door, trying to break in. Then the metal scraping stops. Callie wonders if they were trying to pick the lock. Suddenly, she can hear a louder, rasping noise. Whoever it is, Callie realises they are attempting to slide a flat plastic sheet between the door and the frame. If they are successful, the Yale lock will slide back and the door will open. She knows this because it is something she has done many times herself. The thought of someone doing it to *her* has never once entered her head.

She glances at her phone. It is nearly one a.m. Unlocking it, she taps in 999, but lets her thumb hover over the 'call' icon. Then she creeps down the stairs, stopping when she is halfway. She nestles herself into the curve of the steps. Still hidden in shadow but now with the front door in view straight ahead. She watches, wide-eyed, as the wooden door creaks. There is the sudden sound of a man grunting from the other side.

Reaching forward and down, her fingers slide across the wall until they touch the hard plastic light switch. Callie takes in a breath, holds it, and flicks the switch.

Blinding light floods the downstairs hall. It shines through the window above the door and immediately the scraping sound stops. Callie clears her throat, prays her voice won't crack, and shouts, 'The police are on their way, dickhead, so you better fuck off right now.'

For a long moment, nothing happens. Callie wonders if the man has slunk away without her hearing. She takes a tentative step forward. Her foot is in mid-air when the front door booms.

Callie jumps, dropping her phone. It skitters away across the floor and into the bathroom. The man outside grunts again as he throws himself against the door for a second time. There is the dreadful sound of wood splintering, and Callie knows the door will not hold for a third strike.

She balls up her fists. This is her house. This is her fucking house! She stands up straight and launches herself down the last few steps into the hall and towards the front door, just as it finally gives way and swings open. It batters off the wall, the handle breaking the plasterboard. A man in black wearing gloves with a ski mask pulled over his face fills the doorway, but Callie does not slow. A second after the door opens, she barrels into him with her full force.

He lets out a muffled yell as he is knocked backwards. Three steps to try to right himself but there's only space for two; his left foot comes down on air and he tumbles down the concrete stairs to the pavement. Callie reaches out and grabs the metal railing to stop herself from following.

The masked man comes to a halt in an awkward position. On his front, his legs splayed up the steps behind him. Callie watches, wondering if she's killed him, when he climbs to his feet. One gloved hand on her gate to pull himself up, and that's when she sees it. His arm outstretched, the flash of silver on his wrist. Then he's moving, staggering on to the street.

'Hey!' she yells, and she reaches down to pick up the newly replaced mug by her feet. Hurling it at him, she misses by inches and it explodes on the garden wall. Cigarette butts scatter. He takes off, limping slightly on his left foot, and within a few seconds he's reached the corner of the street and vanished from view.

Chapter Twenty-Two

Afterwards, sitting at her dining room table, Callie recounts the events to two uniformed police officers. One of them takes notes. Painfully tapping out a statement on his cramped smart device using one finger. He keeps asking Callie to slow down so he can keep up. He looks about fourteen.

The other officer is looking over the door frame. She studies the broken lock like she's Sherlock Holmes. Callie half expects her to turn around and announce she's worked out who the masked attacker was.

'So what happens next?' Callie asks.

'We'll get a report started and look into it further,' the female officer says, finally tearing herself away from the door. 'You'll get an incident number.'

'Great. And what are the chances of you finding this guy? Like, genuinely finding him? No bullshit.'

The woman sighs and crosses her arms. 'Well, based on your statement, the man was wearing gloves – so we won't get any fingerprints. We can look and see if any cameras in the area picked him up before or after he attempted to break in, but it'll be difficult to identify him unless he's still wearing his ski mask.'

'Well, I guess I did ask for no bullshit,' Callie mutters. 'He's got a limp, though. From falling down those steps. His left foot, I think. And he was wearing a watch. Something big with a silver strap.'

As she says it, a brief memory hits: Richard adjusting his watch in the kitchen.

'That might help,' the officer says, glancing at her partner, who's finished typing up the statement. 'But I wouldn't get your hopes up here.' She gives a grim smile and sits down across from Callie at the table. 'I know this isn't what you want to hear. But I'm just being honest with you.'

'No, I know. I appreciate it.'

'You want my opinion? We're treating this as an attempted burglary, but whoever tried to break in here might not have been interested in your TV or laptop.'

'What are you saying?'

'I'm saying that maybe there was another reason. Something personal. Do you know anyone that might have had a reason to do this?'

Callie goes quiet. She thinks of Richard, hunched over as he swung a wheel wrench into a man's face. She thinks of Grant Miller, rising off his bar stool with a clenched fist she never saw coming. She thinks of Eddie McCall, sending enforcers round to people's homes to deliver messages. She even thinks of Euan Patton, threatening her on his front step earlier that day.

'Ms Munro?'

'No,' Callie says, shaking her head. 'No, I can't think of anyone.'

The female officer almost looks disappointed. She straightens up and motions to her partner, who moves towards the broken front door. 'Alright. Here's my card, okay? Your incident number is written on the back. If you remember anything else, get in touch.'

'I will.'

'Now, a locksmith is on the way. We'll wait in the car outside until he's done, unless you'd prefer us to wait in the house with you?'

'No, I'll be fine.'

The woman studies Callie for a moment, then nods. She turns to leave, then says, 'You want my advice? You get the locksmith to fit the biggest fucking lock he's got. You invest in a security light and a doorbell camera, and you get someone out here to install a home alarm system. That's a far better deterrent to these assholes than someone like me trying to find them after the fact.'

Callie starts to answer, but something the officer said has struck a chord. 'An alarm system,' she says quietly.

'That's right. I'm sure the locksmith can recommend one, if you'd like.'

'Thank you, Officer.'

The woman nods again. 'Goodnight, Ms Munro. I hope we've been of some help, at least.'

Callie watches them leave, then sits down at her dining table and opens her laptop. *More than you know, Officer*, she thinks to herself. *More than you know.*

Chapter Twenty-Three

It takes Callie less than a minute to find the name. She knows it starts with a 'V'. Can still see the logo in her head. On the white alarm box on the side of Jennifer Patton's house. It was flashing blue. It caught her eye as she looked back at Euan Patton's outline, watching her leave.

Vangelis.

She scribbles the name down in her notebook. It's a long shot, she knows that, but everything is a theory until it's proven otherwise. She loads up the camera footage from Amy Miller's neighbour and scrubs through to a well-lit frame. Hunching forward, she zooms in. There, on the wall, above the front door. The same alarm box, the same blue light. *Vangelis.*

Callie navigates to Google Maps and types in Gail Hart's home address. She jumps into street view, navigates up and down past the house. But the front of the building is obscured. Trees and a parked van block the view. She glances at the time – it's after one a.m. She wonders about phoning Nicola and asking if she knows.

A knock at the front door brings her back. A man's voice shouting hello. Callie steps out into her hallway to see a man in his fifties holding up a toolbox.

'I'm here to sort your lock,' he says, then motions behind him. 'One of those officers outside said it was alright to come up.'

Callie nods, her mind a million miles away. 'Sure, thanks. Can I get you a coffee?'

'Easy now, I'll never get back to sleep.'

'Course. Will this take long?'

'Depends on what you want me to fit.'

Callie smiles a little as she thinks of how the female officer phrased it. 'The biggest fucking lock you've got,' she says.

When Callie finally gets to bed, it's nearly half two. The hall is covered in wood shavings and her bank account is down nearly three hundred quid, but her front door now sports a fancy mortice deadlock with a night latch. The locksmith even tried his best to fix the frame. Regardless, she leaves the downstairs lights on.

She knows it's definitely too late to call Nicola now. She'll have to wait until morning, which despite the hour seems further away than ever. She lies in bed and stares at the ceiling. She can't sleep. Adrenaline buzzes in her system, her ears listening for every gust of wind, every creaking board. She doesn't know how she'll ever sleep again.

After an age she checks her phone. Two-forty-five. It's more than Callie can bear. She thinks about Jennifer Patton's and Amy Miller's houses. She thinks about their Vangelis alarm systems. She thinks about what it might mean if Gail Hart had the same one.

Another check of the clock. Ten to three.

'Screw it,' she mutters, and gets out of bed.

It takes her five minutes to get dressed and into her Mini. Another fifteen to drive through Queen's Park and past the

Commonwealth Pool, her fingers clenched tight around the frozen steering wheel. By ten past three she's pulling up outside Gail Hart's home and killing the engine.

She spots the flashing blue light next to an upstairs window before the car even has a chance to go quiet.

Chapter Twenty-Four

Callie ends up falling asleep on her sofa around four. Still clutching a pen, her notebook open on her lap. She wakes a few hours later in an uncomfortable position. The low morning sun is in her eyes.

She texts Mac as she makes coffee. *Call me when you can.* By the time she's back sitting at her dining table, he does.

'Everything alright?' he asks her. He sounds like he's at his desk in the middle of the station. A hubbub of background chatter.

'Everything's fine,' she says. 'I've got a lead. Can you talk?'

'That was fast. What is it?'

'You ever hear of Vangelis?'

'Sure, he did the soundtrack to *Blade Runner*. You know, everyone talks about Hauer and his tears in rain speech, but it's the music that really—'

'Yeah, not him, whoever he is.' Callie briefly thinks of Richard and *Spider-Man* and how every man in this city seems to be a nerd these days. 'I'm talking about the home security company.'

'Oh. Then sure, I guess I've seen their boxes on people's houses. Why?'

Callie grunts as she takes a sip of coffee. She flicks through her notebook, choosing her next words carefully. 'All three women had Vangelis alarm systems installed in their properties.'

Mac pauses. She can almost hear him frowning down the line. 'And?'

'And it got me thinking. Like, what if the same guy set up the system in each house? It would give him a perfect way to identify his victims and scope their places out. He'd need to check every window, every possible entrance. He'd need to know how many people had regular access to the property. Shit, he'd probably even know how to disable the system when he was ready to break in. I know it's a long shot, but I think it's worth pursuing.'

Again, Mac is silent for a long moment. Callie holds her breath. Somehow, saying it all out loud makes it sound even more ridiculous.

Then he says, 'You might be on to something.'

Callie grins.

'What made you consider the alarm system?' Mac asks her.

'Uh . . .'

'Callie?'

'Someone tried to break into my place last night,' she tells him. She can feel the base of her neck starting to warm.

'What? Who? Are you alright?'

'I'm fine—'

'Did they hurt you?'

'Mac, I said I'm fine.' Callie rubs at her face. 'I'm tired, that's all. Only thing the asshole managed to steal was my sleep.'

'Jesus.' Mac's voice has gone quiet. Callie pictures him hunched over his desk, his brow knotted. 'What did they want?'

'I didn't ask, funnily enough.'

'Do you know who it was? Did you report it?'

'Yes, I reported it.' Callie thinks about the man, standing in her doorway, dressed in black. 'And no, I don't know who it was. Probably some junkie after my TV.'

Even as she says it, however, she knows it's not true. Junkies don't have the foresight to cover their faces. Whoever broke down her front door last night was there for her.

Mac says, 'Maybe we should cool things a little, you know?'

'Absolutely not.'

'Callie, I don't want to put you in danger.'

'Relax, Detective. This isn't the first psycho I've hunted. Chances are, whoever tried to break in last night isn't even related to this case.'

'Chances are that's shite and you know it.'

Callie rolls her eyes. 'Look, I just want to focus on this, alright? I've got the bite between my teeth now. I need to see it through.'

Mac sighs. 'The bit.'

'What bit?'

'Never mind. Tell me what you need from me. If it's a warrant, it might be premature. I don't want to start drawing attention unless we're sure.'

'No, I know. All I need is the name of whoever installed the alarm systems in those properties. If it's more than one person, then fine, the theory is shot. But if not . . .'

'I'm not sure they'll release that information voluntarily.'

'Course they will. With a bit of luck you get some impressionable young thing from their front desk and you make yourself sound important. Ask them to save their bosses a lot of time by just checking the system for you. It's easy.'

'It's inadmissible.'

'Let's burn that bridge when we get to it.'

Mac snorts. 'Fine, I'll see what I can do. No promises, though. Now listen, I've got a meeting about to start. I'll phone you when I can.'

He ends the call before she can say goodbye. Callie sets her mobile down and skims her notebook once more. She drains her coffee, looks through her other cases briefly – even though she knows she can't focus on anything else. The Night Watcher has her now, as surely as if he had sliced through her window and carried her off.

She goes upstairs to shower. Pausing to check the new lock on the way. In the bathroom, she examines her stomach. The bruising has reduced even further. It's turning yellow and fading round the edges. Truth is, Callie forgot about it completely the last couple of days. Maybe that's a sign that it's healing or maybe it's a sign that she's losing herself in this case. Either way, she's not taken a painkiller in over twenty-four hours and that can only be a good thing.

When she's out the shower and pulling on a pair of jeans, she sees her phone light up. It's a message from Mac. Short and to the point. *His name is Nick Fullerton. No priors. Be careful.*

Chapter Twenty-Five

The Red Kite Cafe is a two-minute walk away across London Road. Callie heads there now, her head down, her hands in her pockets. Up the narrow colony street towards the main road. She takes a stool by the window and orders scrambled eggs and a flat white.

Nick Fullerton.

The man's name pulses like a beacon in her head. Callie tells herself that it's just a lead – nothing more than a possibility – but the idea has taken root. It's hard to shift; it blocks out her other thoughts. She realises that she wants it to be him. Too much, maybe.

She sips her coffee as she logs into her various social media accounts. Shell profiles, every one of them. Nothing that can link back to her. No geographical data, no real-life connections. She checks her VPN is working; if anyone tries to trace her location, she'll show up somewhere in the American Midwest.

Callie spends the next hour trawling through Nick Fullerton's online life. His Facebook photos, his Twitter posts (she refuses to ever call it X). Fullerton's a middle-aged man with a receding hairline and a paunch belly. He likes going on holiday to Spain and drinking IPA he brews in his garage. He votes Labour, he drives a Golf, he supports Hearts. She tries to pin down his movements on the dates that each women went missing and finds nothing. Fullerton has no obvious alibi for those three days.

Two coffees down and on to her third. Callie runs through her options. She could confront him, knock on his door and try to catch him off guard. She could surveil him, plant some of Martin's tech around his house and on his car and wait for him to do something incriminating.

The idea comes into her head fully formed. She nearly laughs out loud, it's so simple. She digs out her mobile and dials.

'Vangelis Alarm Systems, how can I help you?'

It only takes a few minutes. She was right about the person manning the front desk: impressionable as hell. All it needs is the right tone of voice and a concocted story about wanting the same installer her friend used, whoever that might be. She's in luck, the young man tells her eagerly. Nick Fullerton has a cancellation in his diary. He can come round later this afternoon. Callie ends the call with a grin.

'You look pleased, Ms Munro.'

A female voice from just behind her left shoulder. Callie turns, sees a woman standing there. A stranger. Tall with short black hair – dyed, going by her piercing blue eyes – and with a pale complexion. A long, faded scar runs down one side of her face, curling in to the edge of her mouth. When the woman smiles, the scar tissue corkscrews upwards.

'Can I help you?' Callie says.

'Is this seat taken?' The woman gestures at the stool next to Callie.

'No.'

'Good. I skipped breakfast this morning and I'm dying. How's the coffee here?'

'It's fine. I'm sorry, have we met?'

Again, the woman smiles. Again her scar twists across her cheek. 'My name's Mia,' she says, settling down on to the stool. 'We actually have a mutual friend.'

'We do?'

'Mr Miller.'

'You know Grant?'

'I know a lot of people, Ms Munro.'

A server comes over with a small breakfast menu. Mia orders a latte and glances over at Callie. 'My treat,' she offers.

'Three's my limit, but thanks.'

'Three coffees down and it's barely nine-fifteen. You're flagging worse than me.'

'I didn't get much sleep last night. Are you going to tell me what this is all about?'

Mia waits until the server is out of earshot. She unravels her scarf and unbuttons her coat. 'I'm here on behalf of Eddie McCall,' she says. 'I understand you want to arrange a meeting.'

'Oh.'

'He knows you're a private investigator, Ms Munro. He knows what you're looking into. He'd like to help.'

'He would?'

Mia laughs lightly. 'If it assists in keeping a dangerous man off the streets, then of course he would.'

The server returns with her latte. Callie watches her thank the man and take a long, slow drink. When she places the mug down, nearly a third has gone. Her lipstick leaves a red rim.

Callie shrugs. 'Okay, then. Great. When can we meet?'

'How about right now?'

Mia nods towards the window. Callie follows the gesture and notes a grey Hyundai Ioniq 5 waiting across the road. The inside is hidden behind tinted windows. It's parked on double yellow lines. She wonders how long it's been there for.

'He better watch himself,' Callie says. 'He'll get a ticket.'

Mia smiles again as she picks up her latte. 'No, he won't,' she says.

Chapter Twenty-Six

As she gets up to follow Mia outside, Callie deliberately nudges her coffee cup off the edge of the table. It smashes on the floor. People around her jump.

'Oh my God,' she says, glancing around and making eye contact with them all. 'I'm so sorry.'

'It's fine,' the server says, smiling, already bending down to collect the shards. 'Happens all the time.'

Callie looks at Mia as they leave. She has a knowing look on her face. 'That was a little obvious,' she says.

'Excuse me?'

'Making a scene, so people will remember you.' Mia starts to cross the road. 'So they will remember who you left with. In case something happens to you later.'

Callie says nothing. She follows Mia over to the waiting car. Even this close, she cannot see through the tinted windows. Her heart rate begins to quicken. The Hyundai's doors unlock and she flinches.

'Please,' Mia says, opening the rear passenger door for her.

Callie nods and enters the car.

Aside from the driver, the only other person in the car is also sitting in the back seat. An older man, with salt-and-pepper hair and a thick beard to match. He's wearing a dark suit with no tie.

The top button of his shirt is undone. He's typing on his phone. Callie recognises him immediately as Eddie McCall.

'Excuse me a minute,' he says to her without looking up. And then, when Mia has sat down in the front passenger seat, he adds, 'Drive.'

The car moves smoothly off into the busy mid-morning traffic. Inside, it is silent. The only sound is the steady clack as McCall types what seems like an extremely long message to someone. Callie reaches up and pulls her seat belt across. When she buckles it in, she realises her hands are trembling a little.

'Now,' McCall says, sliding his phone into his jacket pocket and looking at her for the first time. 'I do apologise, Ms Munro. Or can I call you Callie?'

'Uh, sure.'

'Good. You can call me Eddie.' He speaks with a light Scottish accent, from somewhere outside Edinburgh. Smiling warmly, he holds out a hand. 'It's a pleasure to meet you.'

'Likewise,' Callie says, and shakes it. The man has a firm grip.

'Grant talks very highly of you,' McCall says. He scratches at his beard. He is still smiling. 'Course, Grant would talk very highly of a wheelie bin if it could buy him a pint, but there you go.'

'You should live in my street,' Callie says, forcing her voice to sound light and breezy. 'Everyone shares a communal skip at the end of the road. I'd kill for a wheelie bin.'

McCall stares at her, then bursts out laughing. Callie finds herself joining in, almost in relief.

'Very good,' he says, 'very good.'

His phone chimes. He gives her an apologetic look and checks it, grunting to himself before sliding it back into his pocket.

'My son,' he says. 'Meeting up with him is like a fucking military operation these days.'

Callie smiles and nods. She glances out the window. They're passing the new St James Centre, turning right on to Princes Street.

'Now, where were we?' McCall says. 'Oh aye, Grant Miller and his high praise. So, you're a private investigator?'

'That's right.'

'And you're looking into Grant's missus?'

'I am. Her and another two women. They all vanished under similar circumstances.'

'And the police don't seem too concerned?'

'Not officially, no.'

'Not officially. Well, some things never change, Callie, and police incompetence is one of them. The police, the council, the fucking parliament. Useless twats, the lot of them. The whole public sector's a scam these days. It breeds ineptitude, Callie. It breeds laziness. It forces people like me to rise to the top. To step in, to cover for their mistakes. To help the people they leave behind. See I think we've got that in common, you and me. That need to help.'

'Like you helped Gail Hart?'

McCall pauses his rant. His attention snaps back to the car. To Callie. He frowns and scratches at his beard again. 'Who?'

'Gail Hart. She's one of the missing women. She's actually the reason I wanted to speak with you.'

'Oh? And why's that?'

His tone is hard, accusatory. Callie feels her mouth go dry. She resists the urge to swallow.

'I spoke with her partner,' she says. 'You loaned Gail money after she lost her job.'

'Did I now? Well, isn't that charitable of me. And you, what, thought I maybe kidnapped the woman because she couldn't pay it back?'

Callie shakes her head. 'No, of course not . . .'

'What good would that do me? Taking a woman like that. I'd take her fucking TV, wouldn't I? I'd take her fucking MacBook.'

'I had to ask, Mr McCall—'

'Call me Eddie, for fuck's sake. I told you already.'

'Eddie, I'm sorry. But I had to ask, alright? I'm just doing my job.'

A long moment, and then McCall sniffs. The fight seems to go out of him. He nods and looks out the window. They're turning on to Lothian Road now. Callie sees a bunch of kids coming out of McDonald's. Holding brown paper bags and laughing. Her insides seize with it. A sudden urge to open the door and throw herself back into the world outside.

'Listen,' McCall says, and she tears herself away to look at him. 'I like you, alright? I get the feeling you're trying to do good, and I don't want to get in the way of that if I don't have to. So here's what I'm going to do. I'll ask around, see if there's anything I can find that might be of use. There's a guy out there kidnapping women? I'll talk to my girls, maybe one of them knows something.'

Callie breathes out and nods. 'I appreciate that, Eddie.'

McCall smiles again. It is the same warm smile from when she first got in the car. 'You're welcome. Now, I hope you don't mind, but is it alright if I drop you off here? I'm meeting my son in ten minutes.'

The car slows and pulls in. Callie realises they're at Fountain Park. She sees the large signs for Cineworld and Pizza Hut. 'Oh, of course,' she says.

'I appreciate that. They're re-showing all the Marvel films and we've got tickets for *Avengers: Age of Ultron*.'

Callie thinks of Richard's recent attempts to get her to see *Spider-Man*, and Mac's gushing over *Blade Runner*. 'I really don't get the fascination,' she says.

'More of a DC fan, are you?'

'I'm honestly not sure I could tell you the difference.'

McCall laughs. 'Wait till you have a kid who won't shut up about them,' he says. 'I used to be like you. Now I have arguments with him about what *Avengers* film is the best.'

'Is it *Age of Ultron*?'

'It is most certainly not *Age of Ultron*,' McCall says. 'Even my son and I can agree on that.' He holds out his hand and Callie shakes it once more. 'Goodbye for now, Ms Munro.'

Chapter Twenty-Seven

Walking back into town, Callie calls Grant Miller. It's a little after nine-thirty. His phone rings through to voicemail; she pictures him at The Marksman, slumped over the bar. She considers leaving him a message saying thanks for setting up the McCall meet, then decides against it.

Ending the call, she rings Martin.

'My favourite private investigator,' he sings down the line. 'What a pleasure.'

'I bet you say that to all your girls,' Callie says.

'Only the ones who pay their invoices on time. What can I do for you?'

'I need some kit,' she tells him.

The rest of the morning is taken up by preparations. A trip to the Grassmarket to collect a sports bag filled with expensive recording equipment. Martin can barely contain his glee. Callie tries not to think of the bill when she brings it all back.

Martin's mobile rings three times while she's there. On each occasion he glances at it, frowns, and ends the call.

'Dodging someone?'

'Call centre. Now let me show you how this all works.'

She's finally allowed to use the miniature cameras. Martin isn't so worried about the battery life or storage space this time around. Not when the recording window is so narrow.

'You'll get a couple of hours, tops,' he tells her. 'And it's a horrible fish-eye lens, and it's 720p, it's barely HD—'

'Embarrassing.'

'—but it should work fine for what you're doing.' He pauses then, looking at her suspiciously. 'What *are* you doing, Callie?'

Filming a suspected serial killer, she wants to tell him. But of course she doesn't. 'Following a hunch,' she says, smiling as she zips up the sports bag. 'If I'm right, you'll see all about it soon enough.'

Now, in her flat, she paces the rooms and tries to work out where a home security installer would go, where he would stand. Where she should place each camera to ensure his face is in shot. The devices are too small to capture audio, so Martin gave her a bunch of separate recorders to scatter around. These are easier to place: one in each room, slid neatly out of sight.

She finishes with a half hour to go. Just enough time for another coffee, Callie decides, which she drinks in her bedroom, standing by the window because it has the best view of the street. Her stomach churns as she watches cars. Too much to enjoy her coffee. She's barely halfway through when she sees a van turn on to her street. A white Ford Transit, dirty, the registration plate barely readable, the company name printed in faded type along one side.

Vangelis.

Chapter Twenty-Eight

Nick Fullerton is a big man. He just about fills the doorway, a wide smile on his face.

'Ms Munro?'

Callie nods, smiling herself. She practised it in the mirror a couple of times before opening the door. She knows it has to look convincing.

'Thank you for coming on such short notice,' she says, taking a step back. 'Please, come in.'

Fullerton squeezes past her through the narrow entrance hall and into the hallway proper. She watches him walk. If his left foot's injured, he's hiding it well.

'So, you're looking for a quote for a security system,' Fullerton says.

'That's right.'

'Had any trouble in particular, or just being prepared?'

'Just being prepared,' Callie says. She studies Fullerton's eyes. Tries to work out if they're the same ones she saw under the intruder's balaclava.

'Very sensible,' he says. 'Why don't you show me round?'

Callie spends fifteen minutes or so walking him round her house. Fullerton takes notes as he goes. He checks window seals, he tests their locks. He stands in her dining room and peers down to the street, one floor below.

'You're lucky, being up off the street like this,' he tells her. 'If someone wanted to break into your windows, they'd have to go into your downstairs neighbour's garden and climb their drainpipe.'

'Sounds dangerous.'

'It is. Plus, someone could easily see them.' He turns and nods towards the entrance hall. 'You ask me, your front door's the most obvious weakness. The new lock's a good start, but you should really get yourself a heavy-duty deadbolt.'

Callie smiles sweetly. 'That sounds like a sensible idea.'

After that she excuses herself to check on the washing machine and leaves him to it. She can hear him walking around upstairs. His footsteps heavy as he moves from room to room. She stands in her small, blue kitchen and folds wet clothes over the pulley.

When Fullerton is done, he slides his notebook into his pocket and shakes her hand. 'I'll get a quote put together and someone will give you a call.'

'Great. I appreciate that,' Callie says.

He leaves then. Callie watches from the top step as he hurries down to the road. When he reaches the bottom of her stairs, he pauses and turns back. For a long moment, neither of them moves. Then, at last, Fullerton raises his hand in farewell. Callie does the same, waiting until he's turned away and entered his van, waiting until he's driven away and out of her street, before she closes the door and engages the new lock.

Then she works her way round the flat, collecting every camera and audio recorder. She sits at her dining table and connects each device to her laptop. The files take an age to copy across; she watches the blue bar inch slowly forward. She forces herself to make a coffee just to avoid sitting staring at her screen.

Once she gets going, the mug sits untouched. The first video she tries is her bedroom. She placed the camera on her dresser, giving her a wide-angle view of most of the room. Her window on the right, double bed on the left.

The image on the screen brightens suddenly. Fullerton turning on her ceiling light. She watches him walk noiselessly into the room, reminding herself there's no audio yet. She'll need to pull that from the separate recorder. Somehow, watching this man move slowly across her bedroom in total silence is creepier than she was expecting.

Fullerton goes to the window first. He checks the seals. He tests the locks. He scribbles in his notebook. Then he stands and gazes out the window at the garden below. He stands very still, so still that at first Callie thinks the video has frozen. At last he turns his head. Slowly, deliberately. Callie realises he is now staring at her bed. She swallows as she watches him take four silent steps to stand next to it. He bends forward slightly, as though studying her pillow or her sheets. He cocks his head slightly. Listening, perhaps, for the sound of Callie climbing the stairs.

Finally, he straightens up and walks out. Callie scrubs forward to the end of the video but that's all there is. She realises that she has barely moved the entire time she's been watching.

She roots around in the files and finds the audio recording from the bedroom. She hits play and slides the time tracker forward. Turning the volume up on her laptop, a crackling hiss fills the room. Callie leans closer.

The click of Fullerton switching on her ceiling lamp makes her jump. She listens to his footsteps crossing the room. He's humming something tunelessly. Creaks from the windowpane as he prods the seals; the crinkle of paper as he writes in his notebook. Then the long quiet. Callie pictures him stood at her window, staring out.

When he moves, his footsteps are like thunder. Four depressions in the static; he's at her bedside now. Standing over it, bending towards it. Still, all Callie can hear is the white noise. She turns the volume up further, turns it up as far as it will go.

And there, in amongst the howling gale, she hears it. Rhythmic waves, rising and falling, followed by a long, heavy sniff. Nick Fullerton, looming over her bed, breathing heavily and inhaling her scent.

Callie stops the playback. Her ears pound in the silence of her dining room. Digging into her pocket, she pulls out her phone and dials Mac's number.

He answers on the third ring. 'Callie. Everything alright?'

'You need to bring him in for questioning,' she tells him.

'Slow down. Bring who in?'

'Nick Fullerton,' Callie says, wrapping her other arm around herself tightly. Her skin prickles with goosebumps. 'I think he was the man who tried to break into my flat the other night. I think he's the Night Watcher.'

'Based on what?'

On the fact that he's creepy as fuck. 'Call it intuition,' she says. 'But you take one look at this footage, and then you tell me he's not worth checking out.'

Chapter Twenty-Nine

Callie waits.

Sitting, smoking. Awake in the early hours. A day passes. She spends it doing admin, chasing invoices and looking over cases. She spends it eating shitty Chinese takeaway and drinking. She spends it walking up Arthur's Seat in the middle of the afternoon. She texts Mac while she's sat at the duck pond, watching kids throw pieces of stale bread into the choppy water.

Finally, in the evening, she gets a response.

Are you home?

Callie stares at the message. She's in her kitchen, leaning out of the open window, finishing a cigarette. She balances it on the sill and responds.

Yes.

The three dots pulse on her screen. Callie grinds the cigarette end into a dirty mug, watching them.

Finally:

Be there in ten. We need to talk.

She feels her heart quicken. She tries not to jump to conclusions, tries not to think that Fullerton might have been charged, that he might have admitted to murdering three women. But really, what else can it be? What else would justify Mac coming round in person to speak with her? If Fullerton was a dead end, surely he would have just called?

Eight minutes later, her front door goes. Callie has closed her kitchen window, the smell of cigarette smoke now gone, replaced by the chill evening air. She pulls on a warm hoodie as she goes to answer the door.

Mac stands there, hunched forward. The detective looks grim-faced. 'Sorry to drop in on you like this,' he says. 'Can I come in?'

'Of course.' Callie steps back. She has a sinking feeling in her chest. 'Do you want something to drink? Tea? A beer?'

'No, thanks.' Mac moves inside and closes the door behind him.

'Well, put me out of my misery, then,' Callie says, her hands on her hips. 'What happened with Fullerton?'

'It's not him.'

'What?'

'It's not him, Callie.'

She shakes her head, turning away and moving towards the stairs. She sits down on the bottom step. 'Fuck,' she murmurs. Then, desperately, 'Are you sure?'

Mac nods, leaning against the wall. His cheeks are flushed from the cold. 'He had a solid alibi for each of the disappearances.'

'How solid?'

'We-saw-him-on-CCTV solid.'

'But the footage, Mac. The guy was sniffing my fucking sheets.'

'He says he's got a cold.'

'Seriously?'

Mac shrugs. 'It's not enough, Callie. It's not enough for anything. Dawson says you're reaching and I think maybe she's right.'

Callie sighs and rubs at her temples. She thinks back to Fullerton's visit. She can still hear the sound he made, the way he breathed, stood over her bed.

'I think I need a drink,' she says, standing up. 'You sure you don't want anything?'

'I'm sure. But listen, there's more I need to tell you.'

'Now I know I need a drink.'

Callie moves through to the kitchen. Mac follows her.

'I burned a lot of goodwill, bringing Fullerton in,' he says. 'Joyce is pissed.'

'The chief inspector?'

'Yeah. Said I was wasting valuable police time trying to prove a link between these women.'

Callie grunts as she pulls a can of Deuchars from the fridge. 'But they are connected. Joyce just doesn't want to see it. Or maybe he's keeping you off the scent.'

'Not this again, Callie . . .'

'I still don't understand why you're so quick to dismiss him, Mac. That's all. Because he's your boss?'

'Because I know him. Joyce took me under his wing when I started. He showed me the ropes. I messed up a search warrant application and he sorted it for me, he protected me, he taught me how to be a better officer.'

'So he shielded his department from an embarrassing mistake, big deal. You see him as some father figure, is that it?'

'No, it's nothing like that. This is just . . . it's not him, alright? People at the station would know. I would know.'

Callie shakes her head. He's too close to see what she does, too unwilling to even entertain the possibility. Or maybe he doesn't want to. Maybe the idea of someone close to him being the Night Watcher is just too much for him.

'So what, now Joyce is pissed at you?'

'Not just Joyce. The whole department's freaking out.'

'Because of an angle you were looking into?'

131

'Because I broadcasted it, Callie. I put a man's name against it, you understand? An innocent man. And now the press have gotten wind of it. They've been calling the station all afternoon, looking for a quote. They forced Joyce's hand into opening a proper investigation into the three disappearances.'

Callie cracks open the beer. 'How awful for him.'

'The papers are running it first thing in the morning. A serial killer stalking Edinburgh women, breaking into their bedrooms and snatching them as they sleep. They're even running with the moniker. The Night Watcher.'

'Doesn't mean it's not true.'

'Christ! Will you let up with the antipathy for a minute?' Mac glares at her. His face is still flushed red, only now it's not from the cold. Callie sets her beer down, untouched.

'I'm sorry,' she says. 'It sounds like a stressful day. And I don't mean to be flippant about you getting chewed out. But it's not antipathy, Mac. It's reality. We were never going to be able to keep this kind of investigation quiet, not all the way. And the press getting involved? Shit, maybe that forces Joyce's hand. Maybe now he has to look into it properly.'

Mac exhales heavily and runs his hands through his hair. 'Well, if he does, he'll do it without me.'

'What?'

'I've been reassigned. Dawson, too. We can't be trusted to follow orders, apparently.'

'What's your partner got to do with this? She didn't help you.'

Mac shrugs. 'Didn't stop me, either. Didn't even know I was investigating it, and right under her nose, too.'

They both fall into silence. Callie suddenly feels a little guilty; so caught up in her own momentum, she didn't pause to consider the fallout. She watches Mac as he pulls out a chair from the dining table and sits down heavily.

'Where did you get reassigned to?' Callie asks him.

'Traffic.'

'That sounds . . .'

'Dull as shit? Yeah, it is.' The detective sighs and manages a half-smile. 'Maybe I'll have one of those beers after all.'

Callie opens the fridge and pulls out a can. Passes it to him, says, 'So now what?'

Mac cracks the beer open. It foams a little over his fingers. 'Now we wait and see, I guess.'

'You know, if we're right? If there is a killer out there? Perhaps seeing his exploits splashed across the front page of every paper in the country will rattle him a little. He might make a mistake.'

Mac takes a long drink, setting the can down on the table when he's done. He wipes at his lips and nods. 'He might do,' he says, his voice sounding low and deflated. 'Let's just hope another woman doesn't go missing before he does.'

You are worthless.

Everything you have ever done is meaningless. What is the point of you? What purpose do you serve? What possible value do you bring to the world?

You are an instigator.

Of hurt feelings, of regret. You used to lie in bed listening to your parents fight and know it was your fault. Knowledge as much a part of you as your very bones. A cloying, choking truth: you were your mother's greatest weapon. Born into this world out of spite, out of petty revenge. A leash over your father, the inevitable noose around his neck.

You are unloved.

By your family, by the woman you chose to make a life with. One day she is going to leave you. One day she is going to wake up and realise you are a failure, you are pathetic, you are poison. She lies about moving in with you. She lies about working late. She tells you fairy tales to keep you sane, and she laughs with her friends behind your back.

You are redundant.

You tried to hide it. Tried to bury yourself in your work, tried to make yourself seem busy and important. As though your employers wouldn't see you for what you are. Unnecessary, superfluous. They couldn't get rid of you fast enough. Your salary was a drain; sacking you was the best business decision they ever made.

You are a beggar.

You stand in a queue with other miserable, inadequate drifters. You try not to look at them, lest you become them, and they try not to look at you for the same reason. These parasites, these leeches. Feeding off society and giving nothing in return. Taking their handouts to the abandoned corners, trading them for a bag of mollies or trams, or special k, or black, gooey tar, their pockets forever filled with bent spoons, with rubber tubing, with hypodermic syringes. This is your future. This is your truth. It might as well be written on to your face for all to see. It might as well be branded on to your very skin.

You are ready.

You lie awake in bed and you hear my heavy boots and you watch as I enter the room. You say nothing as I peel back the covers. You close your eyes as I bind your wrists. You want this – on a deep level, you have been waiting for this. For someone to finally see you – the real you. For someone to save you from this wretched life. For someone to wipe your slate clean. You cry, quietly, as I pack your mouth with damp cloth. Tears of joy, perhaps. Tears of relief. You are happy to see me. You are grateful that I've come.

Chapter Thirty

Callie doesn't sleep well after Mac leaves. She drifts, aimlessly, between worlds. Her bedroom is too hot, her covers stifling. She spends the early hours stood at her bathroom sink, drinking ice-cold water straight from the tap. She lifts her top and studies her bruised abdomen. The mark is faded now, but Callie can still see it. She thinks she will always see it, even once it has healed completely.

At first light she is little better. A sleep fragile enough to be woken by the vibration of her phone. She rolls over, fumbling for it on her bedside table. It's a BBC News notification: *Is Edinburgh in the grip of a serial killer?*

Downstairs, she sits in her pyjamas and picks at stale cornflakes and drinks strong coffee and reads online theories about women being taken from their beds.

The story is everywhere. She bounces between websites, hunched forward on her sofa, scrolling on her phone. The morning news on the TV. The same pieces of information, shared and repeated and endlessly amplified. She watches sombre-faced reporters talking to camera, telling viewers that three women have gone missing over the last eighteen months, that the police consider these cases to be linked, that just yesterday they questioned an unnamed suspect before releasing them without charge.

Sources tell us, they say. Callie pictures the bustling station, the throng of people swirling around Mac's desk. She's always wondered about the type of person that leaks information to the press. If there's a certain thrill in it for them, a rush as they watch their words getting picked up and fed into the great maw of the morning news cycle.

Or maybe they think they're doing the right thing. A more understandable angle, given the response. Callie bets these women have had more attention in the last hour than in the last year and a half.

She goes for a shower and a smoke, and when she gets back to her living room she sees Chief Inspector Philip Joyce standing outside the entrance to Corstorphine police station. His face is stern; his brow a thick, rigid line. 'I can confirm,' he tells the reporters, 'that an individual was questioned yesterday afternoon in connection with the disappearance of Amy Miller. That individual was released without charge and is no longer a person of interest.'

'Do you believe that Amy Miller's disappearance is connected with the disappearances of Gail Hart and Jennifer Patton?' someone asks.

Joyce shakes his head. 'I'm not able to comment on an ongoing investigation.'

'But you do believe that the same individual is responsible for all three women's disappearances?'

The chief inspector glares at the person off-camera. 'As I said, I can't comment. What I can say is that the media have a responsibility not to incite panic by reporting on rumours and speculation. I'd ask you all to stick to the facts, not these half-truths.'

He turns away then, scowling. Retreating through the station doors. To his back, just before the feed cuts to the studio, someone yells, 'What half of the truth did we get right then?' Callie smiles a little at that.

She glances at the time; it's just about nine. She isn't sure what to do with her day. When Mac left yesterday, he didn't explicitly tell her to stop investigating – not that she would have necessarily listened to him even if he had. But now the news is out, Callie wonders how the police can afford not to look into it properly. And what use is she to them now? Shit, what use has she been to them at all? Handing an innocent man over to them like that, like she was so sure.

She turns off the TV, takes her breakfast dishes to the kitchen and dumps them in the sink. She tells herself that getting Nick Fullerton brought in for questioning started this whole media circus. That it shone a light on three women, whose names are now being read out and talked about and looked into. She tells herself that if forcing the police to properly investigate these disappearances is all she was able to do it's still a good thing, and that has to be enough.

Callie sits down at her dining table. She opens her laptop and scrolls through her emails. Tries to muster up some amount of enthusiasm for her other cases. They all seem so pedestrian now, so unimportant.

Her mobile phone buzzes in her pocket. She pulls it out. The number is withheld.

'Hello?'

'Ms Munro,' the voice says, and straight away Callie recognises the caller as Mia, the scarred woman from the coffee shop. 'Mr McCall would like to speak with you.'

Callie leans back in her chair. 'Again? What about?'

'About your serial killer, of course,' Mia says. 'He has some information which he thinks might help your investigation.'

'Haven't you seen the news? The police are handling the investigation now.'

Mia laughs. 'I remember Mr McCall making his views on the police clear to you when you met. He doesn't trust them to handle this properly.'

'But he trusts me?'

'So it would appear.'

Callie reaches for her cigarettes, shakes one out as she talks. 'Fine, I'll bite. What's this information that he wants me to have?'

'Are you home?'

'Yes, I'm home. Why—'

'Good. I'll pick you up in ten minutes. If you need to shower, do it quickly.'

'You're picking me up? Where are we going?'

'Mr McCall has someone he wants you to meet.'

Callie sets the unlit cigarette down on the table. Her stomach has started to churn again. 'Who?'

Mia pauses. In the background, Callie can hear the sound of car doors slamming.

'Your mistake was thinking there were only three women,' Mia says at last. 'Mr McCall has found you a fourth.'

Chapter Thirty-One

Her name is Alison. She is one of McCall's girls.

That's how Mia describes her, sitting in the back of the same Hyundai Ioniq 5 that Callie rode in just a couple of days ago – *one of McCall's girls*. Beyond that, Mia refuses to go into any detail. She sits quietly, on her phone, tapping out message after message.

'Are you at least able to tell me where we're going?' Callie asks.

Mia looks up and says, 'Snax Cafe.'

'The greasy spoon? In Newington?'

'What's the matter, not fancy enough for you?'

'I just didn't picture it as the sort of place McCall would go for breakfast.'

Mia laughs, and her scar crinkles across her face. Callie's eyes briefly go to it. Long enough for the woman to notice.

'You want to know how I got this?' Mia asks.

Callie shakes her head. 'I'm sorry, I didn't mean to—'

'I was in a car accident when I was younger. A drunk driver jumped a red light. They had to cut me out afterwards.'

'Jesus, I'm sorry. That sounds awful.'

Mia shrugs. 'It was a long time ago. I barely even think about it anymore.' She runs her finger down the side of her face, tracing the marked skin.

'Well, good for you,' Callie says.

'Yes, good for me.'

Mia turns and looks out the window then, and they ride the rest of the way in silence.

They're sat in the corner, away from the window. McCall and his girl. Alison. She's a slim thing, her blonde hair scraped back into a tight ponytail, wearing a thick coat that must be someone else's because it dwarfs her tiny frame.

Callie catches her eye as they approach. The woman says something and McCall looks over. He smiles warmly and stands up.

'Callie Munro, welcome. How are you, hen?'

'I'm good, thanks. You?'

'Oh, I can't complain.'

'How was your cinema trip?'

McCall laughs at that as they take their seats. 'Fucking awful, Callie. My son spilled his drink over me during the trailers. The trailers! I missed the start of the film trying to dry my fucking crotch in the toilets.'

Callie smiles, despite everything. She wonders if this is how it happens. How sitting down to breakfast in a small, grotty cafe with an Edinburgh gangster and one of his prostitutes becomes normal.

This whole time, Alison has said nothing. She studies the menu like there's an exam later. Callie glances at her. Close up, she can see the woman is wearing a heavy layer of make-up across one side of her face. Her eyes are sunken, her hair greasy, like she needs a hot shower and a good night's sleep.

Maybe McCall senses the shift in focus. He smoothly moves the conversation on.

'Anyway, Callie, I'd like you to meet Alison,' he says, and puts his hand on the woman's forearm. It isn't a threatening move, rather a reassuring squeeze. 'She's a brave lassie, and she's been through a hell of a lot lately.'

Alison looks up briefly. Her tired eyes darting from McCall to Callie and back to the menu.

McCall says, 'Shall we order first then, ladies? I don't know about you, but I could murder a fry-up.'

Drinks served and orders placed, McCall settles back in his chair and cradles his chipped mug of black coffee. 'Alright, hen,' he says to Alison, 'when you're ready.'

The woman nods. She goes to pour her tea and the pot trembles, hard enough to spill on to the cheap plastic tablecloth. Mia reaches across and gently takes over.

'Eddie tells me you're looking for someone,' Alison says finally. Her voice is small, although it doesn't waver. 'The man from the news this morning. The man who took those women.'

'That's right,' Callie says, unsure where this is leading.

'Aye, well, I think he tried to take me too.'

An uneasy silence settles over the table. Callie glances at McCall, who is staring right back at her. Of course this isn't news to him, or to Mia.

'What happened?'

'He picked me up. Started to drive me out to Dalmeny. I said to him—'

'Hold on.' Callie reaches down into her handbag and pulls out the notebook and pen she always carries with her. She flips it open and starts scribbling. 'When was this?'

'Fifth of November. Folk were setting off fireworks all night.'

Callie does some quick maths. November 5th was ten days ago. Amy Miller went missing on the night of the 6th, just one day later. 'You said he picked you up?'

'Yeah.'

'Whereabouts?'

'Maybury,' Alison says. 'Near Cramond.'

'What was he driving?'

'I don't remember. I think it was dark blue though. Electric, too.'

'And he drove you out to Dalmeny?'

Alison looks away. She wraps her left hand around her other wrist. Squeezes it, like she's reliving something. 'Well, he was driving out that way. I saw the Queensferry Crossing. I said to him, I said that it's triple if he wants me to stay over, and then he . . . then he . . .'

Callie says nothing, waiting for the woman to continue.

'Then he stuck me with something,' Alison says. 'He fucking drugged me.'

'He injected you?'

'On my hand. When I woke up, I was . . .'

She falters again, her voice cracking.

'It's alright,' McCall says quietly. 'Take your time, love.'

'When I woke up I was tied to a fucking table, wasn't I? Fucking naked, face down.'

'Jesus,' Callie murmurs.

'I could hear him in the other room,' Alison says. 'He was humming something. Like it was normal for him. Like it was something he did all the time.'

Callie flips a page, trying to make sure she gets everything down. Movement to her left as the waitress returns with their food. A full Scottish for everyone. Callie stares at the plate in front of her. Link sausages, bacon, haggis. She has never been less hungry in her life.

'Can I get you anything else to drink?' the waitress asks.

'We're fine, love, thank you,' McCall says. He squeezes brown sauce over his fried eggs and starts to eat.

Callie slides her plate to one side. She needs the space for her notebook. She rubs at her aching hand.

'You write shorthand?' McCall asks her.

'I wish.'

'Why don't you just use your phone to record it all? Keep your hands free for your breakfast.'

Callie picks up her pen and flips to a new page. 'Tried that for a while. Then I let the battery die halfway through an interview and got fired from the job.' She taps the notebook. 'Paper never dies on me.'

McCall smiles.

Callie turns back to Alison. 'How did you get away?' she asks.

'He hadn't tied one of my arms properly,' she says. 'Stupid twat. I managed to get myself free. Grabbed my clothes and ran.'

'Where were you?'

'No idea. Some house in the middle of nowhere. Near the beach, I think. I could hear the sea. And there was this light.'

'What light?'

'I don't know. Kept flashing on and off.'

'How did you get home?'

'Must have flagged a taxi.'

'You don't remember?'

'No, I don't fucking remember. I woke up in my stairwell the next morning. I didn't even make it into my flat. He fucking drugged me, I told you.'

McCall puts his knife down and gently places his hand on Alison's arm. 'Alright, that's enough. I don't want you making a scene.'

Alison twitches a little but stops talking. Callie watches her take a breath. 'I'm fine,' she says eventually. 'I think I just need something, you know? To take the edge off.'

McCall snorts as he resumes his breakfast. 'I'll bet you do.'

'I'm serious, Eddie, I'm on the fucking edge here, man.'

'Tell you what,' McCall says, scooping beans up with his fork. 'You finish the rest of this conversation without losing your shit, I'll sort you out. I'll even give you the night off. How does that sound?'

Alison nods. 'Aye, that sounds good.'

McCall catches Callie's eye and motions for her to continue. Callie swallows and says, 'Do you remember anything about the man who took you?'

'Not much. It was dark, and I only saw him when he picked me up, and only until he . . .'

'Until he injected you.'

'Yeah.'

'What can you tell me about him? Anything at all, no matter how small.'

'He had dark hair. Short, like. And a bump on the side of his nose. I saw it when I got in his car, before I closed the door and the light went off. I remember telling myself not to stare at it.'

Callie nods as she finishes taking it all down. She looks back over at Alison and says, 'Anything else you want to tell me now?'

'No. I just want to go home.' The woman glances at McCall. 'You said you'd sort me out.'

McCall acts like he never heard her. Says to Callie, 'You got everything you need?'

Callie skims over her notes briefly. 'I think so. Plenty to get started with anyway.' To Alison, she adds, 'I'm so sorry this happened to you.'

'Aye, well, just part of the job isn't it.'

'It shouldn't be,' Callie says.

McCall, setting his knife and fork down on his empty plate, nods. 'No, it shouldn't. Which is why I'm going to find this man, whoever he is, and I'm going to make sure it never happens again.'

He says it looking at Callie. Looking at her dead on, his face hard. She remembers what he told her about the police, about his distrust of them, and suddenly Callie is unsure why she's here. Why she's really here. What she's supposed to do with this information, what he expects from her.

Or what she expects from him. A serial killer is stalking Edinburgh; what would a man like Eddie McCall do if he got his hands on such a person?

The thought sparks uncomfortable ideas. Questions that Callie isn't ready to turn over in her mind – not now, not sitting here. The notion that she would hunt down someone on McCall's orders, that she would hand him over, that he would disappear into the dirt. Worse, that she wouldn't care.

McCall reaches into his inside pocket and pulls out a small plastic bag. Callie catches a glimpse of a handful of white pills.

'You wait until you're home,' he warns Alison, before passing them over.

The woman barely answers. Her hand snatching the bag, quick as lightning. She rises, murmurs of thank-yous and goodbyes falling from her mouth as she pushes out of the small, cramped cafe and into the street.

McCall shakes his head, sighs, then gestures towards Callie's plate. 'You going to eat that?' he asks her.

Afterwards, sitting in the back of McCall's Ioniq, Callie turns to Mia and says, 'How does she move on?'

'Hmm?'

'Alison. After what happened to her, how does she move on? Doing the job she does, how can she go back to work knowing someone like that is out there?'

Mia doesn't answer for a long moment. She doesn't even turn around at first, and when she finally does her eyes are filled with sadness. 'I used to feel the same way,' she tells Callie. 'After my accident, when I knew for certain my face would never be the same. For a long time I didn't think I would be able to go back outside again.'

'That must have been awful.'

'It was, for a while. But eventually I stopped thinking about it.'

'Mind if I ask how?'

Mia smiles and turns away, looking back out the window. 'You simply need to have worse scars somewhere else,' she says.

Chapter Thirty-Two

Back at home, Callie stalks her kitchen. She's starving. Her stale cornflakes haven't touched the sides. Somewhat guiltily, when she thinks back to this morning's meeting with Alison, the first thing she sees is the fry-up, sitting on her plate, untouched.

It's easier to push aside the emotional response. To focus on the food, and not the young girl sitting at the table. The girl who walks the streets every night to find men. Who was picked up and drugged and strapped to a table, and who – in a day and a half – will be out there again, walking.

Callie thinks about Mia's scar, about how it could possibly be worse somewhere else. Growing up, she saw her fair share of wounds. Treated them, too. On herself, on others. She saw the violence that people could do to one another. That children could do. She saw a kid take a beating so bad that his right arm took on a permanent tremor. She saw a girl with scar tissue that never healed, that no one ever cleaned, that oozed blood and pus. Another kid read about it happening in horses. It was called proud flesh.

She heads out. Back towards London Road and the Red Kite Cafe. The same window seat as before. She orders coffee and scrambled eggs and brown toast – devours them in minutes, her notebook open beside her. The scribbled words finally able to coalesce into something more. An avenue of investigation.

Breakfast finished, Callie hunches forward, going over everything Alison told her this morning. She makes further notes: the important parts, the possible leads. He picked her up in Maybury, he drove a blue car. An electric. He took her out towards Dalmeny, towards the Queensferry Crossing. Alison said she saw it before she fell unconscious. Did he stay this side of the river? Did he cross the bridge?

The timing of it all, too; it practically yells at her from the page. Alison was picked up and managed to escape the day before Amy Miller was taken. Two women attacked within twenty-four hours; a sizeable change in this guy's MO. Before Amy – before Alison – nearly six months had passed since Gail Patton. Maybe it had something to do with the fact that Alison escaped. Maybe she ruined whatever he had planned. Callie wondered if it was like sex. If this psycho had gotten himself worked into a lather only to find he wasn't allowed to finish. If he had, would Amy Miller have been left alone?

More notes, more reliving this morning's conversation. Alison said she escaped from a house near the beach. She said she could hear the sea. South Queensferry? Or perhaps he did take her across the water, to Dalgety Bay, to Aberdour.

The light.

Alison mentioned seeing a light, flashing on and off. Near the sea. A lighthouse? Callie opens up a new window and starts searching.

She finds a surprising amount of them. A couple in South Queensferry – both on Hawes Pier, right by the Forth Bridge, but neither of them in use. Moving further out across the Forth, she makes a list of the ones still in operation. Oxcars, Hawkcraig Point, Elie Ness. How far could he have driven her along the coast?

Over an hour passes, sitting there. She sits up, stretching, feeling her back pop. Looking over her notes, she's achieved less than she'd hoped. A list of places along a stretch of beach, a distance of just about forty miles. She needs more information if she's to narrow it down further.

One last scan over Alison's statement. Callie pauses on how the woman got home: taxi, possibly, she couldn't remember. Still, it's worth pursuing. Might be a taxi company has a record of their driver picking up a lone woman and driving her into Edinburgh on November 5th.

Not that they'd give the information up voluntarily. Not to her, anyway. She'd need a cop to make the request.

She'd need Mac.

Chapter Thirty-Three

Callie calls DS Mackenzie Reid's number as she paces her living room. His phone rings out, and she wonders what he's doing. Working traffic, whatever that means. She pictures him parked up in a lay-by somewhere, watching cars flow past, praying for a speeder so he can actually do something.

She sends him a text. *Uncovered some new info. Give me a call.* A few minutes later, her phone rings.

'You know I'm not working this case anymore,' Mac says.

'I know, but I don't know who is.'

'Doesn't matter, you just phone the station.'

'I'd rather talk to you. Why, you too busy?'

Mac snorts. 'You kidding? I've barely moved from my desk all day.'

'How long do you think you'll be in the doghouse?'

'Dunno. A while. Dawson can barely talk to me she's so pissed.'

Callie sits down on her sofa. She's spread her notes out across the coffee table. 'Maybe this'll help get you back in everyone's good books then,' she says.

On the other end of the line, she hears Mac shifting in his seat. A soft clunk as he sets his fancy coffee down on the wooden desk. 'I'm all ears,' he says. 'What've you got?'

Callie tells him. Not everything, of course. She leaves McCall's name out of it. Makes out like she found Alison all by herself. Mac barely speaks the whole time.

'Well?' she says, afterwards. 'What're your thoughts?'

'I think if this woman really was attacked by the killer, then she needs to come in.'

'Mac—'

'She needs to speak to the detectives running the investigation, Callie. She needs to undergo a forensic examination. Whatever he drugged her with? There might still be traces in her system.'

Callie shakes her head even though he can't see her. 'I can tell you right now, she isn't someone who's going to volunteer to get berated by a couple of detectives in a closed room.'

'Fine, they can go to her.' Mac's voice sounds annoyed. 'This isn't some TV drama, you know? They're not going to start screaming at her over a metal table.'

'Alright—'

'This is a murder investigation, and if you've got information that can help, then—'

'I said alright, Mac. I get it. I'll pass along her details, I'm just saying she might not talk.'

The line goes quiet. Then, 'You said you thought she was taken to a house along the coast?'

'Yeah. Somewhere she could hear the sea, somewhere she could spot a lighthouse.'

'Big somewhere.'

'Fuck's sake, why do you think I'm talking to you? I need your help to narrow it down. The taxi companies might have a record of her trip, of where they picked her up from.'

'Callie, there's no way I can do this. Not right now. Joyce gets a whiff that I'm involved and I'll be back in uniform. Best I can do is pass it up the chain.'

'Oh, stop being such a pussy,' Callie snaps.

She knows he's right, but that doesn't make her feel any better. She's used to running her own cases, on her own terms. Small stuff, intimate stuff. She feels suddenly unprepared to handle something of this magnitude. But she can't shake her reservations about Joyce. Maybe it's just McCall's distrust of the police rubbing off on her, but either way she knows there's no one else on the force she'll take this to. No one that's given a shit the way Mac has. And even though she's struggling, Callie knows she isn't about to just hand everything over and walk away.

'Look,' she says, her voice calm. 'I'm not trying to be difficult. You want to pass it along, fine, I get it. But that doesn't stop us from looking into it ourselves at the same time.'

'Callie . . .'

'I'm serious, Mac! Who knows how long it might take for my information to get followed up on? And if they can't track down my girl—'

'*Your* girl?'

'—or she won't talk to them. And yes, she is my fucking girl. I fucking found her, didn't I?' Callie stands up, fast enough to send papers flying from the coffee table. 'Help me look into this. Help me narrow down the search. He's keeping them somewhere on that stretch of coast, Mac. Somewhere across the Forth. Some little shithole shack near Burntisland, or East Wemyss, or Elie. Somewhere they can hear the sea and they can see a lighthouse. Help me find it, please.'

A moment, a long moment. The detective thinking it over. She imagines him hunched over his desk, writing, or maybe sat back in his chair with his hand over his eyes. Finally, he says, 'You really think he might be in Elie?'

'Jesus, I don't know, maybe. There's a couple of lighthouses there right off the beach.' Callie pauses. 'Why?'

'Nothing.'

'No, why Elie?'

'I said nothing, Callie.' Mac sighs heavily. 'Leave it with me, alright? I'll see what I can do.'

He hangs up. Callie stares at her phone, her brow furrowed. The end of the conversation swirls in her head. An uneasy feeling settling over her. She sits down and leafs through her notebook again. All of it, from the very start, and by the time she's done a thought has occurred to her.

She fires off a text to Martin. *I need you to run a background check on someone for me. Stick it on my tab.*

He responds almost instantly. *What you wanting to know?*

Property assets.

Send the details, he types. *Give me an hour.*

Callie spends it cleaning her flat. Headphones in, music loud enough to drown out her thinking. Too wired to do anything else, too full of energy to focus. She's scrubbing her shower when Martin gets back to her. Crouched over the drain, she reads his message.

'Motherfucker,' she whispers.

Chapter Thirty-Four

Callie waits by his blue VW Golf. She rolls a cigarette between her fingers, itching with the desire to light up. A certain perverse satisfaction in making herself wait, in drawing it out. She's only been here a few minutes. She can last.

A couple of uniformed officers glance at her as they enter the station, but neither of them bothers to approach. Callie checks her phone, sees he's read her message, and thirty seconds later the doors swing open and DS Mackenzie Reid emerges.

He nods at her as he approaches. That weird, stilted head-jerk that guys do. She slides the unlit cigarette into her coat pocket and pulls out a sheet of folded paper.

'What's this about?' Mac says, rubbing at his arms. He's not wearing his jacket. 'I've not managed to speak with the DI in charge yet, if that's what you're after.'

Callie hands him the piece of paper. Mac takes it, frowning. She watches his face as he reads it. Sees the crease in his forehead go smooth.

'You told me it was a red herring,' she says.

'What is this?'

'You told me you knew him, that you trusted him. You said this was nothing.'

'Hang on now, I don't understand—'

She jabs at the paper in his hands. 'This is a house just off Ruby Bay in Elie. It's a couple hundred metres from the beach. A half-mile from Elie Ness lighthouse. And it's owned by Chief Inspector Philip Joyce.'

Mac shakes his head. 'I'm telling you, Callie, you've got this wrong.'

'You knew, didn't you.'

'What?'

'This morning, when we talked. You just about shit yourself as soon as I mentioned Elie. You knew Joyce has a property there.'

'You really think Joyce is your man? You think he's, what, taking women from their beds, drugging them and driving them to his Elie holiday home?'

'You think this is something you can just ignore?'

'Callie, I know him!'

'So what? Every serial killer has friends, Mac! Open your fucking eyes!' She grabs the paper back, waves it as she rants. 'This house fits the description given by Alison. It's owned by a man whose car was captured hanging out in Amy Miller's estate for nearly an hour the night she went missing. You can't ignore this. You have to bring Joyce in for questioning!'

Mac stares at her like she's gone insane. 'I can't just bring the chief inspector in for questioning. I'd . . . I'd need to take this to the Investigations and Review Commissioner . . .'

'So fucking do that, then—'

'This is circumstantial, Callie.'

'Bullshit it's circumstantial. It's—'

'It's circumstantial and you know it. I spoke with his wife, remember? She already confirmed she was the one driving.'

'Then she's lying! She's covering for him, don't you see? You need to take her to the commissioner too.'

'Christ, Callie, do you have any idea what you're asking? And even if I did – after Fullerton? The press would eat Joyce alive if they found out he was being questioned.'

Callie presses the sheet of paper firmly against Mac's chest. 'You're a fucking coward, Detective,' she says. She sees hurt in the man's eyes but she pushes it aside. 'And if another woman goes missing then it's your fault.'

She turns and leaves then. Already regretting some of what she said, already wishing she hadn't lost her temper. Digging out that unsmoked cigarette from her pocket, her hands trembling with the confrontation so badly she can barely light it.

Out of the car park now, out of sight. Leaning against the brick wall and closing her eyes, taking in deep lungfuls of smoke, trying not to think about what she has to do next.

Chapter Thirty-Five

It takes Callie over an hour to make the drive. From the Grassmarket out along the M90, across the bridge. It's late afternoon now but it's clear, and the Forth stretches beneath her, the sun glinting along its surface for miles in both directions.

Callie barely sees it. She has no eye for it, not today. This is the same route that Alison and Amy and all those other women were taken, and when Callie turns her head she does not see the postcard view but rather she sees them, slumped in the passenger seat, drugged into unconsciousness.

After the bridge comes Inverkeithing, then Kirkcaldy and Methil and Leven and Upper Largo, and Kilconquhar Loch hidden behind the trees, before finally she reaches Elie.

Callie drives slowly through the small coastal streets. It's not a town she's visited often, never somewhere she's felt much interest in. The type of place she's always associated with golfing holidays and summer homes for wealthy Edinburgh lawyers.

Joyce's property sits just outside the main town, near a stretch of beach named Lady's Tower. Callie parks up on the side of the road and unzips her backpack on the passenger seat. A kit from Martin's bazaar of technology – everything she thought she might need over the next twelve hours. She pulls out the SLR camera and winds down her window.

From here she can just make it out. The lone house standing on the horizon. Painted white, with what looks like a single pane of glass adorning one side. Callie pictures the chief inspector standing there, staring out at the sea. A glass of whisky, a wood-burning stove. Humming a tune – the same tune Alison said she'd heard while strapped down to his table in the next room.

She snaps some photos, then checks the time. It's nearly five. Not dark enough, but getting there. She packs the camera away and turns the car around. Back into Elie proper. She's not eaten since the Red Kite Cafe this morning, and she doesn't feel like breaking into a man's house on an empty stomach.

The next few hours drag by. Callie spends them in her car, waiting. A quick dinner, a sandwich and a piece of fruit, eaten in the driver's seat. Her camera trained on Joyce's house. She uses the viewfinder as binoculars, scanning the property for any sign of life, for movement behind that big pane of glass. But she sees nothing.

As the sky darkens, she prepares. Dark top and bottoms, black gloves, slim narrow-beam torch. Her phone, set to silent. She checks it one last time. Part of her is surprised she's not heard from Mac. A phone call, a text, especially after the way she left.

She wonders how he spent his afternoon. Going over the property details, perhaps, asking himself whether he's right about his chief inspector. Whether it's possible that all the signs pointing to Joyce are coincidences and easily explainable. She wonders how hard he will cling to those ideals, how badly he will want them to be true.

Night falls. Callie steps from her car and into the brisk sea air. The wind rushes up over the edge of the beach wall, making her eyes water. Ahead of her, Joyce's house sits a half-mile or so along a dirt track. She sets off, into the darkness.

By the time she reaches it, she's sweating lightly. Her heart is rattling in her chest. A short fence runs the perimeter of the property; she follows it around to the rear, stepping over it and into Joyce's garden.

Halfway to the back door she hears the sound of a car travelling along the main road. Headlights flash in the distance, growing closer. Callie drops on to her front and holds her breath. The grass is ice cold; it sends a chill spreading through her chest. She listens to the roar of the waves and of the vehicle as it approaches. A steady beat, too slow for her heart – bass from the car radio. It washes over her as it passes by without stopping, the garden around her briefly illuminated before falling into darkness again.

Callie waits a full minute before she gets back to her feet. When she does, her front is freezing, and she rubs at her arms as she reaches the back door. Peering through the small glass panes, she can make out a small utility room. Sink, coat hooks, washing machine. The door to the rest of the house is open, but too dark to see through. Callie tries the handle, just in case. Locked.

She makes an executive decision. Pulling her torch, she turns it over in her hands and then knocks it, hard, against the glass. The pane cracks easily, a large piece falling inwards where it shatters on the floor. She waits for another full minute, holding her breath, but no one comes to investigate.

Reaching her arm through the broken window, Callie feels for the latch and twists it. A clunk as the door unlocks. She takes a breath and steps inside the house.

Chapter Thirty-Six

The click of her torch is a shotgun in the dark. The creak of the floor a wolf's howl. Callie pictures Philip Joyce, silently slicing his way through windows and drifting through people's homes. Quiet enough that they kept on sleeping, right up until he was peering down at them in their beds.

She inches her way out of the room and into the house proper. Keeping her torch beam low, sweeping the hall ahead of her. It's a nice place: expensive wooden floors, plush carpet on the stairs. On a side table sits a heavy-looking sculpture of a woman on horseback. A large mirror on the wall by the front door. Callie catches a glimpse of herself as she passes by. A spectre in the darkness. Hunched forward, her face pale, her eyes mad.

Moving into the kitchen now. A long dining table on one side, a large island on the other. One of those fancy ceramic sinks set into the marble worktop. Brass taps, a wide American-style fridge with an ice dispenser. This place is downright opulent.

She spots a door at the back of the room, but when she tries it, the handle is locked. No glass to break this time, no way to get in other than brute force. After a moment's thought, she goes back into the hall and returns with the sculpture. She sets the torch down on the marble island, pointing its beam at the door as she lifts the ornament and smashes it against the handle.

It takes three swings before it breaks. Callie is sweating again. Exertion, adrenaline. She sets the sculpture down, her hands shaking. Picking up the torch, she pushes open the busted door.

Immediately the atmosphere changes. The room beyond here is cold. No heating, or if there is it's not been on for a long while. She shines her torch inside and feels her stomach cramp. Reaching for a light switch, she flips it and a bare bulb in the ceiling floods the chamber in a harsh, angry glare.

A concrete floor. Callie steps on it, feels the chill rise through her shoes. A smell in the air she can't place but she knows she's encountered before. An awful smell. Tangy and putrid. Coppery, like blood. She doesn't want to but she closes her eyes and the memory takes her and she sees four boys: one on the ground, crying, his hands over his face, his body curled inwards, three others stooped over him jeering, spitting, kicking, laughing.

She remembers it went on for so long it wasn't funny anymore. By the end there was just the sound of them panting as they did it. The sound of them panting and grunting and the sound their shoes made, swinging into the limp boy on the ground. The boy who had long since stopped crying out, who had let his hands fall away from his face.

And now, in Joyce's house, it is the same smell. Blood and piss and shit and sweat and something more, something intangible. Something akin to fear, to pain. Something awful has happened in this room, Callie knows it. She can smell it.

And there, in the centre of the room, is the table. Callie approaches it slowly. It is wooden, and old, and rough-looking. There are score marks in the surface. Callie looks at it and even though she has never seen it before, she can guess how it would work.

Two holes near the top, for your arms. Fed through up to the shoulder. Your face pressed into the hard wood. Your body bent forward, your feet still on the ground. Black leather straps running up the table legs to hold you still.

Alison was here. Tied to this very table. Listening to Joyce in the room next door – in the kitchen – humming a tune. Alison, and Amy, and Gail, and Jennifer. They were all here.

Callie glances away from the table and sees it then. Lying on the floor, tucked away in the corner. Wrapped in a thick bundle of plastic sheets.

A body.

She goes to it. Bends down and unwraps it. Not everything, just enough to be sure. Enough to see the pale skin and the dark hair, the blue lips and the green-skinned Pikachu laughing at her from her shoulder.

'Amy,' she says softly. 'What did he do to you?'

And then, from behind her, Joyce speaks.

Chapter Thirty-Seven

'You shouldn't have come here,' he says.

Callie jumps. Turning sharply, she sees Chief Inspector Philip Joyce in the kitchen doorway. A large man, with the same angry expression he wore while fending off media questions about a serial killer. Red-faced, narrowed eyes. His eyebrows are knotted together so tight they're a single line. There's a knife in his right hand, held low. A long, skinny blade.

'It was you,' Callie says to him. She takes a step back, further into the chamber, one hand still holding her torch, the other sliding into her pocket to grasp her phone. 'All this time, it was you.'

Joyce moves into the room. He closes the door behind him. Callie hears the click of the latch in the pit of her stomach.

'It's over, Joyce,' she says, her voice nearly cracking but not quite. She takes another step back. Away from him. Towards the table. 'You hear me? It's over.'

'How did you know?' he says to her, then shakes his head. 'It doesn't matter.'

'Listen now—'

Joyce runs at her. Callie throws herself backwards, rolling across the table as the knife slashes. She lands clumsily, one hand still trying to get at her phone. She pulls it out just as Joyce hurls himself against the table. It judders across the floor, knocking into her, sending her phone flying. She hears glass break as it lands.

No time to think. Callie moves. Around the table, towards the centre of the room. Joyce panting as he crashes after her. She glances back at the kitchen door, maps her route, then swings her torch upwards.

The bare bulb shatters. The room plunges into darkness. Callie immediately about-turns, skirting back towards the door in a long arc. Even though she can't see a thing, she doesn't slow. She can't; Joyce knows this room better than she does. All she has are these few moments of surprise. A few moments to reach the door, to escape.

She hears Joyce grunting, somewhere to her left. Then the rustle of movement and a sharp, searing pain across her left shoulder. Callie cries out. She drops the torch. Her hand goes slick, warm blood running down her arm. Still she doesn't stop. How many more steps to the door – three, four?

Suddenly it's there. She turns the handle and falls through it into the kitchen, into the light, just as Joyce's hand clutches at her back. His big, meaty fist grabbing her black top. The material bunching around her chest as he pulls her sharply.

With a cry she twists away from him, tripping, sending them both tumbling to the floor. She hears Joyce scrabbling behind her and the sculpture is there, next to her. The naked woman on horseback. Callie doesn't think. She lifts it, rising to her feet as Joyce rises to his. She swings as he slashes.

She's faster.

The heavy ornament thuds against Joyce's head and he grunts, once, his eyes fluttering. He drops the bloodied knife. He rocks to one side. Composure returning to his face as he reaches for her.

But Callie is ready for him. Her feet apart, her back braced. She swings the sculpture like it's a softball bat. Her body uncoiling like a spring. Arms fully extending, ignoring the pain, ignoring the blood. Letting her body twist with the momentum.

It connects with Joyce's head for a second time. A spray of red, hot and warm. The chief inspector's head snaps to the right and he follows after it, plunging to the floor. Callie stands over him, panting, holding the naked woman high, ready to strike him for a third time if he so much as twitches, but he lies still.

Chapter Thirty-Eight

Things move quickly in the aftermath.

Emergency vehicles swarm the property, blues and twos on the dirt track. A sea breeze carries the sound of sirens, of people yelling. Three floodlights on the beach turn night into day.

Callie sits on the edge of an ambulance, holding an unlit cigarette, a paramedic going over her injured shoulder. She has given her statement. She is ready to leave this place now. As the adrenaline fades, her body begins to ache, and not just in her shoulder; in her head, in the tips of her fingers. From gripping the sculpture, maybe.

'You're going to need stitches,' the technician tells her. 'We'll have to take you to A&E.'

Callie nods. The cigarette trembles in her grip. 'Can I drive?'

'I'd strongly advise against it.'

'I don't want to leave my car here.'

The paramedic steps back and smiles warmly at her. 'Don't worry love, they'll get it to you.'

Callie watches her snap off her blue gloves and stuff them into a pocket. 'Where are you taking me?' she asks. 'The Royal?'

'Same place as him,' the woman says, and jerks her thumb towards the house.

Callie looks across the grassy rise. Two medics are wheeling Philip Joyce out on a stretcher. She leans against the ambulance and closes her eyes. In the distance, she can hear the heavy thud of an approaching helicopter.

◆　◆　◆

They give him a private room. Three floors up, handcuffed to the bed. A police officer is stood outside on watch.

Callie hears snatches of all this as she waits for the nurse. By the time her shoulder's sewn back up, the news is clear. Joyce is in a coma.

'Medically induced,' Mac tells her. 'Too much pressure in his brain.'

He sits across from her now. In a crushed suit, in a little plastic seat that he shifts about in, unable to keep still. Beyond the curtain comes the noise of A&E: doors banging, raised voices. Callie has been dressed and ready to leave for twenty minutes.

'I should have hit him harder,' she mutters, massaging her neck with one hand. 'Saved the NHS some money.'

'It's better he's alive,' Mac says. 'It's better he confesses to it all.'

Callie grunts. She studies the detective. His askew tie, his unstyled hair. She remembers that it's four in the morning and he's now working traffic, and she wonders why he's here.

'Tell me what's going on,' she says to Mac. 'At the house. What have they found?'

He shrugs. 'I don't really know anything more than you right now.'

'I assumed that's why you were here. To tell me something.'

'That is why I'm here,' he says, and he squirms in his seat again.

'It's the middle of the night. How did you know any of this was going on?'

'I got a call. Dawson, too.'

'Couple of police cars collide outside Joyce's house?'

He shoots her a look. She holds her hands up.

'Sorry,' she says. 'That was mean. But I thought you and Dawson were working traffic these days.'

'We are. But he was our boss, Callie. News like this doesn't wait until morning to spread.'

Callie nods. She checks her watch. Twenty-five minutes she's been waiting now. 'God I'm tired. I just want to go home.'

'Your car's still at the scene.'

'Fuck's sake, so it is. How long until I get it back?'

The detective shrugs. 'A while. Listen, Callie—'

'And what, I'm supposed to just get the bus home? The bloody night bus?'

'Callie—'

'Joyce'll be out on parole by the time I get home.'

'Callie, I came here to apologise.'

She pauses, feels the rant building inside her dissolving away. 'Apologise for what?'

'For not believing you. For making you go into that house by yourself.'

Callie grunts again and waves her hand through the air. 'Please don't start getting sentimental on me, Mac. I only know how to deal with snark.'

'I'm serious. You flagged him early on and I dismissed you. You asked me about his house and I shut you down.'

'I get it,' she says, her words sharp but her tone soft. 'It's difficult to see what's right in front of us sometimes. But you stepped up when I gave you Fullerton and you lost credibility. That's on me.'

The detective finally seems to relax. He sinks back into his little plastic chair. 'I appreciate that,' he says.

Callie checks her watch again. 'Nearly half an hour now,' she mutters. 'It'll be morning before I get out of here.'

'Night buses might be finished.'

'Small mercies.'

Mac smiles and gets to his feet. 'I'll see if I can find someone,' he says. 'And I'll give you a lift home, don't worry.'

He half steps through the curtain before pausing to look back. An expression on his face like he wants to ask her something, and then he's gone.

◆ ◆ ◆

Whatever's playing on his mind finally works its way loose on the drive home. Mac turns to her and says, 'You mind if I ask how you knew?'

'Hmm?'

Callie is curled into herself on the passenger seat. Her head against her shoulder, her arms wrapped around her waist. All of a sudden sleep has come for her. Sitting here, in the detective's warm car, she has never felt so tired.

'I read your statement,' Mac says. 'You said you knew as soon as you entered the room that something wasn't right.'

'I did.'

'How?'

Callie sniffs and rubs at her nose. They are driving through Newington, past the Commonwealth Pool. This time of night Queen's Park is open, the traffic sparse, and the Golf glides down the sweeping curve by Arthur's Seat. Ahead sits Dynamic Earth and the Scottish Parliament, and just beyond them is her flat. This close to her bed, Callie finally starts to relax.

'Personal experience,' she says quietly. Her mind replays the memory, like it's been doing all night. The inside of Joyce's prison.

Its awful scent. She thinks about the cold concrete floor and the wooden table with its leather straps.

And she thinks about the three boys she stumbled upon as a child. The three boys slowly beating another to death. The drudgery of it. The hard work, the effort.

They didn't manage it in the end, although not because of her. She'd been too transfixed – frozen in the doorway, hands squeezing the chipped wooden frame, her fingers splayed across the countless pencil marks, the countless children's names. Someone else shouted for help. Someone behind her. And a few moments later their foster carer came barrelling into the room, knocking her to the floor in their haste to break up the attack.

The boy lived, or at least he was living when they took him away. Callie cannot remember his name now. All she can remember is his face: the way his eyes were swollen closed, the way his cheeks were puffed, the way his hair was matted with blood.

'Listen, I didn't mean to pry,' Mac says. He half reaches out towards her then stops, letting his hand fall on the gear stick. 'I was just curious, that's all.'

'No, it's alright,' Callie says, and for the second time in recent days, she finds herself telling a man about her childhood.

She doesn't go into detail, and she doesn't even have to reach that far for the words – her conversation with Grant Miller is still warm. Even so, something about it feels nice. Almost cathartic.

Mac doesn't speak the entire time. He pulls up outside her flat and leaves the engine running. He listens to her story about the boy, about how she stumbled upon him. How she was unable to do anything. She tells it to the footwell, she tells it to the glovebox handle. She tells it to the flickering street lamp at the end of her street.

'Jesus,' Mac says when she's done. 'That poor kid.'

'I know.'

'Did you ever find out what happened to him?'

'No.'

The detective shifts in his seat. 'It wasn't your fault, Callie. It wasn't your job to protect him.'

'I know.' She looks over at him. 'But maybe it is now.'

'And your parents? You've never managed to track them down?'

'Closest I got was tracking down the name of someone who worked at the homeless shelter at the time I was dropped off. They'd died a year earlier.'

'Shit. Listen, I—'

Mac's mobile chirps. He digs it out of his inside pocket. In the dim glow of the phone's screen, Callie sees his face fall.

'Oh fuck,' he murmurs.

Chapter Thirty-Nine

Despite everything, Callie sleeps.

It is a heavy, lumbering sleep. It is a physical presence. When she dreams it is of being weighed down, of being pulled under warm water, and when she wakes mid-morning it is with an effort and a gasp of air.

Her shoulder aches. Moving slowly into the en-suite, Callie downs paracetamol and water from the tap, ice cold, to soothe her dry throat. Standing there, stretching, it takes a moment for it all to come back.

Eleanor Joyce is dead.

That's what Mac told her. Last night, in her car. The message on his phone. Callie frowned after he said it, her brain already starting to fog with tiredness and prescription painkillers. It took Callie longer than she'd have liked to realise that Eleanor Joyce was the chief inspector's wife. Uniformed officers found her in their garage, hanging from the rafters.

The death wasn't being treated as suspicious. Someone must have given her the heads-up. A neighbour over in Elie, perhaps, watching the police descend upon the property. Or maybe even someone from the station, breaking protocol to tell a friend that their husband is in hospital. It probably doesn't matter all that much how it had happened. What was important was what Eleanor

Joyce had done once she'd found out. To Callie, the implication was clear: the woman was as guilty as the chief inspector.

Moving downstairs, still half asleep, Callie flicks on the kettle and pats her coat down for cigarettes. She opens her front door and sits on the step, smoking and drinking coffee. It is nearly eleven a.m. When she is done, she makes herself breakfast – cornflakes with three slices of toast, she is starving – and eats it in the living room, on the sofa, in front of the TV. She watches the news.

The top story is the Night Watcher arrest. They don't name Joyce, of course, it's too early for that and he is too important a player, but they summarise the last few hours well enough. A body has been discovered, believed to be that of missing woman Amy Miller, in a house in Elie. Callie makes a mental note to contact Grant, to offer him her support. She doubts he will accept it, but still, it is the right thing to do.

She's halfway through her final piece of toast when the newsreader pauses mid-sentence. The ticker at the bottom of the screen updates itself. *BREAKING NEWS*, it states in a big, bold font. *SIX BODIES NOW DISCOVERED IN ELIE HOLIDAY HOME.*

Chapter Forty

They pull the bodies up from under the floor. They dig them out from the walls. They peel back wallpaper. They rip up floorboards. They break through plasterboard and crack freshly laid concrete.

In the twelve hours since Joyce was carried out on a stretcher, Forensics have torn his holiday home apart.

Callie spends the afternoon following it all online. By early evening, his name has leaked. There's only so long someone's home can be systematically demolished on national television before someone reports who it belongs to. The police are forced to admit that the prime suspect in the murders of six women is one of their own.

They issue a formal statement. Terse, and to the point. *Chief Inspector Philip Joyce is currently the sole focus of our investigations.* When it is announced that he is currently in hospital following an 'altercation', Callie starts to get an uncomfortable feeling in her gut.

It is nearly midnight when Eleanor Joyce's suicide is reported.

Overnight, the story metastasises. Callie wakes to the sound of someone thumping on her front door. A reporter, a small crowd of them. Pressed together at the bottom of the steps, in her small, cramped garden. She watches them from her bedroom window, and they see her, their gazes moving upwards in unison, like a great multi-faced beast. They shout; a babble of incoherent noise. Some of them raise cameras.

Callie drops the blind. Her room goes dark. She steps away from the window and sinks on to the bed. Downstairs, she can hear the hammering on her front door increasing.

She tries to ignore them. She moves round the flat, closing every curtain and blind. She leaves the television off, leaves her phone off. Before she does, she sees she has over a dozen missed calls, from numbers she does not recognise.

She showers and dresses in the near-dark. She makes coffee and cereal, which she barely touches. Acid flares in her guts. They must know she was at the Elie house, that she is responsible for Joyce's injury. For a brief, mad moment, she wonders if Joyce is dead, then tells herself that it would be police – not reporters – coming to her door, and they likely wouldn't stop at knocking.

Callie paces her flat, a caged animal. She wants a cigarette but she doesn't dare crack a window so she swallows down the urge for as long as she can before finally relenting and lighting up, hunched in the corner of her kitchen, blowing smoke into the extractor fan of her cooker hood.

By midday the reporters seem to have given up somewhat. There's still a handful milling around, but they lean against her garden wall with bored looks on their faces. She watches them, carefully, from her bathroom window. Her body angled away from the glass to hide her shadow. They talk to each other, they scroll through their phones. Callie gets a perverse feeling of satisfaction in seeing them waste their day.

Her appetite returns. She makes a fresh pot of coffee and drinks two cups. She fries eggs, taking advantage of the already-running cooker hood to smoke another cigarette. Her phone sits on the kitchen counter. Turned off and on its front. Callie stares at it as she eats.

From outside, there comes a sudden commotion. Car doors and raised voices. Callie pushes her half-finished lunch away and stands up, her stomach cramping. She moves to the window and chances a look: two police cars have pulled up. Uniformed officers move through the small group of reporters, ignoring their shouted questions, their outstretched phones. And there, in the middle of them, is DS Mackenzie Reid and his partner, DI Sandra Dawson.

◆　◆　◆

She lets them in, the door opening just long enough for the detectives and two uniformed officers to slip inside. Behind them, the air is filled with frenzied yelling. Callie hears the shutter of cameras as she closes the door.

'Bloody arseholes,' one of the officers mutters. 'They been there all day?'

'Pretty much,' Callie says.

DI Dawson says, 'I'm sorry you're going through all this, Ms Munro.' The detective's voice has a firm, no-nonsense sharpness that underscores each word. She certainly doesn't sound that sorry. 'My name is DI Sandra Dawson. I understand you've already spoken with my partner here.'

'That's right,' Callie says, her eyes flicking on to Mac. He gives her a short smile.

'I wonder if we could go and sit down,' Dawson says.

They are all still stood around Callie's hallway. 'Of course,' she says, and she gestures towards the dining room. 'What's all this about?'

She asks the question, but she knows the answer already. She tries not to think it though, as they all troop silently through to the next room, as they all pull out chairs. As she clears away her half-eaten lunch and turns off the cooker hood, the smell of cigarette smoke lingering. She tries not to think why two detectives and two uniformed officers have come to her flat the day after she beat a man so bad, doctors had to put him into a coma to try to save his life. An awful, despicable man, but that's not the point, is it?

'Please,' DI Dawson says, and nods towards an empty chair. 'Have a seat, Ms Munro.'

Callie does. Her legs trembling, her heart racing. She keeps her gaze low, suddenly unable to look any of her new visitors in the eye. She pictures Mac's short smile when he entered. Was there pity in his expression? Regret?

'We're here to discuss with you the events that took place last night, at the property owned by Chief Inspector Philip Joyce,' Dawson continues.

Callie nods. She can feel the tension inside her starting to build. She clasps her hands together on the table in front of her.

'Now, you've already given a number of statements—'

'He's dead, isn't he,' Callie says. Quietly, almost to herself. After a beat she looks up and locks eyes with the female detective. 'Joyce. I killed him and you're here to arrest me.'

Dawson blinks, then breaks character by reaching across the table and taking hold of Callie's trembling hands. The woman shakes her head. 'No, Ms Munro, Philip Joyce isn't dead. Quite the opposite, in fact. That's why we're here.'

'I don't understand. He's awake?'

'He is. And he wants to talk.' Another pause, another shared glance between the detectives. 'He wants to talk to you, Ms Munro,' Dawson says, taking her hand back, her mouth forming a thin, hard line. 'He only wants to talk to you.'

Chapter Forty-One

Callie rides with the detectives. In the back of their car, her face flushed. Adrenaline from pushing through the small group of reporters outside her flat. She did what DI Dawson had recommended: face forward, eyes focused on the distance. *Don't engage them, don't acknowledge them.*

Now, as they drive along London Road, past Meadowbank towards Duddingston, Callie leans forward and says, 'What's happening with the investigation?'

Mac twists slightly in his seat to look back at her. 'Forensics are still working the house.'

'And the women?'

'Them too.'

It is the first time he's spoken to her since arriving at her flat. Callie wonders if he prefers letting his partner take the lead.

'Don't take this the wrong way,' Callie says, 'but I'm surprised to see you both working this case.'

Mac smiles at her. 'Don't think we're up to the job?'

She sees Dawson's head twitch slightly, sees in the rear-view mirror her gaze flicking on to Mac's for a moment.

Callie says, 'I didn't think they'd want anyone from Joyce's team on this. Aren't you both too close?'

'We're not leading the investigation,' Mac says. 'We're just assisting. But you're right, most of the department has been shut out. I guess they don't know yet whether he was acting alone.'

'So no more traffic?'

'No more traffic. Although, I don't think it was necessarily a bad thing to show us butting heads with Joyce, given the circumstances.'

'What can you tell me about the women?'

'Very little,' Dawson says sharply, her gaze on Callie. 'This is an active investigation, Ms Munro. I'm sure you understand.'

'It's an active investigation that I'm part of, Detective. You want me to speak to this man? I think I deserve to know what I'm walking into. Were Gail Hart and Jennifer Patton among the bodies you found?'

Dawson pauses. She taps her fingers on the steering wheel as she waits for a light to go green. 'Yes, they were,' she says at last. 'Along with Amy Miller and three other unidentified victims.'

'How long had they been there for?'

'Years, some of them.'

'How did he kill them?'

The detective's fingers curl around the wheel. Callie hears her exhaling. 'He slit their throats, Ms Munro. But before he did he stripped them naked. He stripped them naked, he tied them down and he whipped their backs until their flesh peeled and started to rot. All of them were suffering from hypergranulation to some degree. The wounds had grown so much excessive tissue, it was like . . .'

'It was like an open sore.'

Dawson glances back at her. 'The size of my fucking fist. How did you know?'

'I saw a kid with it, when I was younger,' Callie says. 'Although nothing as bad as that. She'd get into scrapes and no one was around to clean it properly. It took an age to heal, and it bled constantly.' She closes her eyes at the image. 'We called it proud flesh.'

The car falls silent. Mac is still turned around, watching her. He reaches into his inside pocket and pulls out a slip of paper.

'We've written you a list of questions,' he says, and passes it over. 'Topics we'd like you to try and engage Joyce on if you can.'

Callie unfolds the paper. The list looks hastily concocted, a spread of bullet points and general topics. *Number of victims. Did he work alone. What did his wife know.*

She folds the list away and sinks back into her seat. They're almost at Little France now, and the Royal Infirmary is just a few minutes away. She decides to keep quiet until they arrive.

'Do you know why they call it Little France?'

Callie looks at Mac as the three of them, plus the two uniformed officers, ride the lift up to Joyce's room. 'Something to do with Mary, Queen of Scots, isn't it?'

Mac shrugs. 'No idea.'

The doors slide open and the small group steps out. Callie is hustled down a long ward corridor, past nurses' stations and large rooms filled with beds. The air has that horrible, cloying smell to it that hospitals always seem to stink of. From whatever they use to clean the sick and shit off the floors.

Joyce has a room to himself. Right at the end of the corridor, as tucked away from the other patients as you can get in a hospital this busy. A police officer sits on a chair outside his room. Callie can hear her radio squawking as they approach.

The officer stands, nodding at the detectives. 'Ma'am,' she says.

'How is he?' Dawson asks.

'Quiet as a mouse.'

'Good. Officer Howard, this is Callie Munro.'

Callie smiles weakly. She suddenly feels like she's going to throw up. The hospital stench has crawled up her nose and down into her throat, into her stomach. The last twenty minutes have gone so fast, she's not had time to process anything. On the other side of that door is Philip Joyce; the man who attacked her last night – who tried to kill her last night. A man who kidnapped at least six women and tortured them, brutally, before cutting their throats open and letting them bleed to death.

And now here she is, jumping at his request to talk.

'Ms Munro?'

Callie blinks. DI Dawson is staring at her. For a moment, a little of that warmth the detective displayed sitting at her dining table returns, and Dawson puts her hand on Callie's shoulder.

'You don't have to do this, you know.'

'I know.' Callie takes a deep breath. She thinks of Amy Miller, lying in the corner of that cold room, wrapped in sheets of plastic. Just bagged up and waiting to be tossed into a shallow grave, or sealed into a wall, or dropped into the floor, under a layer of concrete. The queasiness comes back strong but this time Callie manages to swallow it down.

'Shouldn't I be wearing a recorder or something?' she asks.

Dawson smiles a little at that. 'This is Edinburgh, love, not *The Wire*. We'll be right outside the whole time. Just leave the room whenever you want.'

Callie nods and forces a thin smile in return. 'Okay,' she says, 'I'm ready.'

Chapter Forty-Two

Chief Inspector Philip Joyce is sitting up in bed.

The left side of his face is wrapped in bandages. The side of his face where she struck him. She remembers the way his body dropped after she did it, like someone had simply switched him off.

Callie pauses by the entrance to the room, the door closing behind her with a soft click. Joyce watches her silently. He looks pale, and unshaven, and when he raises a hand to beckon her nearer she sees it trembling.

'Please,' Joyce says. His voice is low, nearly a whisper. It's barely even a word. It is a scratchy, breathy noise. He beckons her again, towards a plastic chair next to the bed, his fingers still shaking.

She crosses the room and sits down. This close, she can see his eyes are red-rimmed. Like he's been crying, maybe. Tears for his wife, or for being caught? Callie swallows nervously and finds her own hands trembling. She clasps them tightly on her lap and sits up straight.

'Well,' she says. 'Here I am.'

Joyce nods. He starts to speak – another rasping sentence, like he can't catch his breath – before he stops, wincing. Mac told her that they'd placed him in a medically induced coma. That meant mechanical ventilation. A tube forced down his throat to blow air into his lungs. Sounds like the doctors scratched the shit out of him pulling it out.

His gaze slides past her on to his bedside table. Callie looks down and sees a jug of water next to a cup and straw.

'You want a drink?' she asks.

Joyce nods.

'Tough shit. Now tell me why I'm here so I can go.'

The man's face hardens. For a moment, Callie sees a flash of what she can only imagine his victims saw. Defiance, repulsion. Then the look passes, and he sinks back into his bed. He licks his lips and whispers, 'You were the one who worked it out.'

Callie shifts her weight slightly. Something about the way he says it makes her squirm. 'That's right,' she says.

'Clever girl.'

She stares at him. At those red-rimmed eyes. There's presence inside them, more than she'd expected given his physical state. His body might be weak but his mind is sharp.

'I bet they sent you in here with a list of questions,' he says slowly.

'They did.'

'I'm not interested in answering them.'

Callie ignores him. Pulls the folded paper from her pocket, smooths it out across her thighs. Joyce watches her silently.

'Did you work alone?' she asks.

'I told you—'

'Did you work alone?'

'Yes.'

'Was your wife aware?'

'No.'

'How many women did you kill?'

Joyce turns his head and closes his eyes. 'I'm not answering any more of these. That's not why I asked you here.'

185

Callie makes a fist, the paper scrunching. 'Then why am I here?'

'Because I want to apologise,' he rasps, grimacing over the last word. A repulsion at the notion, perhaps, or simply pressure on a raw bit of throat. 'For hurting you.'

'For hurting me?'

'Yes.'

'What about those other women? Where's their apology?'

Joyce pauses, takes a deep breath in and out. Then, 'I don't owe you their apology,' he says. 'I only owe you yours.'

Both of them fall quiet for a long moment. The only sounds in the room the slow, deep breaths from Joyce and the fast, thudding beats from within her own chest. She knows she should leave now. She's already given this asshole more time than he deserves. She'd entertained notions of Joyce confessing to her, of giving her something tangible. The location of other bodies, a reason for why he did it. But this just doesn't sit right. It's a pity play, a plea in mitigation before his trial has even started.

Callie gets to her feet. She finds her hands have stopped trembling. Her nerves gone. 'You don't owe me anything,' she says, and as she moves to the door she hears Joyce shifting around on the bed behind her.

'Wait,' he barks. His voice is like sandpaper. It makes her skin crawl. 'Wait, please.'

She stops, even though she knows she shouldn't. Her hand half reaching for the door handle, for the outside air, for her cigarettes, for the group of people waiting for her on the other side. DI Dawson, Officer Howard. Mac.

She turns, just enough to see him. Joyce is leaning towards her. His face red, the sheets bunched up around his waist.

'I looked into you,' he says.

'What?'

'It couldn't have been easy, growing up the way you did.'

Callie turns around completely. Her hand falling to her side. 'You're lying.'

Joyce collapses back into the bed. His eyes are still on her, his dry, raspy breathing coming faster and faster. 'Your parents abandoned you at the Step One Shelter in Liberton when you were four months old. You passed through six foster homes before you were sixteen, left school the first chance you got. A string of jobs, mostly cash in hand, before becoming a private investigator.' He raises a hand and wipes at his lips. 'Still think I'm lying?'

'Still think you're creepy as fuck. Congratulations on working the internet.'

'I did more than that,' Joyce says. 'I pulled some strings. I got a name.'

'What name?'

'Someone who was working the night your parents showed.'

Callie stares at him. For the first time in a long while, she is lost for words. Or rather the opposite – her brain sending out so much that the words become jumbled and trapped in her throat. She can feel them back there, a physical lump.

In all her investigations, Callie has only ever been able to identify one employee from the shelter. A man who passed away from cancer before she left school. She never managed to get another name.

She shakes her head. Swallows. Says, 'Bullshit, Joyce.'

'You don't believe me?'

Callie realises she has taken a step towards him. Her heart is racing. 'Of course I don't believe you. When would you have done all this?'

'When you involved yourself in this investigation. I had to know who it was that had DS Reid wrapped around their little finger.'

'Fine, whatever. Tell me the name.'

Joyce smiles. 'I'll trade you, instead.'

'For what?'

'You nearly killed me,' he says, and points a quivering finger towards his bandages. 'You tried to, I think.'

'For what, Joyce?'

'I want you to finish the job.' He takes a long, deep breath. Lets it out in a shuddering cough. 'I can do it myself but I'd rather not.'

Callie blinks. The request works its way through her system, her mind cycling through the possible responses.

It takes a moment for the anger to spark, but when it does, it burns.

'You're a fucking coward,' she snarls, marching across the room, Joyce recoiling slightly from the force of her approach. 'Most men like you are, deep inside. A wee bit of power over others, a wee kingdom for you to rule. But it's all just a fucking facade, isn't it? A little pushback and you fucking crumble.' She leers down at him. He looks pathetic now, lying there. He looks halfway to death as it is. Last night, inside that house, she would happily have taken him the rest of the way.

But now, staring at him, in the bright light of the hospital, the thought of more violence turns her stomach.

'You don't have a name at all, do you?' she says. 'You're just a manipulative piece of shit. And you can keep your apology, I don't want it anywhere near me.'

Then she picks up the jug of water from the bedside table and carries it across to the tiny en-suite, where she pours it down the toilet. She sets the empty jug back down next to him.

'I hope you rot inside for what you've done,' she says, before finally leaving.

Chapter Forty-Three

The anger drains from her as she steps back into the corridor. She's left with the aftershocks, the fading tremors and the slight feeling of embarrassment.

The small group is waiting for her, sitting in blue plastic chairs. They stand up as she emerges; the uniformed officers hanging back, the detectives moving towards her. Concern on Mac's face. Impatience on Dawson's.

'Well?' she demands, crossing her arms. 'What did he say?'

Callie sits down heavily. 'Nothing.'

'Nothing? He must have said something. You were in there for nearly five minutes.'

'He wanted to apologise. To me, in person.'

Dawson frowns. 'Did he tell you anything about the women? Did he formally admit to anything?'

'He said he worked alone. That his wife didn't know anything. He . . .' Callie rubs her temples. The thought of a beer and a smoke right now is overwhelming. 'He asked me to kill him.'

'He what?'

'Said he could do it himself but he'd rather not.'

Dawson's eyes flash at Officer Howard. The woman nods and is heading towards Joyce's room when there's the sound of breaking glass.

'Move!' Dawson shouts.

The officers rush inside, the detectives following. Callie finds herself on her feet too, caught up in it all, pushing in behind Mac.

Joyce's bed is empty.

'Bathroom door is locked,' Howard says.

'Break it down,' Dawson orders.

The officer steps back, then throws her weight against the flimsy door. The frame splinters, the hinges buckling, but the door stays largely upright. 'There's something behind here,' she says, lining herself up for a second attempt.

In the end, it takes another three to gain entry. Callie sees the interior of the bathroom in glimpses, over people's shoulders as they jostle ahead of her. She sees the en-suite's mirror, shattered. She sees the hospital gown, and bare feet, and the arc of blood across the walls, and Philip Joyce stretched out across the floor, a piece of broken mirror clutched in one hand, forever clutched in that one hand, clutched so tight it has broken the skin, his face pale, his eyes distant, his throat slit.

Chapter Forty-Four

Mac places two beers down on the table and slides one across. Callie picks it up and takes a sip. It's ice cold and wonderful.

Three days have passed since Philip Joyce killed himself in his hospital en-suite. Three days of answering police questions, of watching the news cycle work itself into a frenzy. It's the sort of story the media love. A police-officer-turned-serial-killer tale. Six women murdered by someone who was supposed to protect them. Six women tortured, their backs whipped until they were bloody. It all seems so senseless.

'We just got forensics back on the last victim,' Mac says, settling into his chair. He picks up his beer and drinks heavily.

'And?'

Mac shrugs. 'Same as the others.'

'You find a name for the unknowns yet?'

'No,' he says, 'not yet.'

'What about the table?' Callie asks. 'Can't be many of those things around. Do you know where he got it from?'

It's called a birching table, that much Callie knows. She looked it up. A form of corporal punishment, used in schools and prisons across the country until the mid-twentieth century. It worked exactly the way she'd feared when she laid eyes on it at Joyce's home. He'd stripped his victims naked, bent them across the table, strapped their calves and thighs to the table legs with thick, leather straps. Two holes near the head of the table for their arms to slot through.

Once they were in position, he'd spend the next several hours, on and off, whipping their flesh with what the forensic reports described as a 'bundle of bare rods'. Traditionally, of course, these would have been branches from a birch tree, but Joyce wasn't a slave to tradition. He'd used whatever he could get his hands on. Willow, mainly. From a tree he'd planted in his back garden.

'We're looking into the table,' Mac says, staring into his pint, 'but honestly, it's not a priority.'

'What is a priority?'

'ID'ing the remaining women, making sure there aren't any others buried on the property. Proving to the public we're able to adequately investigate one of our own.' He looks up at her. 'It's over now, Callie. We've got our guy, you helped us catch him. Now we're just piecing together his story.'

'And his victims' stories.'

'Of course.'

'Be a lot easier if he was still alive.'

Mac makes a non-committal noise. 'Would stop some of the recent headlines, anyway. You picked up the *Daily Mail* lately?'

'Haven't run out of toilet paper yet.'

'They keep pressing this conspiracy angle. Apparently Joyce was murdered in his hospital bed to keep him quiet. Fucking journalists. Honestly.'

Callie grunts and takes a long drink. It's Tennent's, which she normally wouldn't touch with a barge pole, but there's something about finally getting out of her flat, about being able to sit in a pub and have a drink. She feels like she could drink Tennent's forever. She feels like she could drink Foster's.

'Speaking of journalists,' Mac says, smiling slightly, 'I take it the ones camped in your front garden finally got bored and fucked off?'

'I guess there's only so long they can stare at a set of closed blinds.'

'The cycle's getting shorter and shorter. You're lucky if a story lasts five minutes these days. Some politician gropes his aide and suddenly six dead women are yesterday's news.'

'You really think this will move that quick?'

Mac nods. 'I do, yeah. I think if Joyce was alive he'd perpetuate the story, keep it going. His trial, his sentencing.' He lifts his glass. 'Killing himself the way he did? It's an admission of guilt.'

'I hope you're right.'

'Course I am.' He tilts his glass forward and clinks it against hers. 'Here's to being able to walk out your front door again.'

They stay for another drink. The conversation moves away from the case to other, more mundane talk. For a moment, Callie thinks Mac is going to probe her about her childhood – foster care, growing up in the system, what happened to her parents.

Normally it's a topic that she is more than happy to keep locked up inside – her past and her reasons for becoming a private investigator might be one and the same but they are private, and they are complicated, and even now, after years have passed, she is unsure how she feels about them.

Only, Joyce has opened a door to it now. Jammed a crowbar between the wood and the frame and wrenched it apart. She's already told all this to Dawson and Mac, and a half-dozen other people who wore smarter suits but asked the same questions.

And, of course, there is a part of her that wonders about what Joyce said, about his offer. *I'll trade you*, he said. The name of someone who could take her closer to what happened to her parents, closer perhaps than she's been able to get in a lifetime of looking.

But it wasn't true. It wasn't. Six dead women buried in a house by the sea is the only evidence Callie needs: Joyce was a liar, a manipulator. He said and did terrible things, and his offer to Callie was just another for the list. She has no doubt that whatever name he'd have given her would have been fabricated. And how was he expecting her to kill him in any event? With police standing metres outside the door.

The whole thing makes Callie's head hurt. So she focuses on the one thing that she knows to be true: that what Joyce told her was a lie.

A lie.

But Mac doesn't ask about her childhood or her parents. Instead they talk shop, swapping stories, surface chat mainly, although it's just what Callie needs right now. Something to take her mind off the case, off Joyce, off the image of him strapping those poor women to his table.

She gets home late. A gentle buzz from the beers, from being out, from having a nice time. She thinks of Mac as she kicks off her shoes, as she sits cross-legged in her open doorway with a cup of tea, her head curled forward as she lights up. She thinks about what he said. Short news cycles and Joyce's confession, written with a mirror's edge and signed in his own blood. She types out a text message to Mac, saying thanks, not saying a lot more. Her smoke done, she carries her tea upstairs to bed and falls asleep with it on her bedside table, half drunk and next to her phone, the message half written, and in the morning when she wakes, wincing, she sees the news cycle hasn't moved on at all. If anything it's only gotten stronger. It's the top story on every channel, it clogs her notifications, it's everywhere.

A seventh woman has been found. Dumped in an alley. Partially undressed, her throat slit, her back whipped.

Chapter Forty-Five

There are things that are the same about this murder.

The gender, for starters. Another woman. It makes Callie mad, standing in the bracing cold, smoking, soaking it all in. It's practically a cliché by this point. The power dynamic, the Man Who Kills Women. What does it say, she wonders, for a killer who preys on the weak to only prey on women?

The method, too, is the same. The slit throat, the whipped back. She hears people around her murmur as the breeze lifts a flap of the forensic tent. Inside, a glimpse of figures in white boiler suits, hunched over something on the ground. Too brief to truly make it out, but still. Enough.

There are also things that are different about this murder.

The woman was left out in the open. Dumped down at Western Harbour. A stone's throw from Ocean Terminal. Any other shopping centre would have been packed out on a Friday evening – late-night shopping, date night, dinner and a movie – but not here. Here, half the shops are empty, the other half selling tat. A couple of shit restaurants, a Frankie & Benny's, and she can't remember the others. Point being, the place was deserted. A perfect spot to leave a body in the early hours.

Callie watches the scene from behind the police tape. She has become what she has always hated: a rubbernecker, a vulture. She can feel the excited energy rippling through the crowd around her and it makes her feel physically sick. But she had to come here. To speak with Mac, to see it for herself.

The detective sergeant appears then. Stepping out from the forensic tent, snapping off his blue gloves, a long coat over his suit, dressed for the cold breeze that rolls in off the sea. Dark shadows under his eyes. She realises how little sleep he must be running on.

He gestures at the officer manning the tape, nods at Callie. She peels herself away from the group, can feel their gaze on her, the air thick with their unspoken questions. The tape rises and she steps under. Mac falls into step beside her.

'Got your text,' he says.

'What can you tell me?'

He fixes her with a look.

'What?' she says. 'I want to help.'

He checks his watch. 'I can't tell you much.'

'Is it the same killer?'

'Certainly looks like it.'

'Copycat?'

'Maybe.'

'Or someone working with Joyce? Someone going solo now?'

Mac shrugs. A sudden blast of wind carries sand in the air. They both instinctively duck their heads at it. A momentary stab of pain in Callie's forehead. Last night's Tennent's still holding on.

'What's different?' she asks him. 'Maybe that's the best place to start.'

'Callie . . .'

'Just treat me like a journalist, alright? I'm not asking you for everything. Give me enough to do my bit, to work the angles you can't. Like we did before.'

'You were getting paid before.'

'Was I hell. I was doing that job pro rata.'

'You mean pro bono?'

'Alright, Mister Latin. What's the one where I get paid in smug self-satisfaction after I catch this fucker?'

Mac finally smiles. The dark shadows melt away a little. He pulls out his notebook and starts flipping through it. 'I can't tell you her name until we've spoken with the family—'

'Wait, you know her name?'

'Date of birth, too. He took her last night, Callie. She was a rush job.'

'I don't understand.'

The detective glances back at the crowd, at the white tent flapping in the wind. Beyond, the choppy blue of the Forth. 'He killed her like the others, whipped her back and slit her throat, but he did it quick. Didn't strip her completely, left her mostly dressed and with her handbag, too.'

'You find her ID?'

'Driver's licence and bank cards.'

Callie falls quiet. She mulls it all over. No need for notes, she can feel Mac's words burning into her brain.

'It's certainly different,' she says at last.

'I told you,' he says. 'A rush job.'

Mac starts to lead them back towards the tent. He wraps his overcoat around him as another cold breeze hits. Callie barely feels it.

'Anything else?' she asks him. 'Anything concrete I can look into?'

'Nothing yet,' he says.

'You said you found her bag. Did she still have her phone?'

'She did.'

'You check it?'

'Just a preliminary look, but we'll dig into it proper.'

'Mac . . .'

He slows as they near the tent. 'She's missing a shoe,' he says. 'Black high heel, left foot. Might be nothing.'

'Might be something. What else was in her bag?'

'Usual stuff. Make-up, keys. A ten-pound note with a drawing of a dog on it.'

Callie stops. She feels as though she has walked into a wall. 'What?'

Mac glances back at her. 'You okay?'

'The tenner with the dog. Can I see it?'

'Why?'

Callie closes her eyes briefly as she pictures it. The early morning. Richard stood in her small kitchen, smiling, his hands behind his back. His magic trick, the banknote with the doodled dog hidden inside her purse.

Mac repeats himself. 'Why, Callie?'

The world tilts a little but she keeps her balance. In the pockets of her coat, she squeezes her hands together into fists. How could she have been so stupid? The bloodied shirt, the violence he'd brought down on Grant Miller. His own father had beaten his mother and he'd watched, every day he'd watched. She pictures him standing outside her flat in the dark, waiting for her to return home, asking her to lift up her top. She remembers the warning signs she's felt these last six months, the inexplicable moments of unease. She remembers locking the bathroom door as he climbed the stairs.

She looks at Mac and says, 'Because I think I know who drew it.'

Chapter Forty-Six

Callie sits in a small room and waits for news. Hunched forward, her back beginning to ache. A large tape recorder on the table in front of her. A little plastic cup of water. Up in the corner of the room, she can see the video camera watching her, its little red light blinking steadily.

She's been here for nearly two hours now. She's given Dawson and Mac her statement. Nervously, at first. Faltering. A gnawing unease that she was making a mistake. That she was throwing Richard's name into the investigation for the wrong reasons. Because she was still pissed at him, because she desperately wanted to stay involved in the case. What did it say about her, she wondered. If it was Richard, then did that mean he was involved in the other murders? Had he attacked Alison and Amy Miller when they were together? Right under her nose, and she'd never noticed.

And if it wasn't Richard? Then she had just dragged an innocent man into the investigation. Another innocent man.

But then the detectives laid out the banknote. A dirty, crease-marked tenner, tucked inside a plastic evidence bag. There, drawn on one side in blue pen, was the little dog. Callie fished out her own ten-pound note – still in her purse, she barely uses cash these days – and laid it alongside. The doodles were near-identical.

A sharp knock on the door before it swings open at last. DI Dawson enters the room, her face grim. No sign of Mac, and Callie wonders if she should stop thinking about him like that, like he's a friend, and start thinking about him as what he actually is: a detective sergeant. Likely stood in a nearby room, watching the feed from the blinking-red camera.

That sick, uneasy feeling starts to grow again. Her stomach churns with it.

'I apologise for the wait, Ms Munro,' Dawson says, unbuttoning her suit jacket as she settles into her chair. She places a manila folder on the table between them. 'Can I get you anything before we start?'

It's an ominous phrase. Callie stares at the folder, wants to ask what it is exactly they're about to begin, but instead she just shakes her head. 'I'm fine,' she says.

'Alright, good.' The woman reaches over and switches the recorder on. Big chunky buttons that she has to hold down with two fingers. A long, sharp tone sounds, then she says, 'This is Detective Inspector Sandra Dawson, interviewing Callie Munro. It is 3.37 in the afternoon of the twenty-first of November.'

'Hang on,' Callie says. 'This is all getting rather . . . official for my liking.'

'I'm just recording our conversation, Ms Munro.'

'Uh-huh. Feels a little imposing though, don't you think?'

'No, I don't. Not in this case. I want everything on the record, plain as day.'

'Should I have a lawyer present?'

'You're entitled to one, if you'd like.'

'Am I being charged with anything?'

Dawson's eyes narrow slightly. 'You're being interviewed, Ms Munro. You gave us a lead and we followed it up, and now we have some questions for you. Can we proceed?'

Callie almost asks where DS Reid is but holds her tongue. She nods instead.

'I'm afraid I'll need a verbal response,' Dawson says, opening her folder. 'For the tape.'

'Have you spoken with Richard?' Callie asks.

'Ms Munro . . .'

'Yes, Jesus, we can proceed. But have you spoken with him?'

'Officers, including myself, attended the home of Richard Price earlier today. There was no answer, so we obtained a warrant and forced entry to the property.'

'And?'

Dawson pulls a sheet of paper from her folder and slides it across the table. 'Do you recognise this, Ms Munro?'

It's a photograph of a woman's shoe. Black, high-heeled. Left foot. Even though she's never seen it, Callie knows what it is. The partner of the shoe the dead woman was missing this morning. She closes her eyes.

'For the purpose of the tape, I'm showing Ms Munro a photograph of a black shoe. Do you recognise it?'

'No. Did you find this at Richard's flat?'

'In his kitchen. Do you know who it belongs to?'

'I can guess. Where is he?'

'For the avoidance of doubt, this shoe matches the one worn by the woman found deceased at Western Harbour early this morning.'

Callie leans forward, pushing the photograph back towards the detective. 'Where's Richard?' she says. 'Was he inside his flat?'

'No, he was not.' Dawson takes the photo and returns it to the manila folder. 'There was evidence that he'd left in a hurry, however. Tell me, what was the exact nature of your relationship with Mr Price?'

'We, ah . . .' The words seem to have trouble forming. Callie blinks, trying to mentally sort through the information dump she's just been handed. She can see the detective's mind at work, the way the narrative is being framed.

'Ms Munro?'

'We were seeing each other,' she says. 'On and off.'

'You dated him?'

'Briefly.'

'How briefly?'

'I told you, on and off. Six months or so in total.'

'Why did it end?'

Because he was controlling. Because he had a temper. Because I caught him beating a man half to death on a camera I'd planted illegally.

'It just fizzled out.'

Dawson says nothing for a moment, then nods and turns back to her folder. 'Is it fair to say that you've been fairly proactive in this investigation, Ms Munro?'

Callie bristles slightly at the question. 'I was hired to look into the disappearance of Amy Miller,' she says calmly. 'I try to be proactive on all my jobs.'

'You were hired by Amy's husband, Grant.'

Callie nods, then remembers. 'Yes.'

'The same Grant Miller who assaulted you in a pub a couple of weeks ago?'

'That was a . . . misunderstanding.'

Dawson makes a noise in her throat. 'I see. Regardless, my understanding is that Mr Miller brought your contract to an end at that time, is that correct?'

'Well, technically . . .'

'Yes or no, Ms Munro.'

'Yes. But he—'

'And despite this, you continued working on the case. How often did you speak with my partner, DS Reid?'

'With Mac?'

The detective smiles thinly. 'Yes, with Mac.'

Callie can feel herself growing hot. She is sure that her face must be flushed red. Dawson is painting her into a corner, twisting her story into something it's not.

'I think either you come out with where this is going, or I'm leaving,' Callie says. Her voice sounds surprisingly cold.

Dawson gazes into her folder for a moment, and then closes it. She clasps her hands together on top of it. 'Alright, fine. Here's the way I see things. You had a relationship with Richard Price who is now, it's fair to say, a major suspect in the death of a young woman. A woman murdered in a style reminiscent of six other young, dead women. I think it's also fair to say that you inserted yourself into this investigation—'

'DI Dawson—'

The detective holds up her hand. 'Perhaps genuinely at first, but you did insert yourself into this investigation, and you did seek to influence its path by getting close to my partner, DS Mackenzie Reid.'

'This is bullshit—'

'You pushed DS Reid into focusing on a different suspect for a time, a Nick Fullerton, who ended up being a dead end.'

'I also tried to push him into looking into your chief inspector—'

'So you admit that you sought to influence this investigation?'

Callie stares at Dawson in disbelief. 'For what possible end?'

'To run interference for your boyfriend. To keep Richard's name out of it.' Dawson looks like she wants to say more, but then she unclasps her hands and leans back in her chair, waiting.

Callie falls silent. She lifts her gaze from the detective to the camera in the corner of the room. She wonders if Mac is watching.

If he was told to wait outside, warned that he'd overshared, that he'd compromised an ongoing investigation.

She turns back to Dawson. 'If I'm not being charged with anything, then I'm free to go.'

'That's correct.'

'Am I being charged with anything?'

'Not at this time, no.'

Callie pushes her chair back and stands up. 'Then goodbye, DI Dawson.'

You are a bitch.

You tease men, you lead them on. You take what you want and then you discard them. Chewed up, spat out. You rile them and you push them and then you act indignant when they become angry.

You are a fucking miserable cow.

You think you are better than others. You sit at home and you judge people. You drink and you smoke and you eat Chinese food and you fall asleep on your sofa. You follow broken people for money. You take their picture. You watch them as they fuck, as they lie and cheat. You get off on it, deep down you get off on it, it makes you feel superior, it makes you feel powerful.

You are unwanted.

By nearly everyone, you are unwanted. Your parents abandoned you at a homeless shelter. With strangers, with people who might have gone on to do terrible things to a young child. They left you on the doorstep in the rain and they felt nothing but relief.

You have ruined everything.

You creep into places you are not welcome. You break into people's homes. You pry into their lives, into their secrets. You drag innocent men and women into your chaos. You use them. You burn them. You shame them, you drive them to take their own lives. You have blood on your hands and it will never come off.

You will always be alone.

You reject anyone who tries to get close to you. You desert them, you strand them. Your relationships are transactional – money for services, for recording equipment. You were born alone and you grew up alone and you will die alone. Abandoned and abandoning, your life is devoid of meaning. No one knows you exist and no one will remember you when you are gone.

You will be my next.

Soon I will come for you and you will be mine. You know this already, a part of you craves it. The desire from someone like me. Someone who you will not be able to abandon, who will not allow you to push them away. I am your equal, your opposite. I am your opposing force. I will take everything from you, like you have taken everything from me. I will give you space and you will think you are clear, and you will think you are safe, and in your final moments you will know who I am.

Chapter Forty-Seven

Callie spends the evening at home. She paces her small flat. She smokes – two, three cigarettes. She drinks, she orders Chinese food but is barely able to eat it. Sitting at her dining room table in the dark, her mobile rings. It's Mac. She rejects the call.

Later, lying in bed, unable to sleep. Staring at the ceiling as the same thoughts swirl around her head on an endless loop. Richard, smiling as she unfolded the tenner from her purse. Richard, stood waiting at her front door in the dark. Richard, beating Grant Miller so badly that his shirt was covered in the man's blood.

She imagines him doing more. Picking up women, injecting them. Stripping them naked and tying them to a birching table. Whipping them until their backs bleed, then slitting their throats and burying their bodies in the walls.

It doesn't make sense. It's not him, it can't be him. Does he have a connection to Joyce? Access to the chief inspector's holiday home? Richard might have been an asshole, but he was jealous, overprotective. He wasn't sadistic, not like this.

Callie thinks about what Joyce said to her as he lay in his hospital bed. He'd tried to apologise to her. Genuine remorse, or the meaningless words of a man already plotting his plea in mitigation?

But Joyce didn't murder the woman at Western Harbour this morning. And if there is a second killer out there, then it has to be someone who was working with the chief inspector. Too many similarities for it to be random, too much unreleased to the public for it to be a copycat.

Or was it the same killer all along? Someone who had access to Joyce's holiday home, who used it as a dumping ground. Someone that Joyce was protecting. Had protected. Was that why he slit his own throat?

A sudden knock on her front door shakes away her train of thought. She feels her heart rate spike. Glances at her phone. It's past midnight. She suddenly wishes she had one of those doorbell cameras.

Another knock. Hard, like the person is using the side of their fist. Callie tries not to think about the last time someone hammered on her front door late at night. She gets out of bed and pulls on a hoodie over her pyjama top. She flicks the lights on and descends the stairs, presses 999 on her phone, her finger hovering over the 'call' icon.

'Who is it?'

'It's Grant Miller.'

Callie pauses, lowers her phone. 'Grant? It's late.'

'I know, but I need to talk with you. Please.'

She unlocks her door and swings it open. Grant is standing on the other side. Dimly lit by the street lamps, he squints slightly in the dark. She wonders if he's been drinking.

'It's after midnight, Grant,' Callie says, her voice level. 'This couldn't have waited until morning?'

'I found something, Callie. It's been in the fucking garden the whole time. I had to show it to someone, but I . . . I didn't know who else I could trust.'

She straightens up, frowning. 'What did you find?'

Grant holds up a small, black backpack. 'It belonged to whoever took Amy. And you need to see what's inside.'

Chapter Forty-Eight

Callie puts the kettle on. Grant sits at her kitchen table, antsy, his hands grasping that black backpack, his fingers twitching. She watches him as she leans against the counter.

She's sure he's been drinking now. His eyes are glassy, unfocused. A slight sway to his posture. He looks like he hasn't showered in a while, either. His hair greasy, his skin flushed and glistening with sweat.

'How's the head?' she asks him.

'Hmm? Oh, yeah. Fine.' He lifts up a clump of hair to show her. The wound is healing nicely.

'Just make sure you keep it clean,' she says. Behind her, the kettle clicks off. 'For what it's worth, Grant, I'm sorry things ended with Amy the way they did.'

He grunts, still gripping that backpack, his gaze sinking into the floor.

Callie finishes making the tea and sets both mugs down on the table. She sits across from him, cradling her mug lightly. The flat is chilly, this time of night. She has goosebumps down her arms.

'I thought it was over,' Grant says. He looks up at her. 'I thought when you got Joyce, it would be over.'

Callie nods. She isn't sure what to say.

'But it's not, is it?' Grant says, rambling a little, his words slurring. 'That new girl they found . . . He's still out there, isn't he? And then there's this.'

He holds up the backpack.

'I found it in my back garden,' Grant says, placing it on the table. 'It was lying in the corner, by the fence. I reckon whoever took Amy dropped it.'

Callie sits back in her chair. The bag is wet, one side of it covered in soil. She briefly thinks of the dirt that will be collecting on her kitchen table, then chides herself for thinking that.

'Alright,' she says. 'Show me what's inside.'

Grant unzips the black bag and opens it wide. Reaches in and pulls out a small white canister, which he sets down between them. *Advanced Incapacitant*, it states in thick, dark writing. *Police use only.*

'You know what this is?' Grant asks.

Callie nods. 'PAVA spray,' she says. 'Officers use it to immobilise aggressive suspects. Replaced CS gas about ten years ago.'

'Aye, I imagine it'll make your eyes burn.'

'Be careful, Grant. It's illegal for a member of the public to possess that.'

'I know that, I'm not stupid.' For a second, his temper flares. His blank eyes focus on her until the moment passes and he slips away again. 'So why would whoever took Amy have this?'

'In case he got into a fight?'

'Maybe. Or maybe he's a police officer himself.'

Callie frowns, confused. 'But Joyce has already been caught,' she says. 'Doesn't this just prove your theory?'

'Come on, Callie, fuck's sake. You really think Joyce abducted and killed these women? The guy was in his late sixties. No way he could do all that by himself.'

'So he had help. Same person who killed that woman found this morning.'

'That's what I'm saying! Course he had help. But it could be another cop, couldn't it? It probably is another cop.'

Callie sighs, remembering acutely why she has always hated trying to talk to drunk people when sober. She rubs at her eyes, the tiredness like grit. She takes another sip of her tea. 'If that's all that was inside the bag, I'm not sure how much help you think it is.'

But Grant is already reaching inside the bag again. He pulls out a little tin box and pops the lid. Callie leans forward to see better. An item is inside, something small and wrapped in faded material with yellow and white stripes. Grant peels the fabric away with trembling fingers, slow enough that Callie has to stop herself from grabbing the item and doing it herself.

Layer by layer, the item becomes exposed, until finally it is revealed in all its macabre, grotesque glory: a severed thumb, which Grant sets down on her kitchen table.

Chapter Forty-Nine

The thumb is small and shrivelled. Sliced through just below the joint. The skin is black and putrid-looking, the nail opaque.

'Jesus,' Callie says.

'I know.'

She leans closer to study it. The thing has rotted so much that she cannot tell if it belonged to a man or a woman. 'It looks old. Or maybe just badly preserved, I don't actually know. And what's it wrapped in?'

'I think it's a tie. A school tie, maybe?'

Callie looks at the skinny piece of material again, at the pattern running down it. 'I don't recognise the colours,' she says. 'If it is a school tie, I don't recognise it.' She sits back, thinking, her gaze moving from the grizzly item on her table to Grant's flushed face.

'Why do you think he had it?' she asks him.

He shrugs. 'Dunno, do I? It's obviously important to him. You think you can find out who it belongs to?'

Callie's answer is caught in a yawn. She lifts her hand to cover her mouth. 'I don't know, Grant. Leave it with me, I'll see what I can do.'

Once Grant's gone, Callie uses tweezers to wrap the faded material around the thumb and replace the lid on the tin. She picks it up using a tissue and slides the whole thing into a sandwich bag, which she then places in the freezer. When she's done, she glances down at the tweezers and tosses them into the bin.

It's late now. Well after midnight. Callie is knackered but she worries she won't sleep. Grant's story going round her head; the image of the thumb. It's just another piece of the puzzle. Another indication that she's slipping further and further out of her depth.

She knows what she should do. First thing in the morning, she should phone DI Dawson and let her know about her conversation with Grant Miller. About the thumb, the tie – all of it. They'll be able to run forensics on everything. Hell, they might even have the thumbprint on record. It might take them five seconds to get a name, to shut this case down.

But then she looks at the PAVA spray. She knows it's nearly impossible for a civilian to get hold of this stuff. Chances are, whoever broke into Grant's house and left this behind was a cop, or connected to one, at least. Someone who Joyce had been supplying, perhaps. PAVA spray, property searches, who knows what else. Mac told her that the department had actively been discouraged from linking these missing women together, to even consider the possibility of a serial killer. Was that Joyce too? Keeping the real perpetrator in the shadows?

Of course, the other possibility is that Joyce didn't need to supply the killer with PAVA spray because the second person is also a cop.

Callie turns off the downstairs lights and double-checks the front door. Then she climbs the stairs and collapses into bed, tired but wired. She thinks of Mac. She wonders if she should call him. He reached out to her about all this to begin with. Was the only person in the department willing to join the dots. He put his neck on the line when she got him a name – Fullerton, what a bust that was. But surely all of that means she can trust him.

She crashes out then. She dreams in fits and bursts, of blackened skin, of women's faces wrapped in plastic. When she wakes it's daylight, 5.47 according to her clock. She's been asleep for less than four hours.

Her phone is vibrating on her bedside table. Callie reaches for it clumsily, nearly knocking it on to the floor. Bringing the screen close, she squints. The number is withheld.

'Hello?'

'Ms Munro, I know it's early but you need to get up and get out of your house. Now.'

'Mia? What—'

The woman's voice is hard and her tone cuts through Callie's sleep-addled brain.

'Leave your house immediately, Ms Munro. Don't shower, don't dress, don't pack a bag. If you want to avoid a prison cell, you get to London Road in the next sixty seconds. Am I clear?'

'Yes, but—'

'Sixty seconds, Ms Munro.'

The line goes dead.

Chapter Fifty

Callie stumbles out of bed, still clutching her phone. She rushes from the room and down the stairs. Counting down in her head, trying not to think about anything other than the numbers.

Fifty-one.

Fifty.

Forty-nine.

She pulls on trainers and throws on a coat. A glimpse of herself in the hall mirror: Baby Yoda pyjamas and dark circles under her eyes. She zips up her coat and opens the front door. A rush of cold air swirls inside her flat. One foot into the still morning and she pauses.

Forty-two.

Forty-one.

Forty.

Callie hurries back inside. Through the hall, to the kitchen. Throws open the freezer and grabs the sandwich bag. She stuffs it into the backpack Grant brought along with the PAVA spray and races to the front door, swearing.

Twenty-eight.

Twenty-seven.

Twenty-six.

Down the steps to the street, taking them two at a time, praying she doesn't slip. It's still dark, and cold enough to see her breath fog as she hurries along Regent Place towards London Road. In the distance she can hear the faint sound of sirens. Callie tells herself that cars can't drive down her street in both directions – a set of steps at one end is for pedestrians only. They'll have to drive down Easter Road and turn on to Rossie Place if they want to reach her. An extended loop that buys her some time.

Eighteen.

Seventeen.

Sixteen.

Climbing the steps on to London Road, the car comes into view: Eddie McCall's grey Ioniq 5. Windows tinted, sidelights on. The door pops open as she approaches, and she throws herself inside. McCall is waiting for her in the back seat. He gives her a grin as the driver pulls a smooth U-turn. Glancing behind her, Callie sees two police cars swing a hard left on to Easter Road, their sirens flashing silently.

'Bet you never thought your day would start off this exciting, eh love?' McCall says, laughing.

Mia is sat in the front passenger seat. She turns to look at Callie, a hint of a smile on her face. 'You made it out quicker than I thought.'

Callie stares back at her. Her heart is racing, her face sweaty from sleep and the sudden exertion. She feels horribly, hideously underdressed. 'Is that right,' she says.

'Mia and me here had a bet on,' McCall says, waggling his finger towards her. 'She didn't think you'd make it out in time. I, however, had more faith.'

'I'm glad to hear it. But what's going on here, Eddie? Why are there police cars racing to my front door at six in the morning? And how did you know they were coming for me?'

McCall laughs again, scratching at his beard with his thick fingers. 'Because I know everything that goes on in this city, Callie. I'm plugged in, I'm omnipresent. I got a call an hour ago from my man at the *Herald*. Some twat on the force gave him a tip and he passed it straight to me.'

'What was the tip?'

'That the police were about to make an arrest for the murder of Isla Sinclair, the wee lassie they found down by Ocean Terminal yesterday. That they'd found a business card wedged in her throat. Your business card, Callie.'

Chapter Fifty-One

McCall's words rebound inside the silent car. Callie slumps back in her seat. They're driving past Meadowbank, turning at Jock's Lodge. Weaving through housing estates towards Duddingston.

'I'm being set up,' she says at last. The sentence sounds weak and childish. It sounds like something every guilty person in the world says.

But McCall doesn't disagree. 'Of course you're being set up,' he says loudly, angrily. 'How fucking daft would you have to be, leaving your fucking business card behind like that? I've never heard anything like it in my life.'

'Where are we going?'

'We're going somewhere safe, Callie. Somewhere those stupid pricks can't find you. Which reminds me, did you bring your phone?'

Callie fishes it from her jacket pocket with a sinking feeling. She knows what's coming next. McCall takes it from her, opens his window and tosses it.

'Here,' Mia says from the front seat. She hands Callie a cheap-looking black mobile. The thing's like something she had when she was at school. A thick wedge of plastic with chunky keys.

'What's this? A burner?' Callie asks.

'Aye,' McCall says. 'Untraceable, unless you decide to give the number away. Only use it if it's important. Mia's details are saved inside. You call her if you need anything.'

The car is moving down little side streets now. Callie knows they can't be far from the Sheep Heid, a nearby pub with a skittles alley in the back that she used to go to for the occasional Sunday roast. They pull into the driveway of a little house, off a cobbled road and nestled behind a couple of large, bushy trees. A red Fiat is parked in front of the garage. As safe houses go, she's imagined worse.

'What do I do now?' Callie says, staring up at the place. Between the hour, the tinted windows and those two trees, the car is in near-darkness. The driver puts the Ioniq into park and soft, warm lighting spreads through the cabin.

'You're going to catch this fucker,' McCall says. He scowls at her. 'That's what you're going to do. You understand me? The police are so far up their own arse, they didn't know their own fucking boss was in on it. And now someone else is pulling their strings? Incompetence – no, corruption, Callie – it turns my stomach.' He swivels in his seat to face her dead on. 'And if they're targeting you, then it makes me think you're getting close. You're making them sweat. So I want you to keep at it. I want you to catch whoever is killing women in my town, and I'm going to keep you away from the bastard police so you can do it.'

Callie isn't sure what to say. She nods, dumbly, holding on to the burner phone tight.

'There's clean clothes inside,' Mia says, with something approaching warmth in her voice. 'Plenty of food and toiletries, too. Keys to the Fiat in the kitchen drawer. But like Mr McCall said, if you need anything, give me a ring.'

'All right. Thank you.'

'Don't mention it, hen,' McCall says, smiling again. 'And I have to say, I didn't take you for a Grogu fan.'

'A what?'

'Your pyjamas.'

Callie glances down at them. They were a gift from Richard. 'I've always just called him Baby Yoda,' she says.

Chapter Fifty-Two

The safe house is nice. Small, but clean. Callie wanders through, checking cupboards and opening the fridge. Just as Mia said, the place is well stocked. Milk and butter in the fridge, eggs and bread sitting on the kitchen counter. Fresh sheets folded next to the bed. A wardrobe filled with new clothes, the tags still dangling from most of them. A stack of cash inside an envelope on the dining table; nearly four grand in twenty-pound notes. But, most importantly to Callie right now: a large shower in the bathroom.

She stands under the hot water for nearly ten minutes. Washing away the sweat, allowing the absurdity of her current situation to sink in. It is not the first time she has been shunted from one house to another, after all.

Afterwards, she pads through to the bedroom, dresses in dark jeans and a jumper and then goes downstairs to the kitchen. It's nearly six-thirty, and Callie is starving.

She eats at the neat little dining table by the back door. Fried eggs on toast with a cup of coffee. She eats while gazing out into the small garden. It's still dark, and Callie is unsure what direction she's facing. She wonders how far they are from the nearby loch.

A recollection of a trip there, as a young girl. A group of them from the same home. It was a hot day, summertime, the sky blue and the air warm. She stood on the edge of the water and watched the swans, and she ate ham sandwiches on white bread with the crusts removed.

Strange, the things that hide away in your brain. Sensations unfelt, memories unthought of for years, until they emerge without warning, as strong and acute as the day they happened. If Callie closes her eyes, she can just about feel the warmth of the sun on her face.

Once she's finished breakfast, she washes the frying pan and plate and stacks them to dry. She refills her coffee mug and takes it back to the table, and she places the burner phone in front of her.

The phone is the only tool she has now. Her precious notebook is at home, filled with her scribbled thoughts, no doubt currently being pored over by DI Dawson. She thinks of how it will be used. The records she has made of conversations with people like Nicola Mosley, and Alison. Callie will bring the police to their doors in their hunt for her.

She pushes the thought aside. Reaches down and picks up the burner phone. Turning it on, she lets the device slowly come to life. Her jacket is draped over the back of a chair, and Callie goes to it now, searching the pockets until she finds a small, folded piece of card. *Mackenzie Reid*, it says in small type along the bottom, under a police crest. *Detective Sergeant*.

Callie dials his number and hopes she's not making a huge mistake.

Chapter Fifty-Three

Mac answers on the sixth ring. His voice is groggy; he has to clear his throat before speaking. 'Hello?'

Callie almost hangs up there and then. She's withheld her number, of course, although she's not certain Mac can't trace it later on, if he really wants to.

'Who is this?' Mac asks, his voice hardening a little now.

'It's Callie.'

Quiet. Then, 'Jesus. Callie? Where are you?'

'I can't say. I'm actually not a hundred per cent sure myself. The rough area, that's about all I could give you right now.'

'You know Dawson is furious.'

'I can imagine.'

'She just about punched a hole in a whiteboard when they told her you weren't home.'

'I can imagine that, too.'

Callie can hear Mac moving around. Getting out of bed, maybe. Pulling on a hoodie or a t-shirt. Padding out of the bedroom, a mouthed apology to someone still lying under the covers, half asleep.

'Why are you calling me?' he asks her. 'You know I could report you.'

'I know.'

'I should report you.'

'Please don't. I'm reaching out to you because I trust you, Mac.'

The detective laughs lightly. It's not an unkind laugh, but still. 'You don't trust me, Callie,' he says. 'You just need me.'

'That's not true.'

'Isn't it?'

She looks over at the small fridge-freezer in the corner of the room. Pictures the little metal tin nestled on top of the ice cube tray. The shrivelled black thumb lying inside.

'I didn't do it, Mac.' She swallows, the sound of her throat clicking loud in her ears. 'I know they found my business card wedged down her throat or whatever, but I didn't put it there. Would be a fucking weird thing for me to do, don't you think? Stuffing my own business card into someone I'd just murdered? Surely you must see that I'm being set up.'

'What about Richard?'

'What about him?'

'Is he being set up, too?'

'I don't know. I can see him doing it, if I squint. But I go back and forth. Wonder whether I could have missed what was going on.' She pauses. 'Maybe I'm not as good an investigator as I thought, hmm?'

Mac gives a gentle sigh. 'You wouldn't be the first person to miss what someone close to them was up to behind their back.'

Callie realises he's talking about Joyce. 'I guess not,' she says. 'And I get it, Mac. You were all blindsided by the chief inspector even though it should have been obvious, and now you're all shit-scared of being blindsided by the next obvious thing, but I'm too fucking obvious, I know you see that. And so, yeah, actually I do trust you, and just because I also need you doesn't mean both can't be true, it's not exclusive. But yes, I need you. I need your help, all right? You happy now?'

There's a long pause down the line. For a few seconds Callie thinks the detective is going to hang up. She pictures him at the station, handing his phone over to Dawson. Sees them tracing her number, her location. Helicopters and sirens and officers in body armour breaking down the front door.

Then, 'What is it you're after?'

Callie breathes out slow. 'I need you to run me a print. A thumbprint.'

'Whose thumb is it?'

'I don't know, that's why I'm asking you to run it.'

'Oh yeah, sorry. Do you have the print?'

'I have the thumb.'

'The thumb? Is it, like—'

'Severed, yes. Don't ask me where I got it.'

'Okay. So where do you want to meet?'

Callie thinks for a moment. 'There's a Land Rover parked in the street behind my flat, three doors up. Big thing, mustard yellow.'

'How do you know it's still parked there?'

She smiles. 'Because the guy's too scared to move it and lose his space. I swear, it's been sitting there six months now. I'll leave it on top of one of the wheels.'

'What wheel?'

'Front passenger.'

'How do you know I won't have a team of officers waiting to arrest you the minute you show up?'

Now it's Callie's turn to pause before answering. 'Because I trust you.'

Mac laughs at that. 'Fine.' He clears his throat again, and Callie hears him moving about. The sound of a tap running and a kettle's electric click. 'You really don't know where you are?' he asks her.

'No.'

'What can you see from the windows?'

225

Callie gazes out of them now, at the faint outline of trees, at the darkened sky. 'I'll tell you when the sun comes up.'

The kettle boils. She listens to Mac making himself a cup of something. She pins the phone against her shoulder, wraps her fingers around her coffee. The mug is cool.

'Be careful, Callie,' Mac says quietly.

'I will,' she says.

The line goes dead.

Chapter Fifty-Four

It's true, what Callie said. She does trust Mac. He was the sole person to see the missing women for what they really are: an interconnected series of crimes. He felt so strongly about it that when his own side refused to act, he got Callie to help him look into it, off the books. What was that, if not an indication of who he really is?

She tells herself this as she sits behind the wheel of Eddie McCall's Fiat, staring at the mustard-yellow Land Rover parked a few hundred metres away. She forces herself to slowly and methodically scan the area around her. To check every other parked car, every darkened window. Study the face of every person who walks by. It is just about eight a.m., and the streets are in full swing.

In her inside jacket pocket sits the metal tin and its grizzly contents. Still inside the sandwich bag, still cool from the freezer. Callie can feel the icy chill against her chest. A reminder of what she has to do next.

Finally, after nearly ten minutes, she opens the door and climbs out. She moves quickly, crossing London Road and plunging down the pedestrian steps to the narrow street behind her house. She allows herself a brief glance at it, just the once, as she walks. She wonders how it must look inside. Torn apart, most likely. Drawers upended, shelves emptied on to floors. She suddenly wonders if they will find something. Not anything she's aware of, but something nonetheless. An item planted, or its chain of custody later altered. She wonders if that's how it was for Richard.

She sees him drawing a dog on a ten-pound note, sees him laughing, sees him beating a man with a wheel wrench, sees him doing it to a woman, sees him strapping her down and whipping her back, sees him slitting her throat, sees him standing in her kitchen wearing his big, chunky metal watch, sees the masked intruder at the bottom of her stairs wearing the same. She sees it all and she feels utterly, hopelessly lost.

Reaching the Land Rover, she doesn't slow. She pulls the sandwich bag from her pocket and palms it neatly on to the large front passenger tyre without breaking her stride. Then, her head still down, she reaches the end of the street, turns sharply and loops back on herself a block over. It takes her another minute to weave back to the Fiat, and soon she is behind the wheel and driving off. Her heart racing as she keeps watch in the rear-view mirror for any sign of activity, any sign of being followed. But there is nothing. There is just her street, her house, growing steadily more distant until it is gone from view.

Chapter Fifty-Five

Callie spends the rest of the day in a tense mood. She paces the safe house. She makes coffee and drinks it standing by the window, staring out into the well-maintained back garden and wondering who it is that comes to maintain it. The cleaners and the gardeners, do they know the owner of this house? Do they know who they're working for?

Same person I am, Callie thinks wryly.

Turns out, she doesn't have that great a view here, even in daylight. Tall, bushy trees block most of the neighbours and keep any chance of seeing the nearby loch firmly at zero. Callie is sure it's intentional – it's a safe house, after all – but still, it makes her feel trapped.

She wastes away a few hours smoking. Leaning out the kitchen window, chaining cigarettes one after the other, using the dying embers to light the next. For lunch she makes a sandwich from the items Mia has left for her in the fridge. Ham, cheese, tomato. She can barely eat it, forcing half of it down before throwing the rest away. She tracks the sun, watching it inch over the house. She itches for a beer but doesn't want to lose her focus, needs to be able to drive on a moment's notice. She carries the burner phone and turns it over in her hands, again and again, tapping the power button but never pressing it down, telling herself to wait until it gets dark to check in with Mac, to give him time to run the print and leave the station.

Just before seven p.m., Callie turns on the phone. It boots up slowly, spinning a circle in the centre of the small screen while she chews the inside of her bottom lip. The kitchen stinks of cigarette smoke and lasagne; a frozen ready meal in the oven even though she's not hungry.

She withholds the number again when she calls him. A slight hesitation before she does, all that talk of trust swimming in the front of her brain. He answers on the second ring.

'Callie?'

'Yeah. Did you get the thumb okay?'

'I got it.'

'You manage to run the print?'

'I did.'

'Jesus, Mac, this is like pulling teeth.'

'Sorry, hang on.'

He's speaking on his hands-free, Callie realises. Driving, by the sounds of it. A few moments go by, and then his voice comes back stronger. 'There. Was just parking. Let me get my notebook out.'

Callie has already done similar. A fancy ballpoint pen and a stack of printer paper from one of the upstairs cupboards. She starts to scribble as Mac talks.

'I got a match on the thumbprint to a Donna Burnett,' he says. 'She was picked up for shoplifting nearly forty years ago. Doesn't look like her case ever made it to trial though.'

'Who is she?'

'She was a teacher at a boarding school up north. Somewhere called Galbraith Academy in Nairn. It's been closed for years now. But listen to this, Callie. The thumb was taken post-mortem. Burnett's dead. She was murdered nearly a decade ago. A jogger found her naked body dumped on a park bench one morning, her throat slit and her back whipped raw.'

Chapter Fifty-Six

'It's the same,' Callie says softly. 'Burnett . . . all those women, too. The method of murder is near-identical.'

'I know,' Mac says. 'And I have to ask, Callie, I have to ask where the hell you got this thumb from.'

'It was left behind during Amy Miller's abduction.'

'Wait, this guy snatches Amy Miller and drops a fucking thumb on his way out the door?'

'Not quite,' Callie says. She tells him the background. What Grant said to her the previous night. The bag with the PAVA spray. When she's finished, Mac is silent for a long while.

Finally, he says, 'You ever think Grant Miller is messing you around?'

'What?'

'This story about the killer leaving behind a bag with all this stuff. And he finds it now? Days later, when we missed it?'

'He said it was in the garden. I don't know, Mac. I don't know what to believe right now.'

'Okay.'

'You think he's making it up?'

'I might just be overthinking it.'

'You know what I think?'

'Tell me.'

Callie can suddenly smell the sharp, acrid odour of something burning in the kitchen. Through the oven door she can see the blackened crust of her frozen lasagne.

'Fuck,' she mutters, turning the oven off and moving to open a window. She perches on the low sill. The air outside is cool and fresh.

'Callie, you there?'

'Sorry. Dinner mishap.'

'You were about to tell me what you think.'

Callie rubs at her face, stifling a yawn. Her early start is finally catching up with her. She picks up the crumpled pack of cigarettes and takes out the last one. 'I lost my train of thought,' she says.

'You think we're looking for another cop?' Mac says.

'I honestly don't know,' Callie mumbles, lighting up. 'Maybe.'

She pictures Mac then, sat in the front of his VW Golf. The little overhead light on, his notebook open against the steering wheel. Running this side investigation at her behest. Isolated in his own way.

'There's more,' Mac says. 'We finished ID'ing the remaining women found at Joyce's residence. It's not public yet, but we're in the process of informing their families.'

'That's good,' Callie says.

'This is better. Every victim's home address was broken into at some point over the last ten years.'

'Before they were taken?'

'Sometimes years before they were taken. In two cases, the victim didn't even live there when the burglary took place.'

Callie thinks about her earlier hunch. Vangelis and their alarm systems, and Nick Fullerton and the way he stood over her bed. 'You check to see if—'

'I know where you're going with this, but it doesn't look like they all had the same security system installed. At least one of them doesn't have an alarm at all.'

'It's not coincidence, Mac. It means something.'

'Everything means something,' Mac says, 'when you don't know what you're looking for.'

Callie grunts as she finishes her cigarette. 'Where'd you get that from, a fortune cookie?'

'Caught an episode of *Monkey Magic* the other night.'

'I don't know what that is, and I don't want to know.'

She grinds out the cigarette in the sink and drops the butt into the bin. She pins the phone against her shoulder as she opens the oven door, pulling the blackened lasagne out and placing it on top of the hobs.

'What are you going to do now?' Mac asks her.

'I'm going to dig into this Donna Burnett. Might be worth a trip up north.'

'I thought you'd say that. I have something that might help.'

'Uh-huh,' Callie says, digging through the hardened crust of her dinner. She scoops a mound of pasta on to a plate. 'What's that?'

'A photo,' Mac says. 'We found it in Joyce's residence. In a shoebox, tucked away in the back of a wardrobe. Didn't know what it meant. Still don't, not really, but after Burnett . . .'

Callie sits down at the table and pushes dark chunks of lasagne around with her fork. 'What's the photo?' she asks.

'It's a school,' Mac says. 'A class picture, maybe. Four boys lined up on a pitch. Might be the same place Burnett worked.'

'Can you send me over a copy?'

'I'll need your new number. Assuming you trust me enough to share it.'

Callie smiles. 'I'll send you a text now.'

'All right.' She hears him climbing out of the car. She wonders briefly where he lives, what his home is like. 'Please be careful,' he says.

'I'll try.'

'And let me know what you find, or if there's anything I can do from my end.'

Callie starts to say goodbye and then stops. She sets her fork down. 'Why are you helping me?' she asks.

'You're wondering this now?'

'I know you must be running around down there behind Dawson's back. Checking the print, sending me this photo. You're going out on a limb for me, Mac.'

The detective laughs gently. 'Because when I asked you to help me with the Night Watcher case, you jumped in with both feet, no hesitation. And because you've got good instincts. Better than most, better than me. You saw Joyce, from the very start you saw him. So yeah, I am going out on a limb to help you. But honestly? It just feels like the right thing to do.'

Callie smiles, sitting at the unfamiliar kitchen table, staring down at her ruined dinner. 'Thank you. I think I needed to hear that right now.' She goes over to the window and slides it closed, the skin on her bare arms prickling with goosebumps. 'Goodnight, Mac.'

'Goodnight, Callie.'

Chapter Fifty-Seven

Callie finds a stack of road maps in the utility room. She spreads one out across the table, traces the route she'll need to take. It looks like Nairn is almost four hours away by car. A small coastal town to the east of Inverness.

It's another early start the next day, the sky outside still dark. She spoons limp, soggy cornflakes from her bowl. Her appetite still isn't back.

Callie spent the night preparing as best she could. A text to Mac to ask him to source Martin Walsh's phone number, just in case. Packing Grant's backpack with the envelope of cash and the PAVA spray, reading the instructions printed down the side on how to use it. Studying the photo Mac sent her until her eyes started to hurt from staring at her burner phone's small, shit screen. Four boys, aged between fifteen and sixteen by the looks of them, although she's always been terrible at guessing ages. They're dressed smartly – pressed shirts and maroon blazers, striped ties, polished shoes. All of them white, all of them staring solemnly into the camera. A single line of text typed along the bottom border: *Graduation 1985.*

It takes Callie nearly three and a half hours to drive to Inverness, through the receding darkness, under the brightening sky. It's mid-morning when she hits the Cairngorms. The rust-coloured hills rising up on either side of her, the scraggy fields and the long, winding rivers. The A9 carves through the Highlands and she stops for fuel at a small petrol station with just one pump. Across the motorway is a group of cows who stare at her, bored, their mouths chewing continuously.

She arrives at the Highland Archive Centre just after eleven a.m. A large, red-brick building on the edge of the River Ness. Inside, a bored-looking older man is sat at reception, his head down in a book. He looks up at Callie and smiles, his eyes crinkling.

'How can I help you?' he asks.

Callie smiles back. 'I'm looking to find out any information you might have on Galbraith Academy,' she says. 'Including pupil names, if possible.'

The man closes his book and slides it to one side. 'Galbraith Academy,' he repeats, turning to his computer. 'Where is that, about?'

'Nairn,' Callie says. 'It closed in the late nineties. I'm trying to find out the names of any pupils that might have graduated in the class of '85.'

'I'm afraid that's going to be rather tricky,' he says, still typing. 'Access to school admission information is restricted for a century. And no, I did not misspeak.'

Callie feels her hopes fade. 'A century?'

'Data protection, you know how it is.' He peers at her over the top of his computer screen. 'Although I think a hundred years seems a little much, don't you?'

'Yes, just a little.'

'What I can get you, however, is the list of pupils who obtained the Scottish Certificate of Education. Every pupil in the country

236

would have obtained one before graduating.' The man's eyes crinkle again as he smiles. 'You should be able to work out which pupils graduated when, so long as you don't mind doing a little detective work.'

Callie grins. 'I don't mind that at all,' she says.

Callie sits at a desk in the corner of the room and leafs through the thick binder of papers. Rows and rows of children's names, broken down by council area, by school, by the year they achieved their certificate. She spends nearly forty minutes combing through it all until she finds what she's after. Four names for Galbraith Academy, all of whom obtained their certificates in 1985 and dropped off the records thereafter.

She makes a note of each one.

Craig McLaren
John Taylor
James Dalgleish
Paul Brodie

She circles the names in her notebook. These are the four boys in Joyce's photograph. The four boys who graduated in 1985. Who attended a school with an English teacher who would later be brutalised, her body whipped until it was raw and then her throat slit, her thumb sliced off like some sort of trophy. And whoever had done it didn't stop with Burnett. They kept going, murdered seven other women in the exact same manner.

One of these boys is the killer. Callie knows it. Feels it, deep inside. All she has to do now is prove it.

Chapter Fifty-Eight

Behind the Archive Centre sits the Inverness Botanic Gardens. More importantly, Callie sees, is the promise of a cafe. It's past lunchtime now, and after barely eating for twelve hours she's starving.

She grabs a table in the corner. Eats half an almond croissant in just one bite. She phones Mac as she chews. He'll be at work, he might not be able to talk, but Callie has to tell him what she's learned.

'Hang on,' he says when he answers. Callie stays quiet, listens to him as he moves rooms, the background chatter of the station fading out. Then, 'Okay, I can speak. What have you found?'

'His name, I think. Or at least the names of the children in the photograph.'

'You reckon one of those boys is our killer?'

Callie takes another bite of her croissant. She wishes she'd bought another. 'I reckon one of them murdered Donna Burnett, yeah?'

'And our seven women too?'

'Maybe.'

'Maybe. All right, give me the names. I'll run them here and phone you back when I can. What are you planning on doing now?'

'I'm going to stay local. Ideally one of those boys is living nearby. I might go pay a visit.'

'You really think it's wise to approach them yourself?'

'What other choice do I have?'

She reads out the four names, finishes her croissant as Mac writes them down. 'Give me thirty minutes,' he says. 'I'll try to pull their last known addresses and any relevant convictions they might have.'

'Check their family details too,' Callie says. 'Their parents' names, if you can.'

'You think Joyce has got a kid, don't you.'

A sudden commotion near the entrance to the cafe. Callie's head whips up. A large dog is trying to climb on to one of the tables. People laugh as the owner heaves him away.

'Joyce kept that photo for a reason, Mac. Even if the chief inspector didn't murder those women, he helped whoever did. Gave them a killing ground, a place to hide the bodies. And when it was uncovered, he tried to take the blame for it. Slit his own throat to keep us from looking any further.' She gazes down at the four names circled in front of her. She thinks of what it must be like, to have someone looking out for you like that. Your entire life, no questions asked. 'Sure sounds like the actions of a parent to me,' she says quietly.

Mac calls her back less than fifteen minutes later. She's still in the cafe, another almond croissant down and midway through a second cup of coffee.

'I didn't have as much luck as I'd hoped,' he says.

'Tell me what you got.'

'Paul Brodie is dead. Cancer, years back. Craig McLaren and John Taylor are off the grid. Their last known addresses are a homeless shelter and a house that was demolished five years ago. They could be anywhere.'

'What about James Dalgleish?'

'There, you're in luck. Dalgleish still lives in Nairn. I'll text you his address now.'

'What about his folks?'

'They're still alive,' Mac tells her. 'And more importantly, are very much not the Joyces.'

Callie drains the remainder of her coffee and puts her notes away. She grabs her car keys and heads for the exit. 'I'm going to talk to him now,' she tells Mac. 'I'll call you if I find anything.'

James Dalgleish lives in a small, one-bedroom bungalow on the outskirts of Nairn. It takes Callie thirty minutes to get there from Inverness. It's past lunchtime now, and the weather is starting to worsen. Dark clouds have formed overhead, flat and grey, and they stretch out for miles. That charge in the air that comes before rainfall. Callie knows it will be dark soon, and likely it will stay that way until morning.

She bangs on Dalgleish's front door a couple of times and waits for nearly five full minutes. Nothing. She swears, loudly, and then pulls out a cigarette and lights it, hunching forward as she returns to her car. Nothing else to do now but wait.

Dalgleish doesn't show up for another forty minutes. Callie measures it in cigarettes. She sees him ambling up the road in her rear-view. An older man, carrying shopping bags and too much weight around his middle. She waits until he's at his front door, until he's about to slide his key into the lock. Then she pops her door and flicks her cigarette end into the road and shouts, 'Mr Dalgleish?'

He turns, confused. She sees something in his eyes from across the car roof. Unease, unsettledness. She has startled him, she realises.

'Yes?' he calls as she approaches. He seems to shrink back towards his still-unopened front door. 'Can I help you?'

Callie smiles broadly. Hoping that might relax him. 'My name's Callie Munro,' she says brightly. 'I'm looking into the old Galbraith Academy. I understand you were a pupil there?'

The man's face has gone pale. He keeps trying to put his key into the lock, over and over. The blade sliding off the cylinder.

'It's all right, I'm not here to cause you any trouble,' she says calmly. 'I just want to ask you a couple questions about some of your classmates.'

'Who are you?'

'A private investigator. I'm looking into the murder of Donna Burnett.'

'Why?'

'Because I need to understand why she died. Other people's lives may depend on it.'

'And what if she deserved it? What if Donna Burnett deserved everything she had coming to her?'

Callie takes a step towards him. Spreads her hands out wide in front of her in a gesture she hopes means peace. 'I'm only after the truth, Mr Dalgleish,' she says. 'Deserving's got nothing to do with it.'

The man finally gets the key in. He pushes open the front door. 'I suppose you better come in then,' he says.

Chapter Fifty-Nine

Inside, Dalgleish's bungalow is cold and dark. Not enough windows, and the incoming storm above. He shuffles deeper into the house, flicking on light switches, beckoning for her to follow. She pulls her coat around herself and follows him.

He's stood by the cooker now, the shopping bags on the counter. His back to her as he unpacks. Callie watches the items: bacon, frozen pizza, cans of beer. Yellow tags on most of the food. Reduced, about to go off. Just enough to get him through today, to give him a reason to go back tomorrow, to help fill his day. She has just met this man and already she feels like she knows him.

'Would you like a hand with anything?' she asks. The kitchen is quiet. Her voice seems to boom in the space.

'No, thank you,' Dalgleish says. 'You want a cup of tea?'

Callie has studied the room. Seen the grime coating the counter edges, the dark stains in the yellowed paint. 'I'm fine,' she says.

She waits patiently, watching as Dalgleish fills the kettle and flicks it on. She reminds herself of who he is. Of who he might be. One of those four boys is a killer and he is one of those four boys.

As the water boils, he turns to her. 'I've tried not to think about Galbraith Academy in years,' he says.

'I'm sorry to hear that,' Callie says. 'Bad memories?'

'Yes. What did you say your name was again?'

'Callie. Callie Munro.'

'And why do you want to talk to me in particular, Callie Munro?' His tongue darts out for a moment and runs along his lips. 'Plenty of children knew Donna Burnett as well as I did.'

She reaches into her pocket and pulls out her burner phone. Opens up the photo of the four boys and slides it across Dalgleish's dirty counter. He picks it up and studies it closely. His nails are long and his hands shake.

'Christ,' he mutters to himself. 'Where did you find this?'

'In the wardrobe of a dead man. I'm hoping you can tell me who's who.'

The kettle clicks off. Dalgleish sets the phone down and turns back to his tea. He speaks as he pours. 'Left to right, you've got Johnny, then Craig, me, and Paul.'

'I heard Paul passed away.'

'Lung cancer, the poor bastard. He could barely breathe by the end.'

'You keep in touch with them?'

'I kept in touch with him.'

Dalgleish lifts his mug and carries it over to the small breakfast table in the corner of the room. Callie reluctantly follows. She has to lift a stack of newspapers to sit down. She is acutely aware of how the kitchen counter now blocks the straight line to the doorway.

'What can you tell me about Donna Burnett?' she asks.

Dalgleish lifts his mug with those same trembling hands. *It's more than nerves*, Callie thinks. 'I can tell you she was a nasty piece of work,' he says.

Callie feels like she knows where this is heading. Worse, that she's known for a while now. The type of story she's heard about all too often. The type of story she spent her childhood trying to avoid.

'She hurt you, didn't she,' she says. Softly, her voice barely above a whisper.

'Not me,' Dalgleish says. The words coming out before she's finished speaking. Pushing back strong, pushing back too strong. Callie can see the denial for what it's worth, and she lets it be.

'But she hurt others.'

'Yeah,' Dalgleish says, finally taking a sip of tea. 'Yeah, she hurt others.'

'She beat them?'

'Whipped them. Strapped them to a table and whipped their backs. Called it—'

'A birching table,' Callie says.

Dalgleish looks up at her. 'Aye,' he says. 'That was what she called it.'

Callie nods towards her phone, still on the kitchen counter. 'You know where I can find the others? John Taylor and Craig McLaren? I'd love to speak with them.'

Dalgleish coughs, once, and rises to his feet. 'Excuse me,' he says, and ambles back into the kitchen proper. He opens a drawer and pulls out a tissue, dabs it against his mouth as he returns. It strikes Callie as being faintly theatrical, and when he sits down in a different chair she realises why. He is now directly blocking her exit.

'You know, I don't think I've spoken with either of those boys in a number of years now,' he says. 'I suspect they're probably dead too.'

'If you're the only one from that photo still living, I might need to ask you some different questions.'

'You think one of us killed Burnett, don't you,' Dalgleish says. 'And those girls too, the girls they found in Edinburgh.'

'They're women,' Callie says. 'But yes, I think it's all connected.'

'And you came here to see me by yourself.'

'Maybe. Or maybe I've got police waiting outside. Maybe I told them to hang back. Let me try things my way first.'

'Yes,' Dalgleish says, and he licks his lips for the second time. 'Maybe.'

244

He reaches for his tea across the table, his trembling hands making it harder than it should be. The mug catches a little. Hot liquid spills down the side.

'What's the cause of the tremors?' Callie asks him.

Dalgleish shoots her an angry look. 'That's a rude question.'

'Did you kill Donna Burnett?'

'No, but I wish I fucking had. I'd shake the hand of whoever did it, you understand?'

'Might take you a couple of tries.'

'You little bitch—'

Callie's hand snaps out and knocks the mug over. The tea splashes across Dalgleish's knuckles. He yelps and darts backwards, a reflex action. Callie is already moving, pushing past him and out of the kitchen. She snatches up her burner phone on her way to the door.

'I had a stroke,' Dalgleish says, still sat at the table.

Callie slows, pausing in the doorway to glance back.

'Five years ago,' he continues. 'Passed out in the living room and woke up in a puddle of piss. My hands have shook ever since.'

She stares at him. He seems diminished somehow, sitting across the room in his darkened corner. He seems pathetic. Still, just because he would have struggled on his own doesn't mean he wasn't involved. He could have selected them. He could have watched them. He could have taken a turn at the whip, once they were strapped down.

'You really don't know where I can find John Taylor or Craig McLaren?'

'I really don't. Best I can offer you is their phone numbers. But I should warn you, I haven't spoken to them in years.' He looks away. Back to his half-unpacked shopping: the reduced frozen pizza, the cans of beer. 'Give me a minute and I'll look them out for you. Feel free to wait outside, if you want. I promise I won't take offence.'

Chapter Sixty

The sky has continued to darken. The clouds have grown thicker, the atmosphere more charged. Callie flicks her headlights on as she drives off, even though it is still early afternoon. A torn-off piece of paper rests on the passenger seat beside her. Phone numbers for the remaining two boys in Joyce's photograph.

The traffic is bad – an accident up ahead on the A96 causing a tailback. Callie sits on a bridge in a motionless queue. Outside her window she can see the River Nairn passing silently beneath her, a wide expanse of water flanked by thick trees. Rain begins to tap gently against the windscreen.

She picks up the paper and studies it. The numbers are written in slanted, uncertain writing. Dalgleish's trembling pen skittering across the page.

As she inches the car forward, Callie briefly considers ringing the numbers. But what would she say if one of them answered? And if she did get through to the killer? All she'd do is spook him, send him to ground. No, better to wait until she has an address. Until she can confront him face to face.

She calls Mac, her phone on loudspeaker, not wanting to take the risk of getting pulled over for using her mobile while driving. The detective's number rings out, his voicemail telling her to leave a message. She hangs up, sends him a text asking him to call her. Thirty minutes later and she's finally leaving the small town, picking up speed towards the A9. She tries Mac again.

Voicemail.

It's going to be pitch-dark by the time Callie gets back to Edinburgh. She sits her mobile in the drinks holder and tries not to think of the long drive ahead of her. A beautiful route when you've got all the time in the world to admire it, a pain in the arse when you just want to get home.

Her stomach reminds her she's barely eaten all day. No breakfast and a couple of almond croissants for lunch. She puts the thought of food out of her head; she needs to get back. A little over two hours to get to Perth; she'll treat herself to a McDonald's there. That should get her the rest of the way.

Joining the A9 at Aviemore, Callie turns on the full beams when she can. It's four o'clock but it might as well be midnight up here. The road is quiet, at least. The installation of average speed cameras having reduced substantially the number of nutters screaming around blind corners. Once known as the most dangerous motorway in Scotland, it is one that Callie has never enjoyed driving on – especially in the dark. Long, sweeping curves that give the unnerving impression of cars perpetually overtaking.

Her mobile rings.

She jumps slightly. Glances at the propped-up screen to check before answering. She puts the phone on loudspeaker, slowing as she briefly takes her eyes off the road.

'Mac. You there?'

'I'm here, Callie. You okay?'

She refocuses her attention on the motorway. Signs flash past in her full beams; a section of dual carriageway up ahead.

'I'm fine,' she says. 'Where have you been?'

'Briefings,' the detective says. His voice sounds weary, or maybe it's just the connection. 'Did you speak with James Dalgleish?'

'I did.'

'And?'

'I'm not sure. I don't think he did the snatching, but beyond that I'm not sure.'

'Sounds like a wasted trip.'

'Not quite, listen to this. Donna Burnett? She used to abuse some of the children at Galbraith Academy. She whipped them, Mac. Strapped them to a table and fucking whipped them.'

'Jesus.'

'She called it a birching table. It's the same. I think Burnett did a number on these kids, and I think one of them killed her for it, only he couldn't stop after he was done.'

'What else did Dalgleish tell you?'

'He gave me Taylor and McLaren's numbers, although he apparently hasn't used either of them in a while.'

'You call them?'

'Wanted to check in with you first. Maybe see if you could run them, try and get their addresses.'

'Good thinking. But it's going to have to wait until tomorrow, I'm afraid. Station is crawling with brass right now. I've got meetings scheduled until ten o'clock. They've ordered Chinese food and everything.'

'Well, Police Scotland certainly know how to treat their officers.'

Mac snorts. 'I'm not so sure about that. Last time I tried their miso soup I had the shits for a week.'

Callie enters the dual carriageway and keeps to the left-hand lane. Behind her, she sees a pair of headlights approaching. The speed limit is higher here. An attempt to reduce drivers' frustrations by giving them a place to overtake. She flicks off her high beams to let the car pass safely.

'—to give me the numbers,' Mac says, his voice fading in. 'Callie?'

'Sorry, the signal's bad. You want me to give you the numbers?'

'Yeah, please. I'll run them as soon as I can. If I'm able to do it tonight, I will, but no promises.'

'All right, two secs.'

Callie reaches across to the passenger seat for the piece of paper. It flutters a little, caught in the AC's breeze. The car behind her screams past – a dark-coloured Ford Mondeo, its engine giving off a hollow knocking sound. Callie tracks it as it vanishes around an upcoming corner. She glances at her dash, noting the driver must be pushing 90 mph. Clearly, average-speed cameras don't catch every nutter.

She reads out the numbers to Mac, listens as he repeats them back.

'Alright, thanks Callie. Listen, I'm going to have to go. I'll let you know as soon as I get anything.'

'Great. Enjoy the soup.'

The line crackles as Mac ends the call. She thinks she hears him laughing. Ahead, the dual carriageway merges back into a single lane. Callie yawns, stretching her back a little. She turns the heating up and tries the radio, bouncing between static until she lands on a phone-in show. She doesn't focus on what the callers are saying but it's nice to have their voices in the car with her.

She glances at her burner phone. Thinks back over her call with Mac. She gets it – why the detective has to be careful, what he's risking by helping her – and yet it's still frustrating. Callie's made serious progress today, only to now come to a screeching halt as she waits for Mac.

Glancing at the empty road ahead, she picks up her phone and goes into the contacts list. Only three numbers there: Mac's,

Mia's and Martin Walsh's. She calls the latter now, dialling down the volume on the radio.

'My favourite PI,' Martin announces when he answers. 'What can I do for you today?'

'I need you to run some phone numbers for me,' she tells him. 'Anything and everything you can tell me.'

'Done. That it?'

'There any way you can trace a location?'

'From a mobile number?' Martin goes quiet, or maybe it's the bad connection. She imagines him shuffling through his small flat. Making his way to his office, gingerly lowering himself into his fancy leather recliner. The pubs outside will be getting busy right about now. People going for a couple of after-work pints, all that warmth and laughter rising up from the street. Martin's idea of hell, Callie is quite sure.

'Best I can do is send them a hyperlink to click on,' Martin says. 'Once they do, it'll ping me their phone's whereabouts.'

'They have to follow a link? Sounds clunky.'

'It works better when you've got access to their phone already. You set it up in advance and then track them going forward.'

'What's the likelihood that they'll click it?'

'Fifty-fifty. I can dress it up a little, hide it in a text message. Try and entice them.'

Callie smiles. '"Entice them"? I don't want you done for sending dick pics, Martin.'

The man laughs heartily. 'I said I wanted to entice them, not make them fall in love. What's their numbers?'

Callie picks up the paper again, reads them out. 'How long until you can send the texts?'

'Give me ten minutes. You want this added to your tab?'

'Please.'

'You want to think about paying your tab?'

'Not right now I don't.'

'Well listen, I—'

For a moment Callie thinks she's lost signal. Then Martin is back: 'Hang on, some fucker's hammering on my door. Jesus, use the doorbell, mate, the fucking doorbell!'

'Martin?'

She hears Martin muttering under his breath. Pictures him checking the camera feeds from the corridor outside his flat.

'Martin, you alright?'

'I'm fine. Probably a couple of drunks pissing about. I swear this place gets—'

A burst of static from the radio. Callie turns it off. 'Martin? You there?'

When he doesn't respond, she glances at her phone screen: she really does have no signal now. She sighs and checks the time. There's still well over an hour until she reaches Perth. Over an hour until she can get something to eat, until she can get a coffee.

She yawns again and reaches for her cigarettes. As she does so she sees the car up ahead. The Ford Mondeo with the knocking engine from before. It's pulled off the road, parked on the grassy verge. Sidelights only, the interior too dark to see inside. Especially not as she passes at 60 mph.

Callie tracks it in her rear-view mirror. She wonders if the car has broken down, if she should stop and offer assistance. It's what she would want someone to do, she thinks, if she were stranded out here in the middle of nowhere, in the dark.

Just as she begins to slow, the Ford's headlights come to life. Callie watches it bounce back on to the road behind her. An uncomfortable feeling slithers in the pit of her stomach. She glances at her phone again. Still no signal.

The Ford blinks out as she rounds a long, sweeping bend. Callie pushes her speed up. 63, 64 mph. There's leeway in these cameras, she tells herself. In the speedometer, too. Coming back on to a straight, she feels the steering wheel judder slightly. A vibration that travels up both her arms.

A second later, her car wrenches violently to the right. The wheel spins beneath her palms. Callie grips it tight and holds it steady. The Fiat weaves into the opposite lane before she brings it back under control. One of the rear tyres is screaming. In her wing mirror, Callie can see sparks.

She takes her foot off the accelerator. Pulls the car to the side of the road. It limps to a stop on the grass; no hard shoulder here, just stretches of dense, dark forest all around her. She grabs her phone to check for signal.

'Fuck,' she mutters.

Callie opens her door and climbs out. The temperature has dropped, and she shivers as she makes her way around the car. The rear right tyre is shredded. Turning on her phone's flash, she runs the beam over the damage. It's more than just the tyre, she sees. The whole wheel is misaligned. Bending down, she inspects the twisted metal. Most of the wheel nuts appear to be loose. A couple of them are missing entirely.

Callie does not know a lot about cars, but she has changed more than a few tyres over the years. She knows that wheel nuts are designed never to come loose by themselves. In her stomach, the slither constricts into a hard knot.

She hears the knocking then. A hollow sound that builds as the Ford approaches. Standing up, Callie sees the car slowing, its indicator flashing as it pulls off the road. The driver still has their full beams on. Callie raises one hand over her eyes, half turning away to keep from being blinded.

The Ford's engine goes quiet and the window slides down.

'Do you need some help?' the driver calls.

Chapter Sixty-One

Callie screws up her eyes against the Ford's dazzling glare.

'Can you turn off your headlights?' she calls.

'I asked if you needed some help.'

It's a man's voice. Callie raises her phone.

'I've already called roadside assistance,' she says loudly. 'The police, too. They're on their way.'

From somewhere beyond the painful blaze of the full beams, she hears the driver's door opening. Callie turns and looks at the thick forest that runs alongside the road. Her best hope, she knows, is to make a run for it.

'I'm surprised you've got signal out here,' the man says. 'Did they say how long they'd be?'

'Can you please turn down your headlights?'

She can hear the crunch of his shoes as he climbs out. 'Tell you what,' he says, 'why don't you let me have a look?'

'Stay in your car or I'm phoning the police.'

'I thought you already had.'

Callie begins to back away. Moving up the grassy slope, towards the dark thicket of trees. She stuffs the phone into her pocket. She thinks of the PAVA spray in the boot of her Fiat. Wonders if she should have gone for it, evidence be damned.

'Easy now,' the man says, and she can see his outline begin to emerge from the edge of the headlights. A thought occurs to her. Barely formed, she tries to grasp it, but the sound of another approaching car washes it away. Fresh headlights rake the road. Callie holds her breath as a second car pulls in behind them. A second later, its roof lights up blue and begins pulsing silently.

The man retreats into his Ford. The wheels spin on the loose earth as he leans too heavily on the accelerator. Finding traction, the car swings back on to the road and vanishes from view.

'Is everything all right, ma'am?'

A police officer is climbing out of his car, sweeping the beam of a torch back and forth.

Callie breathes out heavily, and the tension in her body seems to leave with it. Relief floods through her. She considers telling the officer to go after the man in the Ford – she even starts to form the words – but she stops herself before she does. What is she going to tell him? That she thinks a serial killer sabotaged her car to force her to pull over? Callie knows how that will sound. Even if she makes something up, gives the officer a reason to call it in, she knows that the second her name is taken down, she's finished. She glances at the Fiat's number plate. Surely Eddie McCall wouldn't be stupid enough to lend her a car registered to a known gangster.

'Ma'am?'

'I've got a flat tyre,' she says, motioning towards her wheel. 'I just need five minutes to change it.'

'Who was your friend?'

'I don't know. He pulled in just before you came.'

'Why'd he run off?'

'I guess you scared him.'

The officer frowns at her. He's a young man, Callie sees. Alone, in the dark, trying to make sense of it all. Finally, he nods at her car.

'Have you got a spare?' he asks.

'Yeah.'

He runs the beam of his torch over the wheel. His frown deepens. 'I'm not sure that's going to cut it,' he says.

'I'm sorry?'

'You're missing a whole bunch of wheel nuts. And your hub looks damaged too. How fast were you going when this came off?'

'I'm not sure. I wasn't speeding, if that's what you asking.'

The officer looks over at her and smiles. 'I wasn't. But I'd be concerned about underlying damage to your axle, maybe even the suspension. Besides, unless you've got some extra nuts along with the spare tyre, you're not going to be able to secure it.'

Callie sags slightly. 'Fuck,' she says.

'You got breakdown cover? Roadside assistance?'

The question almost makes her laugh out loud. 'Unfortunately not.'

'Well, I can radio for someone to come out and tow you to the nearest garage, but it might be a bit of a wait.'

She wraps her arms around herself, feeling the chill in the air as her adrenaline fades. 'I don't think I have much of a choice.'

'Alright, give me a couple minutes.'

The officer returns to his car. Callie watches him speaking into his shoulder-mounted radio. He is eyeing her through his windscreen as he talks. A sudden wave of uncertainty hits her. A nauseous build-up. She thinks back to her conversation with Mac just the other day. *You think we're looking for another cop*, he said. *I honestly don't know*, she told him. *Maybe.*

The officer is climbing out of his car now. His torch back on, the beam low on the ground. 'It'll be about forty minutes,' he says. 'Quicker than I thought, to be honest.'

'Thank you.'

'You want, I can give you a lift down the road. There's a service station at Carrbridge—'

Callie puts her hand up. 'It's okay, I'll just wait in the car.'

'It's no trouble. Better than you sitting here in the dark.'

'I appreciate the offer, but I'm fine. Might be they can get me up and running again. I'd really rather just get back on the road if I can.'

'Well then, do you want to sit in my patrol car with me? I'm happy to wait.'

'Thank you, but no, I'd rather not.'

He pauses. Callie tries to read his face. To see past the surprise and the indignation, past the mask, if he's wearing one. Surely she cannot be the first lone female to feel nervous when a male police officer approaches her. Not anymore, not these days.

'You're really not supposed to wait inside your car on a motorway following a breakdown,' he says.

'I know.'

The officer shrugs and says, 'Well, it's up to you. I'll sit behind you with my lights on until the tow truck gets here, just in case.'

He turns back to his car, giving her a final nod across the roof as he climbs in. Callie waits until he's closed his door before returning to her Fiat. She engages the locks and turns up the heating, holding her hands over the vents. The hot air drifts over her frozen palms. Her fingers tremble as they warm.

She watches the young officer in her rear-view mirror. She's being paranoid, she knows this, and yet she can't shake the unsettled feeling deep in her stomach.

The officer yawns and stretches. He types on his phone. He speaks into his radio. Callie wonders if he's running the Fiat's registration number. She wonders what it would show.

It takes half an hour for the truck to arrive. The mechanic is an older man. He looks over the damage and tells her she should be fine with a set of new wheel nuts.

'What about the hub?' the young officer asks him, but the mechanic waves him away.

'I don't think it was driven long enough to cause any real damage,' he says. 'Although I'd recommend getting it checked out when you're home.'

Callie stands on the grassy verge and watches him change the tyre. He fits fresh wheel nuts, tells her when he's done that he's never seen something like this happen before.

'Sometimes folks forget to tighten them properly before driving off,' he says, returning his tools to his truck. 'But I reckon it's almost impossible for these nuts to come off by themselves.'

She doesn't want to dwell on it. On the fact that someone deliberately sabotaged her car today. When she was in the Archive Centre, perhaps, or when she was talking with James Dalgleish. She's still got a good couple of hours of driving ahead of her; she can dwell on it then.

She pays the mechanic in cash from the stack Eddie McCall left for her. Peeling notes from inside the backpack to keep the true amount hidden. He tells her he doesn't have change, so she rounds it up and gives the rest as a tip. The man's eyes practically jump out of his head.

Waving goodbye to them both, Callie climbs into the driver's seat and allows herself a moment before driving away. She closes her eyes, lets her head droop forward into her hands. She rubs at her eyes, at the sides of her face. Just long enough to feel a little sorry for herself. To miss her old flat, her old bed. Her old jobs – the boring, pedestrian fraudsters she'd grown so tired of chasing. Then she starts her car up, indicates, and pulls back on to the road.

As she does, a thought returns to her. The same one from earlier, still half formed, still unclear. The man in the Ford. The man who blinded her with his full beams and asked if she wanted some help. *Easy now*, he said, and there was something in the inflection of the words that now rings a bell in Callie's mind. She has heard them already – spoken the same way, spoken to her. She cannot place it, but whoever the man was, stood hidden behind the glare of his headlights, Callie knows she has met him before.

You are a lucky girl.

Where were you going to run? Into the woods? In the dark? I would have enjoyed that, I think. The slow chase, the catch and release. I would have done terrible things to you in those woods.

You are a snoop.

You dig into things you should leave well enough alone. You pry into people's histories, into their hidden secrets. You think everything is up for grabs, that nothing is sacred. You think because you are paid to intrude into the lives of others then you are entitled to keep what you find. But you are not the only one who can dig, and I am not the only one with a past. And I know something about yours, Callie Munro.

You are not safe.

You will never be safe. No matter where you go, no matter where you hide. I will find you.

Chapter Sixty-Two

In the end, she doesn't stop. She keeps her foot down. Coasting through Perth, past the signs for fuel and fast food. She doesn't need either. She's got enough to get her home. The thought that the Ford with the knocking engine is out there, still, trailing her somehow, is too hard to shake. Images of being attacked while filling up her car at a quiet petrol station. Of being injected with a tranquilliser as she tucks into a Big Mac. The fucking tragedy of it.

It's late when she pulls into the safe house. Dark now – proper dark, night dark. That chill in the air that only comes around when the sun sets. She's not as hungry as she thought she might be. Adrenaline, maybe, or tiredness. All she can picture is her bed, and she half stumbles into the house, pausing to make sure she's locked the door properly, before crashing out on top of the sheets, still dressed.

When she wakes it's mid-morning. Ten a.m., the sun streaming through the window. She's still lying in the same position. Face down, her arms folded awkwardly around her. She doesn't think she moved once all night.

Easy now.

As soon as she stirs, she hears it. The man's voice. The gentle cadence in his words. It's like an itch in her brain, knowing that she's heard it before.

Easy now.

From somewhere beneath her there's a rhythmic buzzing. Callie rolls over, her arms protesting, and digs out her phone. She peers at the screen, bleary-eyed. It's Martin.

'Good morning,' he says brightly when she answers.

Callie yawns audibly, stretching. 'Morning.'

'You just up now?'

'I had a long day. Don't judge me. How's your front door?'

'Still reinforced. And I'm sorry to wake you, but I thought you'd want an update on your two men.'

Clarity punches through the fog. Callie sits up, crossing her legs beneath her. She scrabbles in her bag for her makeshift notepad. 'Absolutely. What did you find?'

She hears Martin shuffling around. The tapping of a keyboard as he talks. 'I don't know exactly what you're looking into, but I don't think Craig McLaren's your man,' he says. 'Guy's spent more time in prison the last twenty years than in his own bed. He's currently midway through a four-year stint in Addiewell for assault.'

'So it's John Taylor, then?' Callie says, scribbling.

'Hard to say. Taylor's off the grid, and I mean *off the grid*. My guess is he changed his name at some point, started clean. I can keep digging but it might take me a while.'

Callie knows what Martin's really saying. He doesn't do this sort of work out of the goodness of his heart. 'That's alright,' she tells him. The voice replays in her head, on an endless loop. 'I can pick up the trail from here.'

Easy now.

'Whatever you want.'

'Did you send out that text you were talking about? The one that can track their phones once they click on it?'

'I did. Nothing yet though.'

Callie goes quiet for a moment. 'You think you could send the link to me?'

'To you? Why?'

'Because I think having you keep an eye on my whereabouts the next couple of days might not be a bad thing.'

The sound of Martin's keyboard falls away. When he speaks, he suddenly sounds concerned. 'You worried that something is going to happen to you?' he asks.

'Just taking precautions.'

'Callie, if you want to take precautions, you get a bigger lock on your door. A phone trace won't do shit if you're dead.'

'All right, thank you. Can you just send me the text, please?'

Martin sighs. 'Fine. Anything else?'

'No, that's everything.' Callie sets her pen down and unfolds her legs. She slides off the bed and pads over to the window. Outside, it's a beautiful sunny day. 'I really mean that, you know,' she says. 'Thank you, Martin. I'd never have lasted five minutes in this job without you.'

'Five minutes? Five seconds, more like—'

'Yeah, yeah,' Callie says, laughing.

'Whatever you're up to, be careful.'

'I will,' she says, and ends the call.

A few moments later her phone vibrates again. A text from a number she doesn't recognise. *Click here for tracking link*, it says. *Absolutely no dick pics.*

Callie smiles as she taps it. A blank webpage loads up, sits on a white screen. To all intents and purposes, it just looks like some internet site that's failed to load properly. She closes it down and slides the phone into her pocket. Despite what Martin said, there's something reassuring about knowing he has her location.

She yawns for a second time, stretches her back again. Her appetite has finally returned.

◆ ◆ ◆

She eats a late breakfast of yoghurt and fruit. Sitting out in the garden, on the decking. Watching the sway of the tall trees that surround the property. Callie's never been very good with tree names, never been good with nature in general. Not something she's ever had much of an interest in. If it wasn't going to help her survive whatever foster home she was currently in, then it might as well have been ancient hieroglyphics for all the good it would do her.

She thinks about what James Dalgleish told her. Sitting at his kitchen table, his hands trembling as he tried to lift a cup of tea. He told her that he was happy Burnett was dead. Given what the teacher had done to them, she wasn't exactly surprised.

She knows what happens to kids like James Dalgleish, like John Taylor. Kids who suffer, who get twisted and mistreated, who get forced down one of two paths: the introverted, spaced-out loser, dead at nineteen on the floor of some drug den, or the angry, insular ball of rage who just wants to burn everything down.

She thinks of her time growing up. The foster homes, the families she passed through. The violence, the callousness. The unemotional fog that settles over you; a protective layer, no matter how feeble. The two worlds, the lightness and the dark. She understands how the system creates monsters. She understands that the only reason she's not out there burning down the world right now might be nothing more than plain, simple luck.

She phones Mac. Lights up a cigarette, then breathes in deep as his phone rings. He answers with an apology.

'I've not been able to run the numbers yet. Dawson has me on a tight leash. I can barely piss without her watching over me.'

263

Callie exhales slowly. She watches the smoke rise up and fade away. 'You think she knows you've been helping me?'

'No. Or at least, not for sure. I think she suspects it, maybe.'

'Mac, I think that woman suspects everything.'

The detective laughs. She can hear the tension in it though. The strain. She knows it can't be easy, helping her like this. Putting his own job on the line every time he answers his phone.

'Listen,' she says. 'I've narrowed it down for you. The guy we're looking for is John Taylor. He's the only one in the photo it can be. He's dropped off the grid, though. Maybe changed his name, I don't know. Can you look into it?'

'Sure, I can look into it. How did you find all this out?'

'You're not the only man I have running around after me, you know.'

Mac laughs again at that. It sounds a little lighter this time. Callie finds herself smiling.

'Okay, let me go check it out. I'll have to think of a reason to explain to Dawson where I got all this info from.'

'Just tell her the truth. I did all the hard work and sent you my findings, out of the blue.'

'Hmm.'

Callie takes another drag on her cigarette. 'In all seriousness,' she says, 'the guy whose number you gave me?'

'Martin Walsh?'

'If anything happens to me, you ask him to track me down.'

'Callie—'

'You ask him, all right?'

'All right.'

Callie nods, feeling better for some reason. Mac hangs up and she finishes her coffee and her cigarette, still sat outside, still staring at those nameless trees, still feeling the gaze of those two worlds upon her, the lightness and the dark.

Chapter Sixty-Three

She takes a long, hot shower. It's the first she's had in over twenty-four hours. A day's worth of stress, of tension, of sweat and relief. She closes her eyes and lets the warm water rinse it all.

Easy now.

It infuriates Callie, how she cannot place this voice. She can hear it in her head. She replays it, over and over. The inflection, the gentle laugh. A man has said these words to her and he has said them in the same manner because he is the same, because she has met the man who pulled in behind her on the A9, the man with the full beams, the man with the knocking engine. The man who unscrewed her wheel nuts and forced her off the road. Another thirty seconds and maybe he'd have driven a hypodermic syringe into her neck. Just like Alison. Like Amy Miller. Like all those other women.

Afterwards she dresses, towel-drying her hair and letting it fall damp around her shoulders. It's lunchtime already, and even though she's already had breakfast she's starving again. Yesterday she barely ate anything. Today she's making up for it.

She slides bread in the toaster. Makes a mental note that she's going to have to do a shop if she's still here in a few days. Eddie McCall said to speak to Mia if she needed anything, but it seems a little ridiculous to ask the woman to go food shopping for her, especially after having spent a day out of the house already.

She sets out the butter, along with a jar of peanut butter. She's never understood people who don't have both. Peanut butter is so dry by itself. She puts a pan on the hob and melts butter before cracking a couple of eggs in to fry. It's an odd combination, she knows.

She rinses her mug and pours herself another coffee from the percolator. As she takes a drink she hears a faint buzzing sound.

Her phone. She pats her pocket, scanning the room for it. Through the glass of the French doors she sees it sitting on the decking outside, lit up, vibrating. Behind her, the toaster pops – too soon, she forgot to spin the dial. Callie sets her coffee down, replunges her toast, sets the timer properly and retrieves her phone.

It's Mac. Five missed calls and a text message to call back. She does so, drifting back inside. The garden air is chilly on her damp skin and she can feel goosebumps travel along her neck and down the backs of her arms.

'Callie?'

'Mac, is everything all ri—?'

'I need you to stop whatever you're doing and listen to me very carefully.' The detective's voice is low, and flat, and something about it makes her stomach twist itself into knots. 'We just got the forensic report back on your flat. They found a number of very small, very well-hidden recording devices inside.'

'They what? Where?'

'In nearly every room of the house. Behind a bookshelf, under the fridge. But listen to me. They found GPS trackers as well, dozens of them. Stitched into the lining of your clothes, Callie. In your outdoor clothes, your jackets and trainers. A couple of your handbags.'

Callie's gaze moves across the room. Her jacket is hung over the back of a chair. The same jacket she grabbed by the door as she left her flat. She goes to it now.

'Callie? You there?'

'I'm here,' she says, pinning the phone against her shoulder as she inspects the jacket. Turning it over in her hands, running her fingers along the edges of the lining. 'I'm just . . .'

Her index nail catches on a loose stitch. She lifts it, inspects it, works her finger under the thread until she can pick it loose. The slit opens up easily after that. Inside, she digs out a small, black square. It's made of plastic, about the size of a two-pence coin.

'Mac, I think I found one of them here. In my jacket.'

'You need to get out of the house. Callie. Do you hear me? I don't know where you are, but you need to get out of the house.'

The toaster pops. Callie turns to see a man wearing a black balaclava standing behind her. She screams in fright, drops the phone, Mac's voice growing faint as the mobile skitters across the floor.

The man lunges for her. A syringe in his hand and something glinting on his wrist – that silver watch. Richard's watch.

She darts backwards, clattering against the chair. She's still holding her jacket and she whips it out now, around his outstretched arm, pulling it to one side as she flees across the room.

Panic guides her. All rational thought gone. She's boxed herself in behind the kitchen island, the doors to the garden and the hallway on the other side. The man is growling as he rushes towards her. Callie smells eggs and grabs the frying pan, tensing her core as she hurls it across the room. The man manages to lift an arm to protect his masked face, but it buys her some time to push past him towards the French doors.

She's almost there when she feels his gloved fingers in her wet hair. He yanks back – hard – and Callie's head snaps back painfully.

She cries out as she twists backwards. He slams her head against the counter with a grunt. Does it again, then a third time. Callie sees blood splatter across the kitchen floor.

Then comes the sharp prick in the back of her neck. The cold as the plunger is pressed, as the chemicals flood her system.

'No . . .' she moans.

He lets go of her and she slumps to her knees. Her face aches, her nose broken, maybe. She watches as he goes to her mobile phone and in one decisive movement, crushes it beneath his heel.

He lifts her then. Easily, like she weighs nothing. He carries her outside, through the secluded garden towards the Fiat. He sets her on the ground as he digs out the keys – her keys – and opens the boot. She tries to crawl away. Tries to pull herself along the gravelled path. It's like swimming through treacle. It's like that bad dream that everyone has. All your energy into moving forward and barely making any progress. She makes it less than a metre before his hands are on her again, hauling her up, rolling her into the boot of the car.

Callie can feel the darkness closing in around her. The colour fading from the world. The edges of her vision growing small. As he stands looming over her she reaches for him, her fingers grasping clumsily at his balaclava. He lets her take hold of it, lets her pull at the dark fabric. He even helps her a little, peeling it off his head and smiling down at her as it falls away.

Callie stares into his face as she finally slips under. Her last word half spoken, half whispered, slurred, a breath in the cold air as she falls asleep.

'You . . .'

Chapter Sixty-Four

Richard is watching her when she wakes.

She stirs, slowly, rising from the inky black. A smothering fatigue like a heavy blanket over her head. She sheds it as she climbs. Her vision fades in – the dark room, the gentle glow from a lamp in the corner. She feels the thin sleeping bag beneath her. The hard floor beneath that. Something heavy around her ankle, something that clinks when she moves her legs. A chain.

'Finally,' Richard says. 'How are you feeling?'

Callie brings her hand to her face, gently touches her nose. It's sore but it doesn't feel broken after all. A layer of blood on her cheek, crusted over. It flakes away between her fingers.

'Callie?'

'Richard?'

The wooziness is wearing off. The viscous sludge draining from her head. She feels it slide down into her belly, and she rolls over and vomits on to the floor beside her makeshift bed. There's not much to come up – bile and this morning's yoghurt, or is it yesterday's yoghurt, she's not sure. She spits into the darkness, wipes her mouth with the back of her hand. The air has a sharp, acrid smell now.

'Callie, you all right?'

Callie shuffles away from the sick. The chain around her ankle is heavy, and it drags along the floor. 'I feel better now,' she says. 'Although I think I might throw up again in a minute.'

'It's the drugs,' he says. 'I felt the same way.'

She rubs at her face, at her eyes. Forces herself to focus. In the dim light she can see Richard, sat across from her on the other side of the room. On the floor, on his own little pile of blankets. Like her, he has a thick, metal chain strapped to his ankle.

'Are you okay?' she asks him. She shuffles closer but can't move more than a few feet before her restraints go tight. 'Richard, you've been gone for days now.'

'I've noticed,' he says. He gives a flicker of a smile. A taut grimace. He's in pain, Callie realises.

'You're hurt,' she says.

'A little.'

'What did he do to you?'

Richard nods towards something behind her. 'That.'

Callie turns, awkwardly, her muscles still waking up. Against the wall she sees a simple metal table. Her stomach constricts again.

'I woke up strapped to that thing,' Richard murmurs. 'He'd stripped me naked. I shouted for hours until he came back.'

His voice goes quiet. Callie says, 'You don't have to—'

'He whipped me until I was bleeding. Said he was going to slice my throat.'

'I'm so sorry, Richard.'

'He said he was doing it because of you.'

There's no malice in his words. Still, Callie cannot hold his gaze. She thinks about how she gave him up. How she implicated him – worse, how she imagined him doing it. All this time, she has seen him as the possible reason for her life turning to hell these past few days, when in fact it was her who ruined Richard's.

She checks his wrist now. 'Where's your watch?' she asks.

Richard raises his eyebrows. 'My watch?'

'The big silver one you're always wearing.'

'I've no idea, Callie. He must have taken it from me when he undressed me.'

Callie feels a fresh wave of nausea roll over her.

'He's crazy, Richard,' she tells him. 'He's been targeting me too. He's obsessive.'

'Why?'

'Because she killed my father.'

His voice comes from across the room. In the gloom, neither of them noticed the door open silently. Callie stares across at him now. She is barely able to make out his outline, stood in the doorway, staring back.

'John Taylor?' Callie says. Rising to her feet, forcing her voice to sound strong, pushing down the panic, the aching beat of her racing heart. 'You're lucky you took me when you did. I almost had you.'

The man laughs at that. '"Almost" doesn't count, Callie.'

'When you replaced the lock on my front door, you kept a key, didn't you. That's how you do it. You break in and wait for the police to call you to replace the lock. It's so simple. The circle you cut in the glass is just . . . misdirection.'

John claps his hands together. 'I knew this was going to be fun,' he says.

Callie turns away, her brow knotted. She is awake now. She is turning it over in her mind.

'Your father,' she says. 'Your father was Philip Joyce. He sent you to Galbraith Academy. He helped you disappear after you killed a teacher. Gave you a safe space to act out your fantasies. Some twisted guilt, perhaps, for having sent you away in the first place.'

'And you killed him.'

'He killed himself,' she says, looking back at the half-formed man in the dark room. 'As did your mum. I think maybe they wanted to take the blame, give you the chance to disappear all over again.' She pauses, her hands forming fists by her side. 'Like you'd ever be able to stop.'

'Yes, well. Aren't you a clever girl.'

'The police know who you are,' Callie says. 'You hear me, John? It's over.'

Another laugh. 'It is,' he says. 'For you, at least. I'll give it a little longer for the sedative to wear off completely. I'm planning on removing your skin, Callie. Every part of it. I'm going to start with your back and work my way down, tender slice by tender slice, and I want to make sure you're fully present before I get started.'

Chapter Sixty-Five

They are left alone after that. In the dark room, chained to the hard floor. Callie sits down again, more to steady her trembling legs than anything else. She tries not to think of the metal table behind her. She closes her eyes and runs through it all. Every step of her investigation, everything she's uncovered. She finally feels the pieces sliding into place.

'What the fuck's going on here, Callie?' Richard shuffles forward. His chain rattles as he moves. 'I don't want to die down here.'

Callie opens her eyes. 'His name is John Taylor,' she says softly. 'He's responsible for the murders of eight people that I'm aware of. Six women whose bodies he hid in the beach house belonging to his father. An old teacher who abused him as a child. Another woman he murdered just to mess with me.'

'How do you know all this?'

'Because I've been hunting him, Richard. Piecing together his shitty past.'

Callie can see him now, plain as day. The knock at her front door, John Taylor holding up his toolbox with a warm smile and a promise to fix her lock. Less than an hour after breaking it down himself.

She offered him a coffee, she remembers. *Easy now*, he said. *I'll never get back to sleep.*

Easy now.

'So how the hell do we get out of here?' Richard says.

'I'm working on it,' Callie snaps.

She thinks of the trackers John placed around her house. She runs her gaze around the room they're in now. It's possible – perhaps even likely – that he's fitted cameras to watch them in here. Audio transmitters, at the very least. But the room is so badly lit, she can't tell for sure.

'We should try and get some sleep,' she tells Richard.

'Are you kidding?'

'He's going to take his time with this. I don't think he's coming back any time soon.'

'We might be dead soon!'

'What's the matter, can't get comfortable?'

'On this fucking floor?' Richard's chain rattles as he moves around. 'I've barely slept since I got here.'

Callie leans forward and balls her blanket up. 'Then use this,' she says, and tosses it across the room to him.

He catches it in his lap. 'I don't need another bloody blanket, Callie, I need to get out. What's the matter with you?'

'Just use it, Richard,' she says. 'And stop making a big deal about everything, you understand me? Just try and get some sleep. I can't think straight right now. Give me an hour to process all this.'

'An hour?' Richard starts, before falling mercifully silent. 'Fine, whatever,' he says after a couple of minutes.

Callie stretches out on her sleeping bag. The floor beneath her is cold, and she feels its icy tendrils spread across her back. She tries not to think about John's promise to her. *Tender slice by tender slice.* The words make her stomach cramp, and for a moment she thinks she might throw up again.

Across from her, in the dark, she hears Richard lying down too. His breathing slows, the room falling quiet.

'Can I ask you something?' he says suddenly.

'Sure,' she says.

He rolls over on to his side. His chain clanks. 'When we were last together . . . in my flat . . .'

'What about it?'

'The lamb,' he says. 'Was it really that dry?'

Callie starts to laugh. It catches her unawares. Her chest shakes with it, tears prickling at the corners of her eyes. 'It was so dry,' she says, rolling over to look at his darkened shape.

'It was, wasn't it?'

She can hear the smile in his voice, and it makes her laugh harder. 'Honestly I think you cooked it for like an hour too long.'

'I knew it,' he says, laughing now too. 'It was black inside when I cut into it, I knew it.'

Callie wipes at her eyes. 'The wine was nice.'

'The wine was nice. I'll get you a bottle to say thanks once you break me out of here.'

'Sounds good.' Callie rolls over on to her other side and curls the sleeping bag around her legs. She rests her head on her arms.

'You were right to leave the way you did,' Richard says. 'I really am sorry for everything.'

Callie stares into the darkness. 'I know,' she says quietly.

Chapter Sixty-Six

Sometime later, John returns.

Callie hears him unlocking the door. She's not sure how long has passed. She listens to him step into the room and close the door behind him. The sharp click of the bolt sliding home once more.

She's still lying on her side. She rolls over just as he flicks a switch. There's a sudden, painful burst of light from above. Callie screws her eyes shut, wincing. Beside her, Richard gives an audible groan.

She angles her head away from the glare. She can hear John's footsteps as he approaches and she forces herself to open her eyelids a crack. Letting the light flood in. Telling herself that this is how he wants them. Stunned, cowering, unable to fight back.

'Relax,' John says. 'Let your eyes adjust.'

Blinking, Callie slides herself away from him, as far as her chain will allow. She stands up. Her legs shake more than she'd like them to.

John is stood in the centre of the room. Callie stares at him. Remembers his face at her front door, smiling. There is no trace of that smile now. His mouth is firm, a straight line, his eyes hooded. He is dressed in black and carrying a sports bag in one hand. In the other he is holding a gun.

Callie doesn't know exactly what kind of gun it is. She's never had much interest in them. Never even seen one before, not a real one, not in person. But it's a revolver and it's pointed at her. Callie figures that's all she really needs to know.

'Enjoy your sleep?' John asks.

'Rejuvenating,' Callie says. Her voice is low. Quiet but steady.

'I'm glad to hear it.'

Richard is on his feet now too. Callie glances over at him. In the bright room, she sees him properly for the first time. She sees the days-old stubble, the dark shadows under his eyes. She sees the way he stands; hunched forward, like he cannot fully straighten his back. Callie looks across at that metal table against the wall. She tries not to picture him strapped to it, bloodied and screaming. The table is her future.

Only if you let it be, she tells herself.

John moves across the room now. He keeps the gun pointed towards them, despite the chains. Callie tracks the length of hers. It runs to a thick, metal loop, bolted to the floor next to her makeshift bed. Richard's does the same.

'You know, my father talked about you,' John says. He's at the table now. He's set his sports bag down on it. 'He thought we were perhaps rather alike, you and I. Both of us without a strong parental figure growing up, both of us cast out into the world to fend for ourselves. Both of us robbed of that pure, unquestioning love that parents have for their children.'

'I reckon that's where the similarities end, myself.'

John unzips the sports bag and pulls out a set of sharp, gleaming knives. He places them on to the floor by his feet. 'Yes, well. I suppose trauma warps people in different ways, doesn't it?'

'At least you had parents,' Callie says slowly, carefully. 'They sent you away to school but they took you back, too. They let you hide the bodies of those women in their home. What is that, if not love?'

John laughs. 'It's guilt.'

His back is to them both. The gun is on the table, both his hands still busy removing items from the bag. Thick leather straps. Rolls of plastic sheeting.

'The teacher you killed. Donna Burnett. People would understand why you did—'

John lifts the revolver and clatters it loudly against the table. Callie jumps.

'Do not tell me what people would understand,' he says softly. 'I don't care about your opinions, or your armchair psychobabble. It's all bullshit. And you know what, Callie?'

'What?'

'You're right. We are nothing alike. See, my father told me something about you. Right before you broke into his home and beat him unconscious.'

'So now you're offended at my breaking and entering—'

'He told me who it was that took you in.'

Callie blinks. 'I don't . . .'

'The man who was working at the shelter the night your parents left you. I know his name.'

Callie stares at him. All of a sudden she doesn't see the gun anymore. Doesn't see the leather straps, the plastic sheets, the set of knives. She doesn't even see the table. All she can picture is Joyce, sitting forward in his hospital bed, the sheets bunched around him. His face, shining with sweat. His words. *I pulled some strings. I got a name.*

His offer. The name in return for ending his life.

She didn't think it serious. Didn't let herself think it, didn't want to weigh up whether it was an offer she'd be willing to take.

'Bullshit,' Callie spits, shaking her head. 'You're lying.'

John shrugs. 'Maybe. Maybe not.' He picks up the gun. 'We'll revisit it later. On the table.'

'If you think I'm going to—'

He pulls back the hammer on the gun. The click is like a finger snap in the quiet room. 'No more talking,' he tells her. 'I want you to undress yourself for me. I want you to lie down on that table. I'm going to hurt you now, Callie, and I'm going to enjoy it. I'm going to cut you up into little pieces. And I just have one question for you before I do.'

'You're a fucking coward,' Richard says suddenly. He moves forward, dragging his chain until it goes taut. 'Why don't you put the gun down and let me out of this, and let's see who enjoys hurting each other the most.'

'Back off,' John says coolly. He turns the revolver on Richard. 'You'll get your turn. And don't worry, I promise to make it quick this time.'

'Christ, that teacher really did a number on you,' Richard says.

'Enough.'

'You ask me—'

'I said that's enough—'

'What's your question?' Callie says, interrupting. Both men turn to look at her. 'You said you had a question for me, John. What is it?'

John tilts his head to one side. He moves closer. His face is blank, near-unreadable. He looks at her like she isn't really there. Like she isn't really a person. He stands between her and Richard now, less than two metres away from her although it might as well be two miles. He has calculated this, Callie realises. Where he can stand safely, how much leeway the chains give him. He is close enough that she can see the individual beads of sweat that have broken out across his forehead, and yet Callie will never be able to reach him.

'I wanted to ask you how you worked it out,' John says. He has the revolver pointed at her. The barrel aimed at her stomach. Callie's gaze flicks to it. The gun is perfectly still.

'How I worked out what?'

'Galbraith Academy. Donna Burnett. All of it. I thought I was meticulous.'

'You were, for the most part. But you left something behind when you took Amy Miller.'

Realisation dawns on John's face. 'That's where I dropped it?'

'Grant Miller found it in his garden.'

John smiles. 'Well, fair play to him. And he gave everything to you?'

'That's right.'

'So you have my thumb.'

'I do.'

'And my PAVA spray.'

'Afraid not,' she says.

Behind John, she sees Richard pull the canister from the blanket she threw him earlier. The canister she'd removed from the backpack and stuffed down her top just before passing out in the boot of her car.

John catches sight of her gaze. He turns, but not fast enough. Richard jams his finger down on the release and sends a stream of burning liquid leaping across the room. It coats John's face; it splashes into his eyes. He screams.

The spray becomes like a mist in the small room. Callie can feel her eyes start to sting. Her vision blurs, her throat gags. She has to force herself not to look away.

John buries his face in his hands. The gun falls to the floor. He stumbles backwards, towards Callie, across the safety line.

She hears Richard yelling but her eyes are streaming, her skin burning. The room is a blur of movement. Callie breathes through the pain. Short, sharp bursts of air. She shifts her weight off centre, sets her arm like she's doing a push-up. She trusts her body to know what to do.

Elbow behind the wrist.

Shoulder behind the elbow.

Callie fires her palm heel upwards and straight into John Taylor's throat. Something in her arm pops, pain flaring along her bicep. She hears John choking and then the scrape of metal, and when her vision clears enough she sees Richard has him now, on his knees he has him, his chain wrapped tight around the man's neck.

'Richard,' she gasps. The word barely more than a whisper, her throat on fire. 'Wait . . .'

She sees John's face turn red, his fingers scrabbling to get under the metal links. His eyes are red and streaming from the PAVA spray, and they bulge in their sockets.

Callie tries to move forward but her chain is already taut. Her foot connects with the fallen revolver. It is an ink stain on the white floor. She scrabbles for it.

'Richard!' she croaks, loud enough that he looks over at her this time. His face is almost as red as John's. His skinny arms bulging as they hold the struggling man in place. 'Richard, I have his gun, let him go!'

But Richard doesn't stop. Spittle comes from his mouth as he grips the chain tight. John's scrabbling has started to slow, one of his hands falling limply by his side.

Callie raises the gun. Adrenaline and blurred vision and that pain in her elbow – the revolver swings, wildly, the barrel dancing between the two men.

'The name,' she barks, her voice hoarse but getting stronger. 'Richard, he knows who took me in. Please, you have to let him go!'

Richard is gone. His breathing loud, his arms shaking. His gaze on the metal table against the wall. He stares at it and he does not stop. John's other arm has gone limp now. The man's eyes have started to roll upwards.

'Richard,' Callie whispers, the gun becoming more steady, her aim becoming more precise. 'Please.'

But he makes her choose. Between the killer and his prisoner. Between her past and the innocent man. The sudden unfairness of being dangled an answer to the question she's spent so much of her life asking.

What happened to my parents?

Callie lets the gun drop. She sinks to her knees. Richard takes another few seconds, just to be sure, and then he lets John go. The man slumps to the floor, dead, his killings finally brought to an end, his secrets lost forever.

Chapter Sixty-Seven

Callie carries this one with her. She worries for how long.

A set of keys in a dead man's pocket. She watches Richard fish them out and unlock his restraints, then come over and unlock hers. He does not speak; he barely looks at her. His fingers tremble. It takes him ten full seconds to slide the key into the lock.

The room has taken on a sour, foosty smell. The odour of a place where a man has been kept prisoner. Where a man has died. Sweat and blood and shame. Callie didn't notice it before, but she does now. Now it is nearly overwhelming. Now she rushes from the room to escape it.

The rest of the evening passes in a series of moments. Retching again on the side of a busy road. The feel of the cold night air on her warm face. The sight of twirling cruiser lights in the distance, the changing wail of their sirens as they approach. Callie has never been so happy to see the police.

DI Dawson appears. Later, after Callie has given a statement, after she has been placed in the back of a car. A small crowd has gathered by then; onlookers and officers, crime scene tape and white boiler suits. Callie recognises the blue VW Golf as it pulls in. Dawson climbs out just as Callie is driven away. Their eyes meet briefly, the detective's face drawn and unreadable. A glimpse of Mac beside her, but he does not see her.

◆ ◆ ◆

Her home is a mess. The drawers ransacked, her wardrobe emptied. Someone even tossed her mattress, like they do in prison. Like she was keeping a home-made shank in the frame of her bed. She imagines DI Dawson keeping watch as SOCOs searched every inch of the place. Callie stands in the middle of her flat and doesn't know where to start. She sinks to the floor and hugs her knees tight against her chest.

She doesn't think she'll sleep what's left of the night but she does. With a chair wedged against the front door and a knife on her bedside table. She manages a few hours.

She sees the dawn in. Stood outside her front door, smoking. Abbeyhill waking up alongside her. The shadow figures behind mottled glass, the car doors, the steady thrum of traffic along London Road. The real world moving on like nothing ever happened, and Callie playing along. Two doors down, the man in his pyjamas stoops to collect his dog's shit from his front garden. She wonders if he saw the police officers break down her door. If he was stood right there, in that very spot, holding his little bag of warm dog shit when it happened. He straightens and sees her, and he nods. Callie lifts her cigarette and blows smoke.

By the end of the day, things are better. The flat is tidied. Clothes refolded. Fresh sheets on the bed and the carpets hoovered. The little stuff that feels like progress. A phone call to Martin and he sends someone he trusts to sort her home security. New locks, a camera above her front door, every window alarmed.

'Maybe now you won't laugh at my set-up,' Martin says.

'Maybe.'

'You know, sometimes it takes a near miss before we realise how dangerous the world is,' he adds.

And Callie smiles and continues to play along, and listens to the instructions on how to run her new system from her phone, and she thinks of being chained to the floor as John Taylor prepared to skin her alive, and she wonders if that counts as a near miss.

Mac comes to visit her later that evening. Callie is washing her dinner dishes when her phone buzzes on the kitchen counter. The detective's face looms large on her screen. She makes her way to the front door and slides back the three deadbolts before swinging it open.

'Hello, Detective,' she says.

'Hello, Callie. This is all very fancy.' He motions to the CCTV system. 'And did I hear three deadbolts? Or was it just two?'

'It's almost like I don't want a serial killer kicking in my front door again.'

'Fair enough.' He stands against the railing that runs down the steps to the street. He isn't dressed properly for the cold: a thin-looking suit and no overcoat. When he smiles it looks half-hearted and tired. 'How are you?'

'I'm fine,' she says.

'Really?'

'No, probably not. But I will be.'

Mac nods. *He looks spent*, Callie thinks. *Like he hasn't slept well for days.*

'I just wanted to tell you that I'm sorry,' he says.

'For what?'

'For everything that happened to you. For everything I wasn't able to stop.'

Callie folds her arms and leans against the doorway. 'You're sweet, Mac, but none of this was your fault. I went after it on my own.'

'Doesn't mean you deserve it.'

'Doesn't mean you could have stopped it, either.'

'I could have tried.'

Callie rolls her eyes. 'Men,' she mutters.

The detective looks away. He buries his hands in his pockets. They must be freezing.

'I'd ask you in but I'm just about to head out,' Callie says.

'Oh. Anywhere nice?'

'Just another job.' She watches him shiver slightly at a gust of wind. 'How are you doing?' she asks him.

'I'm fine.'

'Really?'

Mac smiles. It seems more genuine this time. 'I will be,' he says. 'Department is getting gutted. I don't know where I'll end up.'

'Ministers making an example of you all?'

'The public need their scalps.'

'Will Dawson protect you?'

'She'll do what she can.'

'Then you'll be fine,' Callie tells him. 'That woman's a Rottweiler.'

'That she is.' Mac takes a step back. 'Listen, I better go. I don't want to keep you if you're busy.'

'Sure. Thanks for popping round. I'm sorry I can't talk longer.'

'That's okay. It was good to see you.'

'You too, Mac.'

Halfway down to the street, the detective stops and turns back. 'Richard's not going to be charged with anything,' he says. 'After everything he went through, the fiscal doesn't think it would be in the public interest to try and prosecute him. I thought you'd like to know.'

Callie thinks briefly about the last time she saw Richard – a glimpse through curtains pulled around a hospital bed. His pale face and his skinny body, just lying there, staring up at the ceiling. She tried to speak to him but wasn't able to find the words. The PAVA spray still clamping her throat tight. Or perhaps something more.

'Thank you, Mac,' she says now.

Mac nods and continues down the stairs. Callie watches him hurry along the street, his suit jacket pulled tight around him, until he vanishes from view.

Chapter Sixty-Eight

Callie wasn't lying. She really does have somewhere to be. Her phone buzzes in her pocket as she relocks her front door. A text from Mia. *Be there in 10.*

She finishes up in the kitchen and does a final check of the flat, testing the windows to make sure they're locked. Then she grabs her sports bag and quickly goes through its contents. An array of recording equipment, mostly. Martin's kit that she still has to return. She plans on heading over later tonight. Once her meeting with McCall is done.

Mia called her an hour ago. Told her that Eddie wants to meet her, see how she's doing. Callie didn't exactly feel able to say no. Not after everything the man has done for her. If he hadn't kept her away from police custody, John Taylor might still be out there right now, killing women.

Her doorbell goes. She waits for Mia's face to appear on her phone before swinging open the front door.

'Good evening, Ms Munro.' The three deadbolts barely seem to register. 'How are things?'

'They're fine, Mia. Thanks for asking.'

She thinks back to their earlier conversation. About how all it takes to get past something is to experience something worse.

'Good.' Mia smiles. Her scar tissue twists. 'Then let's go.'

It doesn't take long for Callie to realise where they're headed. Corstorphine. Signs for Edinburgh Zoo.

'You're taking me to see Grant Miller,' she says.

Mia turns from her front passenger seat and nods. 'Yes. Mr McCall is there now.'

'Oh.'

Callie tries to hold the woman's gaze, but Mia's piercing blue eyes prove too much. She turns away, stares out the window instead. A sick feeling has started to build in her gut.

They turn into the estate and park outside. Callie has barely undone her seat belt when the driver opens her door. He makes it seem like maybe he's just being polite, but Callie figures it's more than that. He's making sure she doesn't try to run.

Inside, the house is much like she remembers it from before. That same patterned glass on the vestibule door. Same light from the kitchen spilling into the darkened hallway.

Mia leads the way. Callie follows, the driver close behind. He shuts the front door after them. The sound of the lock turning makes her stomach hurt.

'Callie! I'm so happy to see you're all right.'

McCall is sat in Miller's kitchen. At the table, a beam on his bearded face. He looks genuinely pleased to see her. Grant is across from him, his face pale. On the table between them is a hammer and chisel.

'Thanks, Eddie. How are you?'

'Ecstatic, Callie. Ecstatic. I can't tell you how pleased I am that you've made this city safer and managed to embarrass Police Scotland at the same time.'

'All in a day's work.'

She smiles, awkwardly. The atmosphere in the house is strained. Tense. Grant Miller looks like he's about to throw up. Mia sits on a bar stool, off to one side. She's on her phone. The driver stands by the doorway. McCall gestures to the empty chair next to Grant.

'Please, Callie, take a seat.'

She sets her backpack down on the floor and does as she's told. She tries not to look at the tools but she can't help it. They are old and well used. Their handles are paint-splattered.

'I wanted to ask if there was anything else I could do for you,' McCall says to her. His voice is light and friendly. That same Scottish sing-song to it. A little bit Aberdeen, a little bit Glasgow. 'I wanted to make sure you're doing okay after everything you've been through.'

All these men, Callie thinks to herself, *coming to check on me.*

'I'm doing fine, Eddie,' she says. 'I'm doing fine.'

'And how's work?'

'Work is good.'

'Wonderful.'

McCall sits back in his chair, still smiling. Grant is staring at the hammer and chisel. She can hear his breathing growing loud. Movement in the corner of the room; a skinny cat drapes itself across the counter, watching.

'What's going on here, Eddie?'

'Oh, just a wee matter for Grant and myself to sort out. Isn't that right, Grant?'

'Aye.' Grant's voice is faint.

'Actually,' McCall says, snapping his fingers and sitting forward. 'Actually, maybe there's something you can help clear up for us, Callie love.'

'What's that?'

'How you first heard about me. About my involvement in all this.'

The question catches Callie off guard. She pauses, thinks back to her conversation with Grant. Sat in this very room, at the island where Mia is now. 'Your name came up as part of my investigation,' she says. Choosing her words carefully, unsure where the danger might lie. 'I asked Grant whether he knew anyone that might want to target Amy.'

'And he named me?'

'He didn't say anything incriminating, if that's what you're worried about.'

McCall places his hands on the table, interlocking his fingers. 'Did he happen to tell you why he thought I might have something to do with Amy's disappearance?'

'Not specifically, no.'

'Did he tell you it was because he'd stolen five grand's worth of coke from me, and he was worried about how I might respond?'

Callie wants to close her eyes but she looks over at Grant instead. The man is sweating. His large nostrils flare with each great lungful of air he noisily sucks down.

'You know the part that really gets me the most, Grant?' McCall says, switching his focus. 'It's the fact you only stole five fucking grand from me. That's pennies, for fuck's sake. Where's your fucking balls, big man?'

Grant says nothing.

McCall says, 'You sent her to investigate me, Grant. In the name of your wife, you sent her. Were you hoping she'd find something on me? Something to put me away? Were you hoping maybe I had taken your wife?'

Callie says, 'He was just trying to find her, Eddie. Please don't take it as an insult.'

McCall looks at her. Same smile in place. 'I'm not going to kill him, Callie, if that's what you're worried about. And Grant here knows that. Because Grant knows that everyone who works for me gets ten chances.' He picks up the hammer. 'Five chances on one hand.' He picks up the chisel. 'Five chances on the other.'

Now Callie does close her eyes. Just briefly. Just enough to lock down the dread that's rising inside her. She doesn't want to be here. She wants to go home, to lock her front door and crawl into bed.

'You can go now, love,' McCall says quietly. He's still staring at her. Still smiling warmly. 'Mia can drop you off wherever you'd like. And if there's ever anything you need, you just let me know. I always look out for my people.'

Callie nods. His parting words hang thick and heavy in the air. She gets to her feet, the chair legs scraping against the tiled floor. Beside her, Grant flinches. The sole acknowledgement of her presence this entire time. His gaze is still on the table, which is good, because Callie doesn't think she could bear to meet his gaze right now.

Mia is at the door, and Callie forces her trembling legs to move her away from the men. To carry her out of the room and into the long hallway. Behind her, she hears McCall placing the tools down on the table again. They make a heavy thud.

'Now choose your chance, son,' McCall says, 'and let's get this over with.'

Chapter Sixty-Nine

Mia drops her off at Martin's flat. A wordless journey; Mia isn't here to make Callie feel better. A tight smile for a goodbye. Those sharp blue eyes, that twisted scar. It seems like everyone in the world is carrying scar tissue right now. Inside and out; their own proud flesh.

Callie hits Martin's buzzer. Waits but gets no response. She hits it again, holds it down this time. Still nothing.

It's late. She checks her watch. It's after ten. No chance Martin is out right now. Around her, the Grassmarket is swarmed with tourists, with drinkers, with groups of smokers stood huddled outside pubs. She watches them light up and feels an urge to join. To be amongst the bodies and the noise. Anything other than standing alone outside Martin's block of flats in the cold.

The door suddenly swings open. Callie steps back as a young man leaves, his head down. She catches the door before it clicks shut. Slipping into the stairwell, Callie climbs the three floors. The outside world fades away with each step. By the time she reaches Martin's front door, there's only a trickle of it left.

She goes to knock and sees it's ajar. A sliver of light from inside cutting across her raised fist. A warning bell sounds in her head. In all the time she has known Martin, he has never left his flat open like this. She thinks back to her earlier phone call with him, when she was driving down the A9. The person hammering on the door.

'Martin?'

The door swings open on a light touch, the hinges well oiled. Callie pushes it inwards just enough to poke her head through. The hallway light is on, the narrow space bathed in white. She calls his name again. Still nothing.

It doesn't take her long to find him. Down the tight corridor to the spare bedroom. To his command centre. The room here is lit up too. Spotlights in the ceiling giving the place hard shadows.

Martin is sat at his desk. His hands are in his lap. His eyes open, his head at an uncomfortable angle. A little blood has pooled in the corner of his mouth. Whoever killed Martin Walsh did it with a single bullet. A small-calibre round through the centre of his forehead.

It sparkles now, in the spotlights' shine. Nestled in the back of his chair. Callie stares at it, at the spray of red across the fancy leather, at the brain and bone that surround it. The bullet seems to wink at her. It smiles. It glistens like something beautiful.

ACKNOWLEDGEMENTS

This was a book of firsts for me, in a lot of ways. The first time I've written something set in the UK rather than in the US, for instance. And set in my home city of Edinburgh, no less. We're not shy of a crime novel or two round these parts, but hopefully there's still space for Callie and her journey into the city's dark underbelly.

This was also the first time I've written anything as part of a larger series. I had a lot of fun with this aspect – throwing in teasers to future books, leaving some character stuff unanswered, and of course, ending on a cliffhanger. Who shot Martin Walsh? Will Callie catch them in book two? Have I planned any of this out? Find out next year . . .

As always, it takes a whole load of people to write a book, even though it's only my name on the front cover. Thanks to my agent, Harry, for his ongoing support. Thanks to everyone at Thomas & Mercer – primarily my wonderful editor, Vic, who I have enjoyed working with for a number of years now. Thanks to Russel, whose developmental edits really helped flesh the book out and added all those lovely layers to everything. Thanks to Gemma and Sadie for their excellent copyedits too – so many little details would have slipped through if not for you both!

Thanks, as always, to my wife, Lucy, for kicking ideas around with me and reading various bits. You taught me what proud flesh is (gross), and your hatred of Elie helped me decide exactly where to set my serial killer's holiday home.

And finally, thanks to my son, Isaac. Your brother, Sami, got a book dedicated to him when he was born, so it only felt fair that you get one too. When you're older, I look forward to hearing your thoughts on the book. Perhaps afterwards we can all take a drive out to Elie and find out why Mum hates the place so much.

ABOUT THE AUTHOR

Photo © 2025 Michael Rummey

Tariq Ashkanani is a solicitor and co-host of the writing podcast *Page One*. His debut novel, *Welcome to Cooper*, won the Bloody Scotland Debut Award 2022, as well as being shortlisted for both the CWA John Creasey (New Blood) Dagger and Capital Crime Fingerprint Award. His second novel, *Follow Me to the Edge*, was published in 2022. His third novel, *The Midnight King*, was published by Viper in 2025. He lives in Edinburgh with his wife, two sons and dog, Scout.

Follow the Author on Amazon

If you enjoyed this book, follow Tariq Ashkanani on Amazon to be notified when the author releases a new book!
To do this, please follow these instructions:

Desktop:

1) Search for the author's name on Amazon or in the Amazon App.
2) Click on the author's name to arrive on their Amazon page.
3) Click the 'Follow' button.

Mobile and Tablet:

1) Search for the author's name on Amazon or in the Amazon App.
2) Click on one of the author's books.
3) Click on the author's name to arrive on their Amazon page.
4) Click the 'Follow' button.

Kindle eReader and Kindle App:

If you enjoyed this book on a Kindle eReader or in the Kindle App, you will find the author 'Follow' button after the last page.

Printed in Dunstable, United Kingdom

73656464R00173